AN EL CHANGE

The Otherside and Beyond

Book 7

LINDA TUBB

Copyright © 2017 Linda Tubb

All rights reserved.

ISBN: 10:1541342526
ISBN-13:978-1541342521

DEDICATION

To Brian

Always

And Forever

xxx...

Chapter 1

Eleanor Harrington took off her straw hat and fanned herself with it. It was hot and she was feeling too lazy to move from her deckchair. She had found the one patch of shade on the patio and was taking a well-earned break from decorating. The room she was working on in the attic was like an oven and she was reluctant to return to it just yet. Maybe she should stay here just a little longer.

Oh well, she thought, this bedroom isn't going to decorate itself but the thought of picking up her paintbrush again made her fingers curl with cramp and set off a pain in her neck. Maybe she should get up and get a cold drink.

Bella appeared just inside the French windows and tapped on the glass. She squinted out at Eleanor.

"You mind you don't go gettin' sunburnt," she cautioned. "I thought you'd like some o' that Elderflower cordial that Miss Emma left."

Eleanor heard the clink of ice against glass as Bella put the tray on the console table beside the open door.

"Thank you Bella, you must have read my mind."
Bella gave her a knowing smile. "I'll just leave it in 'ere for when you're ready."

Eleanor had tried to insist, many times, that there was no need to wait on them but Bella was going to do it anyway. Her need to be useful was deeply ingrained and she enjoyed it after all those years of haunting the place without anyone knowing she was there. Had she been able, she would have brought the drinks all the way out to Eleanor but in life, as the lower housemaid, she had been forbidden to go out onto the patio and her ghostly form was unable to leave the house – at least, not by that door.

"Oh, an I fort you ought to know, there's a strange little person comin' up the garden. I saw 'er from upstairs. Looks like a funny little fing, ... 'er frock's covered in leaves an' she's got twigs in 'er 'air," Bella added.

Twigs and leaves sounded like a dryad. There was really only one dryad who ever paid her visits. It was not long before Alsea arrived at the patio.

"Hello Alsea. How lovely to see you. Is everything alright?"

"Yes, everything's fine," she said airily and hugged Eleanor.

"I was just wondering… have you seen my son and his wife lately?"

"Simon was here yesterday, working in the garden, but I haven't seen Marianne for a couple of days. Why, is there something wrong?"

"No… I just thought… it might be nice… make sure they're well and see how they're settling back in… you know." She smiled a little too brightly. Something told Eleanor that this was more than a simple social call.

"I'll give them a ring and let them know

you're here," Eleanor said.

Meanwhile, elsewhere in the multiverse, in the Land of Faerie, Thanir, Chamberlain to the Elven King, was waiting for a visitor to King Branchir's castle. As the Elemental of Air, Sylvestri had always been given a welcome appropriate to her status, which had grown higher now that a recent spell had given her the choice to be visible at will.

It made Sylvestri smile to see Thanir coming towards her and her heart gave a strange little flutter. She had no particular reason for being there at that moment in time but there was something about this darling man that kept drawing her back. She really had tried to resist but well, here she was again.

"Welcome to the castle of the Elven King. I do hope you will enjoy your visit," he gave his standard formal welcome and then his tongue tied itself into several knots and seemed to glue itself to the roof of his mouth. "It's ah... lovely to um... see you... again,

Madam... Miss!" He blushed furiously as he held out his hand to help her from her carriage. He could only hope that it was not sweaty or clammy.

"Thank you darling." She gave the poor man a dazzling smile and he almost swallowed his tongue.

"There are... er... rooms... rooms to ah... to um... to refresh yourself after your travels... if you... only if you wish..."

"Oh poor dear Thanir, I do seem to make you rather nervous, don't I?" Sylvestri flirted, fluttering her eyelashes at him.

Thanir closed his eyes and took a deep, calming breath. He called upon his years of experience with protocol – not that he had experienced anything or anyone like Sylvestri before – and stiffened his spine.

"I can assure you, I have everything under control."

"Yes you do darling," she gave his hand a small squeeze as he realised he had not yet let go of hers.

"Dear Thanir, would you be so kind as to direct me to His Majesty please?" Sylvestri thought it best not to do too much damage to the poor man's reason and stability. This was going to need a much softer approach than she was used to.

"But of course Madam... Miss... um... If you would be so kind as to follow me..." and he turned on his heel and set off towards the inner gate. With the Lady Sylvestri behind him, he could no longer see her and therefore it became easier to ignore her, so long as she did not speak... in that velvety purr that made his heart beat too fast.

He left her in the library. "I shall let Their Majesties know you have arrived and arrange for refreshments to be brought in."

Elsewhere in the castle, Their Majesties, King Branchir and Queen Daewen, were deep in conversation with Sardo and Aurelia or, to give them their proper titles, the Duke and Duchess of Carrinburgh. They were discussing the jewels, which had been stolen many centuries ago by the wizard John Dee. He had been known by many names throughout his life, one of which was the god of the Ancient Greeks, Zeus. Dee's daughter Emma, a close friend of Eleanor's was one of the wise women who had recently uncovered Zeus's hidden hoard and returned them to their rightful owners in Faerie. They were something of an enigma – the jewels and the women, but it was the jewels that commanded their attention right now.

"I only have a vague memory... it was a bedtime story... there was a queen and some jewels and a challenge or contest of some sort... but I was very young," Aurelia said. "May I touch them?" The gems lay on the table on top of their black velvet bags. Branchir nodded and she picked up the largest of the torcs. It was not as heavy as she had imagined. It was made of fine strands of gold wire twisted together and at each end, a delicately scrolled loop held a milky white stone that would sit on the wearer's collar bone. As she picked it up it caught the light and she could see delicate shades of opalescent green, blue and lilac. The colours shifted subtly as she moved it and she noted pale pink, peach and deep inside, the silvery white of moonlight.

"Oh goodness me, I think these are moonstones. I didn't think they actually existed," Aurelia said.

"And what do you think these stones are?" Daewen asked. "They're not as pretty as the moonstones." She picked up one of the smaller torcs. "These are too big to wear as bracelets so they probably go here," she said patting her upper arm. They were smaller versions of the moonstone torc but the stones were a deep velvety green, marked with vivid splashes of red that resembled fresh blood.

"I'm just guessing but I think these must be what they call bloodstones," Aurelia told them.

"I've seen similar bands to these before but not with gem stones in them," Sardo said. "Worn by warriors, they're usually much bigger," he tapped his bicep. "These are much too small for a man. The size does imply they were made for a woman."

Branchir picked up the other armband and before he thought about what he was doing, he took his wife's hand and slid the torc slowly and gently up her arm. It was a perfect fit. Daewen slid the other one on. She now wore the pair and they felt right, somehow.

"Oh my!" she gasped and stretched her hands out before her. "It tingles… no, no, no," she said hurriedly when Branchir moved to take them from her. "Not in a bad way. It feels… good… invigorating," she smiled.

"In the story I recall them being called the Queen's jewels and Daewen is the Queen, so…" Aurelia pointed out. "I wonder what would happen if you put the moonstone torc and the crown on."

"I don't think that would be a good idea just yet. Not until we know more about them," Branchir said. "I think we should consult further with Cousin Eleanor's friends, the Wise

Ones who returned them to us. We must be sure there are no spells or undesirable magic attached before we proceed any further. I would also like to know more about this John Dee character or Zeus as he would have been. He may have... I'm sorry my darling, I shouldn't have put this on you. We have no way of knowing if it's safe." He took his wife's hand and slowly drew one of the torcs down her arm, watching for any adverse reaction the whole time. Daewen smiled and Branchir breathed a sigh of relief when nothing happened.

"I should like to keep the other one on, just a little while longer," she said.

"How do you feel?" he asked her.

"Fine... still good... really good." She grinned.

"That's good," Sardo's gruff voice made Aurelia smile. He was not comfortable around magic. He preferred a foe that he could defeat with a blade or better yet, his bare hands.

There was a discreet cough from the doorway.

"Sire," Thanir bowed. "You have a guest. She is currently in the library and I have arranged for refreshments."

"Guest you say... and who might that be?"

"That would be the Lady Sylvestri, Sire."

Branchir noted the slight flush to Thanir's cheeks and the tiny hitch in his voice.

"Stand down, General Sardo," Branchir chuckled, giving the Duke his previous title. "I don't believe that the lady has come to visit us."

Thanir's face went from pink to white as if all the blood had suddenly drained away. He looked as though he was about to collapse. Daewen was suddenly at his side and took his hand in hers. She patted it soothingly.

"Are you unwell, Thanir?" she asked him.

"Indeed no, My Queen," he gasped. "I... um... merely um..."

"That's all right," Daewen smiled at him.

"You are happy the Lady Sylvestri has come to see you, aren't you? Everything will be fine, I'm sure."

"Why yes, it will," Thanir's face smoothed out and he took a deep calming breath. He smiled and wondered why he had been feeling so nervous.

Chapter 2

In a different part of the multiverse, in the Land of Aldamar, Fyr and his companions were eager to get home to the Boroviche territory within Faerie and share with their families and friends tales of their many adventures such as their meeting the Elven King. On their outward journey, they had encountered a tollgate on their road out of the known Boroviche territory. The guard said he was collecting taxes for the King but King Branchir had assured them it was nothing to do with him, despite what they had just been told. He gave them a demonstration of his magic by removing the tollgate and associated buildings and then he sent the guards back to their homes. So it was with some surprise that, on their way home, they discovered a similar gate flanked by several small wooden buildings and a pair of heavily armed guards blocking their way.

As they approached the gate, the two guards stood warily. They were tall, well-muscled and dressed in leather armour with round metal helmets that looked rather like cooking pots. They might have looked comical but for the short swords strapped to their hips, the knife sticking out of their boot and the long pole arms, twice their height and topped with bill-hooks, which were pointed in the direction of Fyr and his friends.

A third man came out of a nearby building. He was short, round, bald and sweaty and he did look comical. He was dressed in a dark red cloak that clashed with his florid complexion and a medallion around his neck, which labelled him as 'OFFICIAL'. He did his best to look down his nose at them but they were all taller than he was.

"Stop right there," one of the guards took a defensive stance behind the gate with his pole arm lowered menacingly. The second guard had slipped around behind them before they had time to realise what was going on and now had his weapon pointed at them.

"Welcome to the land of Boroviche, folks. What can we do for you today?" The round, ruddy-faced, little official gave them a smarmy, insincere smile.

"We'd like to pass through this damn gate and go home." Kedros, being the eldest of their small party, took the lead.

"Home? And where would that be exactly?" The official took a small notebook and pencil out of his pocket. "Can I see your papers please?"

"Papers? What papers?" Kedros frowned.

"Exit permits, travel permits, re-entry permits, identity cards..." the official began to make a list and tick them off on his stubby fingers.

"Since when has that been necessary?" Kedros did his best not to shout. "We weren't told about any of this before we left."

"And when did you leave?" the Official licked the end of his pencil and waited with it poised to take notes.

"Must have been about eight days ago, maybe nine," Kedros said. The others nodded their agreement.

"Uh is everything huh... uh huh!" The official nodded imperiously while leafing back through his notebook. "Sorry folks. Not had anyone leave through here in a couple of months. I'm going to have to take you all into custody until we can get this little misunderstanding sorted out. I'm sure it's just a little mix-up." He bustled around the gate and up to the women. He did his best to elbow the men out of the way and invaded their personal space. He peered lecherously at each of the women in turn as he asked them; "Names, please." Spittle dotted his lips when he spoke. Having written their names down in his notebook, he beckoned to the women. "This way please, just the ladies..." He began to walk away but turned when no one moved. "This way... Come along now." He nodded at the guard who had somehow managed to place himself so that the men were now separated from the women. Letty, Cemara, Kesia and Loria were shepherded away and forced to follow the official. "We just need to get you processed and then you can be on your way... probably."

"What do you mean... processed?" Kedros demanded.

"Don't you worry," the official waved dismissively. "if you'll just wait there, I'll be back to take your details shortly."

The men looked at one another. This was not right. What had been going on while they were away?

"Who ordered this?" Kedros demanded of the guard that had his long hook-ended pole pointed at them. "Why are you threatening us?"

"Wait, I know you, don't I?" the guard demanded. "Ain't you the baker from just out west of the river?"

"Yes..." Kedros admitted.

"You went off with them strange, foreign

types ..."

Kedros nodded slowly. It was an odd way to refer to the King.

"But that were nearly three months ago," the guard told them.

"Three months? But that's not possible. It's only been a week."

"Nope! No one's been allowed to leave for weeks. Least, not through this way... and there ain't many other ways out now."

"Right then, gents." The official came bustling back out of the building where he had taken the women." That's all the ladies attended to..."

"Where is my wife?" Kedros demanded.

"They're quite safe. Now, do you have any proof of your claim?"

"My claim? What claim?"

"To be married to one of these ladies. Do you have any paperwork?"

"Paperwork? I don't understand." Kedros turned to his companions but they were none the wiser.

"Do you have a marriage permit? As it happens, I might be able furnish some of you with the proper paperwork... for the appropriate fee of course."

"I see... it's like that is it?" Kedros growled. Fyr grabbed his arm and Tanne stepped up to the other side of him. He was making the guard twitchy.

"Now then, if you would step back... let me see," the official consulted his notebook. "Which one of you fine gentlemen is Farris?"

"That would be me," Farris said stepping forward. The official made a few marks in his notebook and waved Farris through the gate.

"Not that door sir, the other one," the guard called out.

"But my wife went in there."

"That's right sir... and you go in here." With the hook-tipped pole barring his way, he had no choice but to go through the other door.

"And which of you is Tanne?" the official looked up from his notebook. "Could you tell me your wife's name?"

"My wife is Cemara. I don't have any papers and don't want to buy any. We've been married for fifteen years; she wears my ring and I wear hers, look." He held up his left hand. "And we've both our names inscribed inside. Would you care to see?" He moved to take his ring off.

"No, no, no need, I've seen hers... you're fine. Go on through." He waved Tanne through without looking up from his notes.

This time the guard sent him through the same door as the women.

"Now... which of you is Kedros?"

"That would be me. My Letty and me, we've been married nigh on twenty five years." He planted his feet and crossed his arms over his chest.

"Have you any proof of this claim?" the official said with a sneer.

"My Letty will tell you the same. What other proof do I need?"

"Do you have any children?" The official

appeared to be engrossed in his notebook.

"We have two children, twin boys."

"And where are they?" He still did not look up at Kedros.

"They're at home, running the bakery for us while Letty and I were away."

"And why…"

"That's enough!" Kedros shouted as he loomed over the official. "I'm going to join my wife." And he stormed off towards the wooden hut.

"But you can't prove…" the official began to raise his voice.

"He knows me and Letty," Kedros pointed a finger at the guard who had recognised him earlier and kept walking.

"Is this true?" the official demanded of the guard.

"Yes sir. My family come from the next village to the baker and his family. We've been getting our bread from them for years."

"Oh very well," the official sighed loudly and waved a dismissive hand in Kedros's direction but he had already disappeared into the hut so he turned his attention to the remaining men.

"Name?" he demanded.

"Gould."

"And do you lay claim to any of these women?"

"No sir."

He moved on. "And you… name?"

"Thorn."

"Married?"

"No sir."

Finally, he arrived at Fyr.

"Name?"

"Fyr, younger brother of Elder Fenyo," he said.

"And your current abode?"

"With my brother and his family." He had not asked Thorn or Gould where they were living.

"And what about Mistress Kesia? Where does she currently reside?"

"With me," Fyr said quickly.

"And how long have you been married?" The official's smile was sickly sweet and smug.

"Well, we're not actually…"

"Just as I thought," the official sniffed haughtily and made more marks in his notebook. "The young lady's name will be added to the list."

"Which list?" Fyr asked.

"The auction list," the man smiled unpleasantly.

Chapter 3

Just as Eleanor reached for the phone, it rang. It was Marianne. "Hello sweetie, has my mother-in-law arrived already?"

"You knew she was coming?" Eleanor asked in surprise.

"No," Marianne laughed. "But Simon sensed her when she crossed through the gate."

"Well… do you have time to pop round and see her? She seems a little out of sorts." Eleanor said. "I've offered her the phone but she looked at it as though I was holding out a poisonous snake. She's waiting out in the garden, won't come into the house."

"We'll be about half an hour. Will you be alright till we get there?"

"I'll be fine. Not sure about Alsea though. Bella's keeping her company and they're regaling each other with all sorts of stories."

"Really," Marianne said. "I didn't think Bella could leave the house."

"She can't. She's on the inside of the French window and Alsea is on the outside. I just hope Bella doesn't frighten Alsea off."

"Or Alsea send Bella into shock," Marianne laughed. "Simon's ready now. We'll be there soon. Bye."

Less than twenty minutes later, Simon and Marianne arrived.

"There you are, my darlings," Alsea skipped across the patio as they came around the corner of the house.

"Hello Alsea," Marianne gave her a hug.

"Mother!" Simon gave her a smile but he did not move towards her.

"Don't I even get a small kiss?" she pouted and patted at her cheek.

Simon sighed and knelt down so that she could reach him.

"Ahh, don't be cross with me," she stuck out her bottom lip. "I haven't seen you in such a long time."

"It's only been a few days," Simon said. "Oh!" He suddenly remembered the odd time discrepancy between their two worlds. "So how long has it been for you?"

"It's been almost a whole growth ring." Dryads had a rather unique way of measuring time. "So how have you both been? Have you settled back here now?"

"We're fine," Simon said. Marianne shared a quick glance with Eleanor. It was not like Simon to be quite so brusque, especially with his mother.

"And how is your business? Still have plenty of work in other people's gardens?"

"Yes…" there was an edge of suspicion creeping into his voice. "Why all the questions? You've never shown any interest in what we do here before."

"Well I… you know… after everything… I thought I should make sure you're both…"

"And yet a whole season of tree growth has passed and it only just occurs to you now."

"I wanted to give you some time to

heal."

"Simon!" He heard Marianne's calming voice in his head as her hand touched his arm. He blinked and turned to look at his wife. Then he dropped his gaze back to his mother.

"I'm sorry, Alsea. I didn't mean to snap. I just haven't been sleeping too well lately."

"And before you ask," Marianne jumped in. "I've tried numerous potions, tisanes and remedies but so far nothing has worked."

"What about dreams, anything at all?" Eleanor asked.

"I'm sure that I have but, infuriatingly, I never remember anything."

"I don't think you've been dreaming properly though. Mostly what you've shared has been a few jumbled flashes of Hob," Marianne said. She did not miss the look that passed across Alsea's face at the mention of Hob, King of the Gnomes and Elemental for Earth and neither did Eleanor.

"Alsea? Is everything all right with Hob?" Eleanor asked.

"Um..." She took a little too long to answer. "Well... he's not been around much lately. Rumour has it that he's at the Gnome Homes but he seems to have gone to ground. No one from the outside has seen a whisker of him for many turnings of the day. He hasn't come to see you has he?" Alsea asked with a hint of desperation in her voice.

"Last time we saw Hob was in Aldamar, complaining about getting too old for all this," Marianne said. "I'm not sure he was joking."

"But too old for what?" Alsea asked.

"Not sure... to be gadding about possibly." Marianne shook her head. "I didn't pay an awful lot of attention. We were a little distracted at the time but now that you mention it, he did seem a little... off. I just thought he was being his usual cantankerous self."

"So what do you think the old boy is up to?" Simon asked. His temper had calmed somewhat and he now sat cross-legged on the ground and held his mother's tiny, child-like hand in his large one.

"I'm worried," Alsea admitted at last.

"Worried about Hob? Why?" Eleanor asked.

"I can't put my finger on it. I haven't seen him in so long and..." Alsea began but Simon cut her off.

"I'm sure this isn't the first time he's taken off to have some time to himself."

"But this feels different. Don't ask me how, I don't know but I think you need to come back with me." She got up and prepared to head back towards the gate. She stopped and looked back, obviously expecting Simon and Marianne to follow her.

"Whoa there, just a minute. Marianne and I have lives here... jobs... responsibilities. We can't just drop everything and go rushing off because you've got a feeling."

"If you think Hob is ill or in danger, then of course... but..." Marianne added.

"Well no, I don't think he's in danger, or ill as such but..." Alsea looked desperately from face to face. "Something is changing. I can feel it coming. It's like the turning of the seasons but more… much more… oh, I don't know," she let out a great sigh. "More something but I just don't know what."

"If you're dreaming about Hob, it could be important. Maybe I can help you to find out what's going on in your dreams," Eleanor offered.

"Could you try scrying for him first?" Marianne asked.

"We can try." Eleanor placed her bowl of water in the middle of the table on the patio so that Alsea could be involved as they gathered around. It came as no surprise to Marianne or Simon that the bowl of water looked just like… a bowl of water.

"What are you going to do with that?" Alsea asked.

"Well, Marianne asked if I could find Hob by scrying for him," Eleanor began to explain. But Alsea looked at her blankly with her head on one side, which made the oak leaves in her hair rustle. "I use the water, or sometimes a mirror, as a focus to help me find people. Sometimes it will show me where they are and what they're doing. I warn you though, if Hob doesn't want to be found, I might not be able to see anything."

"Just do your best, sweetie." Marianne smiled and gave Eleanor's arm a gentle squeeze.

Smiling back, Eleanor turned her attention to the bowl of water, the surface of which began to ripple. The image that formed was one Eleanor recognised from the map in Branchir's library and she found herself flying across the undulating landscape of Faerie. Eventually, she came to an area dotted with oddly rounded, grassy hills. No houses or buildings of any kind were visible as the gnomes lived underground. Nor were there any obvious entry points, but then the gnomes had no need of them. They seemed to travel through the earth as easily as water. Eleanor's view panned to the left and then to the right and then up and down but that was as far as she could get.

"Sorry guys but I can't get any closer. I can see the area around the outside of the Gnome Homes. If Hob is inside, I can't get to him." Then she had an idea. "Hold hands... if we make a circle I might be able to tap into something that could help."

Marianne took Eleanor's left hand and nodded at Alsea for her to take Eleanor's right hand. Simon closed the circle by taking Marianne and his mother's hand. All at once, Eleanor staggered slightly as the ground seemed to rush up to meet her with the sensation of vertigo. Clinging tightly to the hands, she expected the sense of movement to stop once they reached the ground surface but was horrified to find herself sinking into the ground. A flash of claustrophobic panic washed over her until she heard both Simon and Alsea inhale sharply and remembered that this was all an illusion within her scry.

"I can see it," Alsea gasped.

"Really? What do you see?" Eleanor wanted to know.

"I see the soil... sands and silts and rock... layers of organic matter." Simon's voice was full of wonder.

"I can see the roots of so many trees," Alsea added. "And there are tiny creatures, sleeping peacefully... apart from the worms, they're always busy... Oh! Pardon me!" she said moving out of the way of a passing worm. The worm did not respond because, of course, they were not actually there.

One moment they were sliding slowly through the earth and the next they were standing in a tunnel, lit by a green, phosphorescent glow from the walls. The tunnel opened into a large cavern; the walls were honey-combed with openings framed by huge timbers. They were at the lowest level and from all the comings and goings it appeared that the nearest openings led to a variety of shops: food, clothes, furniture and tools for sale and through one of the larger doorways, alcohol. It looked like a pub and quite a noisy one, with raucous singing accompanied by an accordion-like instrument. It was soon joined by the skirl of pipes and rumble of a drum. It looked like something Hob would enjoy but he was not there because their journey continued as they drifted into another tunnel on the opposite side of the cavern.

Eleanor began to wonder if they had somehow been turned around or they had gone in a circle because this tunnel looked just like the first, but then it led them into a smaller cavern. Here, the only other doorway was barred by a pair of heavy oak doors. Two people stood outside the door as though waiting for permission to enter. As the doors opened, Eleanor and her little group slipped through.

This cavern was much smaller the others they had seen; small but somehow opulent. The walls glowed as light was reflected from gemstones that were embedded here and there. Flowing curtains of limestone stalactites hanging from the roof sparkled and shimmered in the light of hundreds of small lanterns. It was a spectacular and rather overwhelming display. It was so magnificent and distracting that they had to look twice to see the small figure hunched in the corner of the jewel-encrusted throne.

Before Eleanor could speak to Hob, the image vanished and she was once again aware of her actual surroundings. She dropped the hands she had been holding and expected the water to clear but it was still rippling and it snagged her gaze. Someone was trying to get in touch.

Chapter 4

Eleanor was about to apologise to the others for losing the scry when Branchir's face appeared in her bowl.

"Dear cousin, how are you?" he asked breezily.

"Fine thanks, and yourself?"

"Who is she talking to?" Alsea whispered with a frown.

"No idea but I'm certain it's not Hob," Simon whispered back.

Marianne shook her head, she could not see or hear anything now either. She patted Eleanor's arm then she and Simon led Alsea away so she could continue her conversation in private.

"We are all very well thank you." Branchir took a quick breath and continued. "I'm glad I was able to contact you. I have a favour to ask."

"How can I help?" Eleanor asked.

"I would like you to contact the ladies who returned our lost treasures, on my behalf." His tone was light and jovial but Eleanor thought he sounded a little anxious.

"Of course, I can do that. Is there a problem?"

"Not exactly," Branchir frowned. "We have been discussing the treasures and wondered if they had any more information about them. One of the ladies said she thought Faerie was their place of origin, but we know very little beyond a story that Aurelia half remembers from childhood. There is most definitely magic within the pieces, I can sense it. I would like to be certain that there is no danger or malicious spells attached to them. I would have asked the ladies when they were here but they had to rush off and... Look, you can tell me to mind my own business if you like but I would like to talk to them about John Dee too. Was he the same Zeus from our legends? If he is, there are still cautionary tales told about him. He was known to be a stubborn and jealous ruler. This man, Dee seems to have had a hand in so many disasters… in your world, my world and probably, many others too… and if he really is Zeus, it has been going on for a long time. I believe there should be consequences…"

"You're right, something does need to be done about him. He has affected so many people. To be honest, James and I were just happy to be home that I think we've tried to put him out of our minds. It is about time he faced up to what he's done. Repercussions are long overdue. I don't know how he managed to escape the three-fold return backlash all this time. I'll contact the sisters for you and get back to you as soon as I can."

"Thank you dear Cousin. I am ever hopeful that we shall see you and James here in the not too distant future." He bowed and disappeared from the bowl.

"What was all that about?" Alsea asked.

Eleanor had not seen her come back. Simon and Marianne had done their best but

Alsea had got the bit between her teeth and wanted to know what had happened to Hob.

"We were there with him one minute and then there was nothing... but you spoke to someone... was it him?" Alsea asked.

Eleanor shook her head. "I'm sorry about Hob, but I did say, if he did not want to be found..."

In Faerie, Branchir waved his hand over the surface of the mirrored table and Eleanor's face disappeared. He took a deep breath and stepped away. Time was marching on and his presence was expected in the Great Hall. Protocol said that the main meal of the day for those within the castle could not start without the King's presence.

Branchir strode up to the top table and stood beside his wife. He smiled, nodded and gave Daewen's hand a gentle squeeze as he took his place at her side. He turned his attention to the people in the Hall who were all waiting in eager anticipation.

"Friends and good people of Faerie," he

held up his goblet. "Eat well, drink your fill and may you never go hungry." With a small sip from his goblet, he gave the signal for the feasting to begin.

As he sat, Daewen murmured behind her goblet, "Is everything agreeable my King? Did you speak to the Lady Eleanor?"

"I did, everything is in hand."

"Maybe now you can tell me what ails thee?"

"Truly, my heart, I am feeling uncertain and unsettled by recent events." He smiled as he spoke. He may have been able to use his magic to hide his words from everyone but his wife but they could all see his face. As King, he had to put on a show.

"How so, my love?" Daewen matched his smile. It would not do for the people to see their King and Queen so troubled.

"How is it that all knowledge of these treasures disappeared into the mists of time? And how did they become little more than a children's story, especially as we have so many stories about Zeus and his exploits?"

"That I do not know," she said taking another sip from her goblet.

"And why is it that Aurelia remembers this story and yet I do not recall ever having heard it before?"

"You should eat something," she reminded him and held up a small piece of fruit to his lips. It would not do for the King not to eat, everyone else would have to stop as well. Branchir nodded and licked her fingers as he took a bite of the fruit that she held.

"I confess to being more than a little confused by these events," he murmured. "I begin to wonder what else is there yet to be revealed. So many things have been lost and forgotten. A whole race of people, the Boroviche, disappeared, had been forgotten. We knew nothing of them, yet they existed under our very noses, hidden by powerful spell to live within the doors to our Great Hall until Simon, the one they call their Forest Mage, set them free. And now, we have these jewels, also lost and forgotten for generations..."

Daewen looked thoughtful for a moment then said, "I suspect the reason Aurelia was told the stories was because she was female. She said they were called the Queen's jewels and from what I can gather her mother was a little delusional in wanting her children to take over the rule of Faerie from your father's line." Her voice was calm as she spoke but Branchir could see the pain behind her eyes at the thought of Aurelia's brother, Morfinnel. The mere thought of what he had done to Daewen made Branchir's blood run cold. None of it was Daewen's fault... or Aurelia's, but it made him feel helpless and angry to know of the abuse that his Queen had suffered at the hands of that sadist. He did not want to think what could have happened if Sardo and Aurelia had not rescued her. It could have broken her completely, and it almost did, but she was strong, his Queen, his heart. Branchir's stomach turned over. If Morfinnel had not already been dead... it was a shame he could not die more than once... With some difficulty, he managed to swallow another bite of fruit without gagging and did the only thing he could. He leaned over, wrapped his arms around her and whispered his love in her ear. It took a few moments before he realised that a hush had fallen over the Hall.

"Everyone is looking at us," Daewen whispered.

"Uh huh," he whispered back, but did not let her go. He needed to hold onto her for the sake of his own sanity. "Let them look. A man should be allowed to hug his wife, even if they are the King and Queen."

"Sire," Thanir's hushed voice came from somewhere over Branchir's left shoulder. "I believe everyone is waiting upon you to eat so that they may continue with their meal."

Branchir pulled himself together and gave Daewen a kiss on the end of her nose. He took her hand and smiled. Then he stood and looked down the long tables that stretched before him.

"My apologies for the interruption to your meal my friends but I find myself..." he turned and smiled down at Daewen again. "...ever more in love with my wife, your Queen, as each day passes." He bowed over her hand and could not resist pressing a kiss to it. As one, the guests stood and spontaneous applause and cheering broke out.

"I do believe your people approve, Sire." Thanir was forced to raise his voice over the noise. The noise died down as Branchir raised his hand.

"Please, continue to eat... drink!" He took his seat and the feast continued.

Towards the end of the meal, Thanir approached the King once again and bent to speak quietly into his ear.

"If I might presume Sire, I have been pondering this current dilemma with regard to the return of the lost property. I do not wish to presume but I thought I might make contact with Brother Ambrosius at the Guild of Brothers.

It is possible they may have pertinent information within their archives."

"Of course Thanir, that is an excellent idea. Please, get a message to the good Brother as soon as possible."

As Thanir bowed and backed slowly away to comply, he bumped into someone. He began to apologise when a sultry voice purred in his ear.

"Hello, darling. Where are you going in such a hurry?"

He gave an unintentional little squeak. "Oh beg pardon Lady Sylvestri… how lovely to… um, I mean I… I didn't see you there… I mean…" He bowed quickly and began to back away. He did not get very far before she hauled him upright, threaded her arm through his and began to lead him away from the hall.

"It's quite alright, darling. I'm quite used to people not noticing me, although, being visible is such a novelty. Now then, where are we going?"

Chapter 5

Fyr had returned to his home town less than half an hour ago along with Farris, Gould and Thorn. They needed answers. Surely, his brother and the other Elders had to know something. "How long have you known about this? What happens at these auctions?" Fyr demanded of Fenyo as he stormed into the house.

"What happens to the women... the ones put up for auction?"

"It depends on who's buying..." Fenyo winced.

"And what are the Elders doing about it? Its barbaric, how could you all let this happen?" Fyr demanded.

Fenyo grabbed his brother's arm and drew him out into the garden. His eyes scanned the area as he said, "We can't talk in there, Bor and Sosna are too young. They'll ask questions or talk and might let something slip."

His voice was barely above a whisper.

"But I don't understand..." Fyr dragged his hands through his hair.

"I'm sure it won't be that bad. I'm sure someone will buy the young woman's services as a maid or a farmhand and not for… "

"No! Not happening… not that!"

"I'm sure she'll be fine …" But he did not look at all sure.

"Don't… how can you say that? They took Kizzy and Loria away. The others had to prove, to that pompous little git, that they were married before they were allowed to leave together. Farris and Loria had no proof and Kizzy and me…" he gulped in air but it did not help.

Fenyo was no more comfortable with the situation than his brother was as he tried to calm him down and defuse his anger. "You haven't known this girl all that long…"

"That is not the point. How long had you known Frea before you knew she was the one?" He shook his head and took another gulp of air. "The official at the border... there shouldn't even be a border... said that as Kizzy and Loria were unmarried they had to return to their own villages to participate in the local auction. It's beyond barbaric... they're going to be sold to the highest bidder... I can't..."

"Keep your voice down," Fenyo had to keep his brother calm.

"How can you be so...? You're an Elder. What about the other Elders? Surely they...? Are you telling me you all agreed to this? Did you even know...? Apparently, living together without being married is now against the law? Who's law? Who voted for that?"

Fenyo put his hand on Fyr's shoulder. "Keep your voice down, they may be watching us." He pretended to be pointing out something in the vegetable patch. "Come and look at these cabbages, best I've ever grown," he said over-loudly. Then he dropped his voice again. "There are so very few of us now. Most of the old ones have retreated up into the high grounds. They were finding this new world order too difficult to cope with. But..." His eyes darted furtively. "Those few of us who remain dare not be seen together... I can't say anything more now." He picked up a watering can and passed it to Fyr and pointed to the cabbage patch again "You must be careful what you say and who you speak to. There are eyes and ears everywhere."

Fyr played along and played the water back and forth over the vegetables. "Does King Branchir know about any of this?" Fyr murmured as he bent to pluck at some weeds beside his brother.

"You've met him. What do you think?"

"I don't know why I'm asking. Of course he doesn't know." Fyr was sure that Branchir was not the sort of King, or the sort of man who would condone such abuse, the sale of people to the highest bidder, like livestock. "I need to get word to him... but I can't go, not while Kizzy is in danger. I've got to find her."

"Come inside for dinner, boys," Frea called from the back door. "Come and eat before it gets cold."

Fenyo stood up and a warning look passed between husband and wife. Fyr gave a quick glance around beyond the garden but there was no one in sight.

Later that night, Fyr lay on his bed staring up at the ceiling, unable to sleep. His mind constantly replayed the things that Fenyo had said... or not said. He could not believe how much had changed in the short time that they had been away. How was it that although they had only been in Aldamar for what? Mere days! Time here, in Faerie had run on so much faster? How was that even possible? As far as he could see, none of these changes they had come back to were for the better. How had all of this happened under their very noses without them being aware of it until now?

It was not so long ago that life had been so much simpler. The stories of being trapped within a magical spell inside a door had been... just that, stories that people told one another to pass the time during the long winter nights. Not real... And then it was real. A stranger had appeared, as if by magic - the Forest Mage. Legend promised that he would release them from the sepia world they inhabited into one of light and colour. But that act alone could not have changed their way of life. They could have gone on the way they always had. There was nothing wrong with the old ways, so why change? The Boroviche people were mostly farmers, used to cultivating the land. They kept animals and grew food to support their families and their villages. The Blacksmiths made ploughs and spades to cultivate the fields. They made scythes and flails to reap the harvests. They made pots and pans for cooking and tools to chop wood for their fires. But now, they were making weapons and armour – no good for growing, harvesting or cooking. Why were they being forced to make weapons of war? The Boroviche had never made war, they were a peaceful people, or had been until now.

Coming home should have been a

cause for celebration. Whilst travelling home, Fyr and Kizzy had talked about their future. Now they had returned to this alien place. This was not home. He felt more foreign here than he ever had in Aldamar.

Gould and Thorn had been the only two unattached men in their group. They were not able to return to their own villages as they had been denied travel permits. Maybe they could do something to help Fyr and Farris.

The two couples who had been allowed to leave together: Kedros and Letty, Tanne and Cemara, had been allowed to travel home but trying to pick up where they left off was not easy with all the new rules and regulations. Farris had gone home but without Loria – he was lost without her and did not know what to do. The only information they had about Loria and Kesia was that they would be returned to their home villages.

Most of the people the men tried to speak to were too afraid to say anything. The wrong word overheard by the wrong person could get them into trouble. Whilst large quantities of ale loosened the tongues of a few, stories told by drunks needed to be taken with a hefty pinch of salt. Gould and Thorn had managed to find employment and lodgings at the inn and brew house and listened to every tale no matter how far-fetched. There had to be a grain of truth in there somewhere. They shared with Fyr when they could.

The more Fyr discovered, the more he was sure that King Branchir knew nothing of this situation. There had to be a way to get a message out to him but all the roads were blocked and guarded. Fyr's priority though, had to be Kesia. Guarded roads or not, he was going to find a way to her village and... and... He did not want to think about what might be happening to her while he was stuck here.

"I have to go soon," Fyr murmured to Thorn behind his tankard. "She shouldn't have to face this... not alone."

Thorn made no comment as he made a show of cleaning the table next to Fyr.

"Loria has to be here somewhere. Farris said this was her home town too. We've not heard anything about an auction though." Gould murmured as he put a plate of bread and cheese in front of Fyr and then he was gone again.

"So they lied," Fyr said. "I've only got a vague idea where Kesia's father lives but I've got to start somewhere."

"What about going through the trees like the dryads taught us in Aldamar?"

Fyr blinked in surprise. Why had he not thought of that? All this worry about Kesia had him seriously rattled. He was about to comment on it when a hush settled over the inn. The door opened and three rough looking, heavily armed and leather-clad men came in. Fyr thought he recognised one of them as a local field labourer – lots of muscle but very little brain. They took up an intimidating stance at the bar and stared at all the patrons and staff with smirks and sneers.

The first man called out to Thorn "You

boy! Ale for me and my men... quick as you like.

Fyr suddenly realised that he was the only one staring back. Everyone else had found somewhere else to look, somewhere else to be. An old man stumbled as he passed by his table. As Fyr helped him up the old man muttered in his ear.

"Them is 'is Lordship's bully boys. You might want to try and be a bit more... invisible."

Chapter 6

Once they had been split up, Kesia had been taken to a small hut with the other women. The Official was an oily, creepy, little man with clammy hands and he kept touching them... patting them on the arm or the knee or lingering on their shoulder. She tried hard to suppress a shudder.

"Now my dear," he moved in closer and gave a wet little chuckle. "Full name, age and place of birth."

She gave him her information and tried to move further away but he kept leaning in closer, pretending he was having trouble hearing her, which was ridiculous. She wanted to shout at him but the guard at the door frowned and stood with his hand on his sword.

The official moved on to Loria and Kesia found herself guided to a seat by Letty.

"I'm sure they'll get this sorted out soon and then we can all go home," she smiled at

Kesia. The older woman was trying to reassure herself as much as the young woman.

Kesia gave herself a chance to look around the small hut. There were two doors: one they had just entered by and one directly opposite it. This second door had a small, square window, the only one in the building. There was a table covered in piles of paper, pens and a large ink-stand at one end of the room and three chairs along the end wall.

After what seemed like an interminable age and a barrage of ridiculous questions the official left by the door they had entered. He had been gone a long time before anything else happened. When the door next opened however, it was not the official but Tanne. Cemara flew to him and he held on to her tightly.

"It's alright. We're going home now," he told her. He turned to speak to the others but the guard was right behind him with his bared sword.

"No discussion. Move it along." Tanne

and Cemara were hustled out of the second door without the chance of a backward glance.

Moments later Kedros stormed in. Letty stood and put a comforting hand on Kesia's shoulder.

"Shouldn't be long now," she whispered.

"The man's an imbecile," Kedros thundered. "I'll have his badge for this piece of corruption. Come, wife!" he said to Letty, with extra emphasis on the word wife. He took her hand and gave it a little squeeze and they left by the same door as Tanne and Cemara. The guard watched them with eyes like a hawk as they walked off down the road after the other couple.

Only Loria and Kesia were left. They sat together, holding hands, waiting to see who would be next to leave. When the door opened again, it was not Farris or Fyr but the official. He stood for a moment and studied his notes with lots of head nodding and muttering to himself. Eventually he looked up and smiled at them. It was not a friendly smile.

"So you two ladies," he made the word ladies sound like something unpleasant, distasteful. "Your stories have been confirmed and as neither of you have any proof of ownership..." there was that smile again, "the law states that you have become tainted and unmarriageable."

"That's ridiculous," Loria exploded. "I am married, to Farris and Kizzy here is going to marry Fyr."

"I'm afraid that it is no longer possible, nor permissible to arrange one's own marriage. Therefore..."

"Why will you not listen?" Loria cried.

"Miss, if you continue to speak when you have not been given permission to do so you will be considered a scold on top of everything else and bridled."

The guard took a step forward with a nasty grin but the official held up his hand. "She has been duly warned." The guard took a step back. "As I was saying; as unmarried women you should have been living with your parents or, if your parents are dead, then an approved guardian."

Until the recurring dreams had sent her on a journey, Kesia had been living with her father but she was not willing to be forcibly gagged for speaking up.

"You were wandering about the countryside with people who were not family, not related in any way and therefore you are now considered to be fallen women and, as such, eligible for auction." Eligible – that was how the official worded it, as though it was some great privilege. It was no such thing. It was obscene.

Before they had time to consider what to think or feel they were both shunted out of the door by which they had entered, to a waiting horse-drawn wagon. The back of the wagon was little better than a large livestock crate with a door at the back, straw on the floor and small round air holes near the top.

There were no windows.

Loria helped Kesia to climb in and then, "In you get, love," the guard grabbed her bottom and squeezed while supposedly helping her in. She turned and glared at him but he just laughed. "Better get used to it, 'specially if you get bought up by a Comfort House... you could do worse."

Loria squeezed Kesia's hand while Kesia bit her lip and tried not to cry. Less than an hour ago, she and Fyr were discussing plans for their future, now all of that was gone and she had no idea where Fyr was or where they were being taken. The wagon gave a lurch as the horse moved off and all Kesia and Loria could do was sit side by side in this little box and wait to see what was going to happen to them.

Chapter 7

Hob had lost count of exactly how long he had been an Elemental but he knew the years had to be measured in the hundreds. It may have been closer to millennia. The passage of time had become a little blurred. It had now come to the point where he had to put those difficult choices he had made, about the two halves of his life, Earth Elemental and Gnome King, into practise.

It was never supposed to have been this tough but then, that's what you get for falling in love with the wrong person. Though now, even that was a far distant memory. People joked that he was older than dirt but that was probably closer to the truth than anyone knew. He had spent so long trying to put off thinking about this and his memory was not what it once was... He was no longer sure what was real and what was myth any more. It was all so tangled. He closed his eyes and tried to force the memories to take shape in the right order.

He saw himself as a nipper... a cheeky, little scamp, full of curiosity, wanting to know the ins and outs of everything. Being so damned nosy was what had got him into this position in the first place. He had become King of the Gnomes by accident. He had never meant to be the Earth Elemental either. Talk about being in the wrong place at the wrong time... twice!

In those long gone days, Faerie had been awash with magic of every kind. Everyone took it for granted. Every species of Faerie folk had their own specific place within the magical spectrum. The driadi had their affinity with the trees and plants, the naiadi had the water, the sylphi had the air and the gnomes had the rocks and soils. When magic disappeared from Faerie, it was the big Elven folk that were affected the most. For those who could tap into the natural magic of the elements, it never really went away. It was probably why the gates stopped working.

Gnomes had little use for gates. They could create their own links from one place to another through tunnels they called wormholes. Though Hob rarely had any need for tunnels. If he could visualise the place he could drop down into the earth and pop up again just where he wanted to be much like the driadi had been able to with the trees but then one day the driadi disappeared too.

Hob raked his fingers through his beard. He should have known then that having extra magic would come with strings attached. He frowned. He probably should have stayed at home that day all those years ago.

Although neither he nor anyone else had been aware of it at the time, he had been the only link between Faerie and the outside worlds for centuries. So it was probably just as well that Eleanor and her friends had come along and fixed things when they did because his grip on it all had been slipping for some time now.

He opened his eyes, surprised to find

that he had been dozing and startled from his stupor by a noisy group of young gnomes as they filed through the throne room with their teacher.

"What do they think I am... a museum exhibit?" he grumbled under his breath. "Huh! I s'pose I'm old enough to be one."

"Stragglers at the back there... do keep up," the teacher called out. One of the younglings at the end of the line who had stopped to gawp, open-mouthed suddenly piped up;

"Why've they given the King a red face?"

"Well I... Do hurry children... lots still to see through here." The teacher had assumed, like the children that this was a wax effigy of the King and was mortified when he winked at her. "Do come along..." The teacher hurried down the line to nudge them in the right direction.

"Can we go and see the jewel caves, Miss?" another child hollered.

"Yes, yes... do come on... let's leave the King alone."

The last child in the line gave Hob a toothy grin and a little wave as she ran to catch up with her classmates.

So, the throne room was not the quiet place for serious thinking that Hob had remembered - at least not today, nor was the jewel cave apparently. Whose idea had it been to have tours of his palace? Maybe he should just open a random wormhole, see where it took him. But then, maybe not. That was what got him into this position in the first place. What he should really do was sit down and talk to his great-Grandson, sort out their options.

Options, what options? He could not talk to Simon yet. It was not the right time. He and Marianne had suffered enough traumas recently. This might just be the 'thing' to tip the balance and balance was everything. The Great Powers had to be aware of what Simon and Marianne had been through and they promised to give them some time but they could not wait forever, any more than Hob could. There were more trials ahead for Simon before he could take the mantle of Earth Elemental from Hob's shoulders - and poor Simon had no idea it was coming. Hob could only hope that the young Fire Elemental, Salamander, had been able to start the ball rolling without giving the game away.

Hob pulled up his knees, wriggled into the corner of his throne, and pulled his hat down as far as it would go. It muffled his groan. He was being cowardly and he knew it but a few more hours wouldn't matter - would it?

Meanwhile, far away in another place...

Eleanor tried to contact Dorcas several times but was having no luck. She decided to leave it for a while and try again later. Right now, she was more concerned with the friends sitting at her kitchen table. Alsea had disappeared back to Aldamar to see if anyone there had heard from Hob. Marianne and Simon sat side by side in identical poses, with hands wrapped around mugs and eyes staring into the black depths of rapidly cooling coffee. Neither of them could scry, so that's not what they were doing.

"That coffee must be cold. Can I make you fresh ones?" Eleanor spoke quietly but the sudden intrusion into their thoughts still made them both jump. Simon's coffee mug went flying and the black puddle spread across the scrubbed wooden surface of the table and began to drip onto the floor.

"Oh... sorry ..." he leapt to his feet looking around for a cloth.

"Don't worry..." Eleanor began. "It's fine..." And then Bella appeared with a cloth in her hand and began quietly mopping up the mess.

"No! It's not fine, Eleanor." Simon dropped back into his seat. Marianne reached out to hold his hand. She did not say anything but then there was no need to, Marianne's face spoke volumes.

"Simon, are you ill?" Eleanor asked.

"No… I don't think so…"

"I'm sure it's nothing… physical," Marianne added. As a healer, she would know.

"I just feel… I don't feel… Oh! I don't know how I feel… Just, not myself lately… sort of weak… no energy…" Simon sighed.

"You said you weren't sleeping properly?" Eleanor queried.

"I seem to lay there awake for hours but I must be getting some sleep because I wake up… always on the edge of a dream but I can't catch it and it's gone before I can…"

"And you said you get flashes of these dreams?" Eleanor turned to Marianne. "Do you think this has anything to do with Hob and why Alsea is so concerned?"

Simon and Marianne both nodded and shrugged at the same time.

"I'm beginning to wish I had some of Emma's tea handy," Eleanor murmured to herself.

"I've tried all the potions I've gathered

from Aunt Addie and those that Emma was willing to share and..." Marianne shrugged helplessly. "Nothing."

"Maybe you should consider seeing your GP. It might not be anything magical..."

"No, I'm almost sure it is. It feels as if something is blocking him." Marianne said.

"Even the soil feels wrong... I can't ... draw from it like I used to..."

"Do you think it could be more of John Dee's mischief?" Eleanor wondered.

"Before we came home from Aldamar, Hob suggested that we visit Evie and Salamander."

"We went but it felt like more of a compulsion than a suggestion," Marianne said, remembering it.

"True," Simon said pensively. "I think there was something we were supposed to learn from our visit."

"But beyond having a good time with our friends and their crazy daughter... I didn't sense anything out of the ordinary. But now I'm wondering if we missed something important."

Chapter 8

Thanir and Sylvestri left the Great Hall together but once they were in the narrow alley between the hall and the kitchens, Thanir put on a burst of speed. Sylvestri found herself running to keep up with him. It had been a long time since she had last exerted this much physical energy and it was an odd sensation. She was used to flowing and floating on the breeze these days. It took a little while to acclimatise to being corporeal again.

A quick wave of her hand and a sharply sucked-in breath strengthened the stiff breeze that was funnelled between the high walls. It slowed him down so that she could catch up. The sudden gust almost knocked Thanir off his feet.

"Careful darling," Sylvestri purred as she placed a supporting hand on his arm. The strong air currents had no effect on her.

"Pardon me, Miss," Thanir stepped back

a little too quickly. His face flushed and he made a strangled gulping sound.

Sylvestri's mouth curled into a little pout. "Oh dear, have I done something to upset you darling?"

"No Miss... begging your pardon My Lady..." His face grew even redder.

"Are you trying to run away from me?" she grinned to take the sting out of her question.

"Oh no M... m'Lady," He looked down at his feet. "I'm... I'm currently on a mission for His Majesty. The Brotherhood will be locking their doors for their nightly contemplations very soon. I must be quick."

"Well, yes, I suppose you must," she sighed. "I think it would be better if you went on alone." Another smile to soften her words. I should not like to hold you back from your duty to the King."

"Oh no Miss!" Thanir's face was both horrified and relieved at the same time. It was an odd look.

This was probably not the time to be teasing him with her flirting. She could wait. "Good luck with your search." She could not resist one last tiny flirtatious gesture and brushed a butterfly kiss across his cheek just to see him blush again.

"Oh dear me… I must umm… I should… yes…" Poor Thanir almost tripped over his own feet in his eagerness to get away.

By the time Thanir reached the front door of the Brother House and knocked, his pounding heart had calmed sufficiently that it no longer felt as though it was trying to escape from his chest. It was just as well that he had come alone. It might have been awkward trying to explain that ladies were not allowed within the Brother House. He could see that she might not have taken kindly to that. He was sure that Lady Sylvestri was used to going wherever she pleased.

The door was answered by a young brother wearing the simple habit of an apprentice. Thanir did not recognise him but the apprentice obviously knew who Thanir was and he bowed, stepping aside to allow the King's Chamberlain to enter. He led the way to Brother Ambrosius Tertius Decimus's office. He opened the door without knocking and bowed Thanir into the room. Brother Ambrosius was not there.

"His Eminence will be with you shortly," he said and left Thanir alone.

There was very little furniture in the room. A small iron stove in one corner gave off just enough heat to take the worst of the chill from the stone walls and floor but not enough to make it comfortable. A simple trestle table, piled high with books and manuscripts, stood against one wall and a low, uncomfortable looking three-legged stool sat near the stove. Above the table was a small lancet window that let in very little light even during the daytime. The only light in the room came from the two candles in their iron sconces on either side of the window and a small orange glow from the stove. The walls were bare, whitewashed stone without any decoration or embellishment.

Thanir heard the shuffling footsteps and tap of a cane, moments before Brother Ambrosius appeared at the door.

"Good evening to you, Brother Ambrosius." Thanir gave the old man a smile and a deep bow. The Brother shambled into the room, hunched over his cane and unsteady on his feet. He raised a hand in greeting and gave a slight nod of his white head but once he had closed the door behind him and slid the bolt into place he straightened his back and stretched. His bright blue eyes twinkled at the King's man.

"Shuffling around like an old fool is getting somewhat tiresome but it's expected of someone of my advanced years," he chuckled. "It means I can get away with all sorts. So, to what do I owe the pleasure of this visit?" The old man rubbed his hands together in anticipation of a little – if not excitement then at least relief from his current boredom.

"Might we speak somewhere a little more...?" Thanir began but Brother Ambrosius put his finger to his lips and winked. He double checked that the bolt was secure then walked across the small room to the candle holder to the right of the window. He removed the candle and gave the iron bracket a quarter turn to the left then he pushed on the wall and a section of it swung open to reveal a door and a dark space beyond. Brother Ambrosius winked and beckoned Thanir to follow.

"If I had not seen that for myself I would never have believed that there was a door there."

Brother Ambrosius put his finger to his lips with a smile and closed the secret door behind them. There was not even a chink of light to show where the door was. In fact, the only light they had was the single candle in Brother Ambrosius' hand. A long barrel-vaulted tunnel led into the other set of archives, the ones known only to Brother Ambrosius and his predecessors. As Brother Ambrosius Tertius

Decimus, he was the thirteenth incumbent of this office and Keeper of the Secrets... which in itself was a secret.

The tunnel opened out into a circular cavern with a domed ceiling. Bookcases were arranged like the spokes of a wheel with a large circular table at the centre. The padded chairs arranged around the table looked rather more comfortable than the stool in Brother Ambrosius's office.

The old man added his candle to the candelabra standing in the centre of the table.

"Now then, let me find us a good bottle and then, what shall we discuss this fine evening?" Ambrosius said as he invited his friend to sit.

"Well... where should I begin?" Thanir was thinking out loud.

"I find the beginning is usually a good place."

"Would that I could. The beginning of this story is tangled within the mists of time."

Thanir frowned for a moment and then asked. "What do you know of the ancient, mythical Queen's Jewels?"

Chapter 9

"Help me out of here boy," The old man whispered as he clung to Fyr's arm with all the appearance of the frailty of great age. Fyr could feel the lie of it. They almost made it to the door before one of the three guards spoke.

"Do us all a favour boy and chuck that useless, weak-kneed old serf in a ditch on yer way 'ome… afore he pisses on yer feet… it'll rot yer boots quicker'n anyfin that will." The thuggish brute fell about laughing at his own wit.

Fyr and the old man almost made it outside but found their way barred by the broad girth of the largest of the three guards.

"Wassa matta wit' you boy? Our jokes not good enough for yer?"

"Beg pardon sir," Fyr kept his head down and his eyes on the man's heavy boots. "But Grandfather has been taken ill and I need to get him home."

"Ill?" Fyr sensed the man fold his arms and settle in for a contest of will and words. He was not moving. "'e ain't sick... had a bit too much o' the old sauce, I reckon. You wanna watch he don't puke on ya too." The huge man was almost doubled over now. "Go on... get outta here... just remember," he was not laughing now. "You serfs need to know your place in this new land."

"Yes sir," Fyr nodded rapidly, still keeping his head down and not entirely sure what he was agreeing to. The old man sagged on Fyr's arm and, stumbling and limping, they made their way out of the inn and down the lane to a small isolated cottage.

"Better come on in son," the old man said. As he opened the door, the smell almost knocked Fyr off his feet. The old man chuckled. "Bit ripe... but yer soon gets used to it and it keeps nosy neighbours away a treat."

Once Fyr had got his innards under control and managed to ignore the worst of the smell, he discovered that the ground floor of the house was more like a small barn. There was a scrawny brown cow, a couple of goats and several chickens pecking around at the rushes on the floor. The old man's living quarters were on an upper level that only made it halfway across the length of the building and a small fenced off area beside the hearth.

"You'd be surprised at how much heat them do give off. Saves on firewood... 'cep when I needs to cook." The old man's smile was a little sad now.

"Do you live here alone?" Fyr asked.

"No... I 'as me animals still... least... the few of 'em that's left."

"But you've no one to look after you? No family?"

"Not now. I 'ad me granddaughter 'ere for a while. Then the changes happened and she 'ad to go an' work up at the big 'ouse."

"Big house?"

The old man's eyes were far away and he carried on as though he had not heard Fyr.

"I used to 'ave some land. My son worked alongside me but they took 'im away first... then me land... all gone now apart from a little bit o' garden... so I can't grow much food now... an' they took away the common for that fortress so there's nowhere for me animals to graze." He patted the skinny old cow on its side. "I 'ad to bring 'em in 'ere or lose 'em. Still... I got a little bit o' milk an' a few eggs to barter..." It sounded to Fyr as though the old man had forgotten he was there and was talking to himself.

"Hey..." Fyr touched the old man's arm and he looked up in surprise, he had forgotten.

"Sorry lad, miles away." The old man blinked. "I know who you are. You're Fenyo's little brother aren't you?"

Fyr nodded.

"Good. My name is Barras. I'm the only other Elder left in this town. Most of the other's retreated to the mountains. There's Harac and his wife, Wilga in the next valley but they're ancient." Fyr decided it was best not to ask. If this old boy thought the others were ancient - just how old could they be?

"You said those men in the inn were soldiers for his Lordship. I don't understand who is this Lord? Lord of what?"

"Hedeon's 'is name," Barras whispered. "But not too loud now, he's got watchers an' listeners out all over the place. Can't be heard talking about him... or saying his name. T'was prob'ly a good idea that those soldiers didn't know who we were... who you were... you and your friends are the ones who went travellin' abroad ain't yer? You've seen the outside world. You know it's real. You know what's out there. That man and his followers are trying to say that there is nothing out there. They don't believe we was trapped in the dark lands of the doors. Us Elders, we were the keepers of the stories. We knew there was another place, we knew about the magic." He stopped speaking for a moment and Fyr wondered if he had forgotten what he was saying, but then he started again. "Long 'afore we was freed, there was some who were opposed to change of any sort. They was afraid of magic and wouldn't believe the evidence of their own eyes. They say it's impossible that we were freed by users of magic cos magic ain't real. They's the ones Himself 'as gathered about 'im."

"So how long has this been going on?" Fyr asked.

"Prob'ly far longer than we know. They managed to keep it quiet until it was too late for anyone to do anything. Oh, he wasn't doing anything illegal that we could tell. Not at first anyway. Listen boy, you've got to get a message to the outside world, maybe that King you went to see or the Great Mage. Someone needs to tell them what's going on." Barras's words were little more than a whisper.

"I know... I wish I could but I can't go now. I have to get to Kizzy. They're going to sell her." Fyr scrubbed at his face helplessly.

"Now, now lad, don't take on so. It's pointless either way. No one can travel anywhere without a permit, and they ain't givin' those to no one."

"But I've got to get to her village… let her father know what is happening… I've got to save her…"

"Needs a permit just to walk down the road to the market these days," Barras muttered as he pottered about gathering eggs from all the ledges and nesting boxes. He lowered his voice and Fyr had to lean in to hear him. "I might be able to do something… might have a contact who can get you a permit. I get a permit to take my eggs to the markets here and in the next village. If I was too ill to go… or maybe you can come and be my helper… he might be able to get you permit of your own. It'll only be as far as the next village, won't get you all the way but it'll get you out of 'ere."

Fyr followed the old man and helped him to gather the eggs, putting them into the basket of straw.

"Now, one step at a time, lad. What

about your friends at the inn. Maybe they could find a way out. They're not from round here are they? Prob'ly won't be missed as easily, most like."

Fyr was beginning to feel as though there was a plan forming, but there were an awful lot of hurdles in his way.

The wagon rumbled on for what felt like hours. From the sounds, they had passed through one village without stopping. Kesia had no idea what that village was but Loria thought it was her home. They had tried to get a look through the holes in the wall but they were too high, too small and too close to the ceiling.

"I thought that man said we had to go back to our home village," Kesia whispered.

"He did say that but I have a feeling they won't stop at my village because Farris will be there and we have friends…"

"Maybe they'll take us both to my village."

"Maybe…"

The wagon trundled slowly onward. Loria gave Kesia a wink and banged on the wall close to where she knew the driver would be.

"Hey... are we going to get any food or water? And I need to go... you know..."

The wagon slowed and then stopped. They heard someone moving, coming around to the door, then the sliding of the bolt and the door opened a crack. It was getting dark outside and there was not a lot to see beyond the grizzled face of the driver. Loria edged closer to the door.

"Please... I need to... you know..."

"You wanna pee? Here!" He shoved a bucket through the gap. "You'll get fed and watered when we get to the next stop." And the door was slammed and bolted.

"Charming!" Loria said prodding at the bucket with her toe.

"I can't use that in here," Kesia whimpered.

"No, me either. Let's hope it's not too far

to the next stop. Why don't we try and get some sleep?"

They lay down and closed their eyes. Kesia did not think she would be able to sleep but she did and when she awoke, she was alone in the wagon. Loria was gone. Having managed to hold off the tears for this long it had suddenly become too much and now she sobbed and they flowed freely. She did not think she would ever be able to stop.

Chapter 10

"Do you think Hob sent you to see Salamander for a reason then... other than a social visit?" Eleanor asked.

Simon shrugged his shoulders and slumped further into his himself. Eleanor had never seen him like this before. She turned to Marianne who dragged her concerned gaze from her husband to her friend with great difficulty.

"What do you think?" Eleanor asked.

"I think there was something but..." she frowned. "I haven't a clue what we talked about."

"Hmm, I wonder. Could that be deliberate or maybe it's a hangover from Dee's memory spell..." Eleanor murmured as she began searching through her kitchen cupboards.

"What're you looking for?" Bella asked. "I might be able to 'elp."

"Umm, not sure… but I'll know it when I find it," she muttered.

"Right oh! Not sure I can 'elp wiv that." Bella shrugged. "But shout if you need me."

Eleanor nodded distractedly.

"Ooh… tells you what though," Bella continued as a thought popped into her head.

Eleanor was not really paying any attention to the ghostly maid as tins and jars, bottles and boxes came out of the cupboard to be piled haphazardly on the worktop beside her.

"Sorry, what's that?"

Bella sighed. "I said I'll put the kettle on."

Marianne watched as the kettle floated to the kitchen sink, filled itself with water and returned to its seat. She groaned as the little blue light came on.

"Oh I couldn't possibly drink any more coffee."

"Tell 'er I ain't makin' coffee," Bella huffed. "I am makin' tea… fer 'im." Eleanor was the only one who could hear and see her right now… if she had been listening.

Eleanor stopped what she had been doing and turned to Bella.

"Sorry, what?" She snapped - a little more sharply than she intended.

"I got some talents too…" Bella crossed her arms in a defensive 'I'm not moving' stance. It was rather spoiled when the kettle boiled and she had to unfold her arms to pick up the tea caddy. She then reached up to the shelf and brought down a single teacup and saucer.

Eleanor frowned as she watched Bella but said nothing.

Bella gave the teapot a small swirl and poured the barely brewed tea into the cup.

Eleanor could not help herself. "That's a bit weak… and you forgot to use the tea-strainer…"

"Nope… it's fine," Bella gave her a knowing smile as she picked up the cup and saucer.

"What's this?" Simon asked as the

teacup appeared to float across the room and land gently on the table in front of him.

"Looks like it's for you," Marianne said, suppressing a smirk.

"Tell 'im," Bella said, "to sip it slowly and carefully down to the dregs."

"Why don't you make yourself visible and tell him yourself?" Eleanor said, trying not to sound impatient.

"Sounds better coming from you."

"What does?"

"All that witchy stuff," Bella wrinkled her nose. "Sorry, prob'ly shouldn't have called it witchy." Still, she did what Eleanor asked and made herself visible to Simon and Marianne. She bobbed them a little curtsey and gave Simon a nervous smile. "You're the gard'ner chap, ain'tcha?"

"Yes..." Simon acknowledged cautiously. Not really knowing what he was owning up to.

"Don't know if you're s'posed to be upstairs or downstairs. See, bein' Miss Eleanor's friend an' all that makes you upstairs... but you's trade too..." She gave a nod as though she had decided something. "So you can be downstairs and that makes it alright to do this, don't it?"

"Err?" Simon looked to Eleanor to explain but she just shook her head and looked just as confused as he felt.

Bella was looking at him earnestly, obviously waiting for his answer.

"Okay... I guess I can be downstairs..." He saw Marianne's smile out of the corner of his eye.

Bella nodded. "Good... I c'n read the tea-leaves for ya, see? Well, I used to... Cook and some of the other girls used to get me to do it for 'em." She sounded a little apologetic now but Simon nodded so she carried on. "Right, so, you 'ave to drink the tea slowly until there's only a little drop left in the bottom... and don't go swallerin' any o' the grouts cos it makes the reading wonky."

"Am I allowed a splash of milk in it or will

that make the reading wonky too?" He smiled to show he was teasing then did as instructed and sipped, slowly and carefully at the weak brew while Eleanor went back to her cupboards with more purpose.

"This should do," Eleanor said and placed the box, she had just found, on the table. She paused for moment in thought before dashing out of the room muttering, "Oh, I know..." They could hear her rummaging around in one of the many small rooms in the passage beyond the kitchen, and came back in with a large department store carrier bag. Rather more mundane than magical at first glance.

"I knew this would come in handy one of these days."

"What is it?" Marianne asked.

Eleanor pulled a woven willow hoop from the bag.

"Okay... and what's that for?" Simon asked, peering at it askance. He was beginning to feel a little out of his depth and miles away from his comfort zone.

"I was going to use it make a Christmas wreath for the front door one year but never quite got around to it," Eleanor smiled. "So I'm going to make you a sort of dream catcher."

"Have you finished that tea yet?" Bella demanded.

"Nearly..." His eyes flitted between Bella and Eleanor. "You got any idea what they're up to?" He thought to Marianne.

"Not a clue," she thought back.

Eleanor began binding small bundles of dried flowers and herbs to the hoop with green ribbon.

"Need a hand, sweetie?" Marianne asked.

Eleanor was grateful and handed her some of the flowers.

"Chamomile, lavender and rosemary," Marianne noted approvingly. "Although, we've tried the first two several times already without much success... but not like this," she added hurriedly.

"So I was thinking, poor sleep could be the cause of you not dreaming properly, although it could be the other way round. Either way, it seems to me that you've got yourself into a bit of a vicious circle. I think there's a blockage and your magical fuel tank, for want of a better word, is running on fumes," Eleanor tried to explain.

"Magical… no… I don't have any magic… I'm not like you and Marianne," Simon gasped at the ludicrous idea.

"Of course you have magic my love," Marianne stroked his arm. "Why do you think they call you the Forest Mage?"

"Yes, but…"

"You have power over all the green, growing things. Believe me other gardeners, even those with green thumbs, can't do what you do."

He still looked a little sceptical until Marianne laughed and said.

"Simon, your mother is a dryad for goodness sake."

"Ah… yes… I hadn't thought of that…"

Eleanor picked up her train of thought again. "It's all about balance and harmony. When we dream, it recharges our psychic batteries. Dreams can also show us the different paths before us, letting us walk them in the dream-world to try them out before we have to face these things for real if you like. This is all in our subconscious of course and most people aren't even aware of it – magic tends to make us see things a little differently. I think that whatever's causing this blockage, it's preventing you from seeing all your options and might even be pushing you towards a path that you wouldn't normally take, given free-will."

"Right… I'm not sure I understood any of that…" He glanced at Bella out of the corner of his eye. It was difficult to concentrate on what Eleanor was saying with the ghostly maid hovering at his elbow, quivering with anticipation. He gave his tea another sip.

Opening the box that she put on the

table, Eleanor showed them that it was full of candles: all different colours, shapes and sizes. She picked out two tall candles, one green and one white and a small purple, lavender scented tea-light.

"Okay Bella, is this enough?" Simon asked, picking a tealeaf from the tip of his tongue.

Bella nodded and took a seat opposite Simon. Looking up she asked, "Is it alright if I say a little prayer 'fore we start, Miss Eleanor? Cook used to insist before we did a reading and it wouldn't feel right doin' it wivout."

"Of course, Bella. Nice idea. Tell you what, let's light this candle too." Eleanor held up the green candle, flicked her fingers and transferred the little flame that appeared on the tip of her index finger to the wick. "Green is the colour that represents the earth and things that grow within it. We've got green ribbon and a green candle… it's a shame we haven't got some green crystal or stone too. It might add…"

"How about these?" Marianne asked as she took out her earrings. "They were my grandmother's... her birthstones... peridot I think it's called."

"Perfect." Eleanor put the candle into the holder, placed an earring on each side and set it on the table between Simon and Bella. "Okay Bella, say your prayer."

Bella gave a small nod, closed her eyes, bowed her head and put her hands together.

"Dear Lord, Guide this man's hand to turn the cup. I pray it shows his fortunes up. Amen." She looked up at Simon. "I know it ain't much, but they always said it 'elped. Now, put the saucer over the cup... like this. Give it a good swirl then tip them both over together." She mimed the actions with her hands. "Now turn the cup on the saucer thirteen times, clockwise. Mind you count carefully."

Simon did as he was told and then looked up at Bella to see what to do next.

"Now, carefully turn the cup the right way up and pass it to me." Bella took the cup and cradled it between her hands, peering inside and turning the cup this way and that until eventually she gave a nod and looked up at him.

"So can you actually see anything in there?" Simon asked.

Marianne peered over Bella's shoulder. Wet tea leaves stuck around the inside of the cup in messy clots. She had no idea what she was looking at.

"Right," Bella said. "We always start at the bottom of the cup cos that's going to be about the distant future. It tells you where you're going. Then we work up to the top to see how you're goin' to get there. The bit nearest the top of the cup is right now or maybe it's som'fin that's already 'appened." She looked up to check that they were with her then peered closely into the cup again. "Right there see?" she pointed to the blobs at the base of the cup. "There's a tree... and that looks like an acorn... so it must be an oak tree."

"Alsea's tree is an oak," Marianne said quietly.

Bella nodded. "Oak trees are a good omen; means good fortune, long life and happy marriage." She held up a silencing finger before Marianne or Simon could speak. "Ah! See that there on the side? If it's high on the side, it means it's the near future. That looks like an anvil... you know... one of those things the blacksmith uses...?"

They all nodded. They knew what an anvil was, but none of them could see it the way Bella did.

"...and those are bees..."

Marianne tried again. No, she could not see an anvil or bees but wait... what was...

"Are those footprints?"

Bella turned the cup to look it the blobs from Marianne's point of view.

"Yep, looks like feet to me. But... the anvil and bees..." Bella was not going to be moved from her own reading order. "So this is going to happen soon. It says you 'ave a lot o' friends and you'll be working together because of your special strength and energy. Your labours will meet with great success." She flicked a quick glance to Marianne who was now furiously scribbling down what Bella was saying. "Now, those feet..." She looked back at Simon to make sure he was paying attention. "You will be called upon to walk a certain path – you have to make a decision that's going to lead to great changes in your life. And that bit there..." she pointed to the last remaining blob that looked like it was trying climb out of the top of the cup. "It's a great worm."

"A worm?" Simon asked.

"Not a worm like an earthworm... it's another name for a dragon," Bella said.

"A dragon... I'm going to see a dragon? And why not!" Simon decided he should not really be surprised by anything these days.

"No, not a real actual dragon. Dragons just mean there'll be something a bit tricky and maybe even a little bit dangerous… doesn't mean it's bad though," she added hurriedly.

"That's good… but how can something be a little bit dangerous?" Simon asked.

"Right, so this," Bella said, as she tapped the edge of the cup, "is happening now… or very soon. The footsteps are heading towards the dragon so whatever choice you have to make, that's got to happen soon too and there are going to be great changes in your life."

"So what does that all mean when you put it together?" Marianne asked. Simon had gone very quiet. She could not even hear him though their link.

"So to find out what it means we have to read it backwards – top to bottom," Bella said. Marianne wrote down everything she said.

"The dragon here says you have to face great changes and a little bit o' danger quite soon. You have to make a choice that will change things - not just for you but your friends too... that's the bees, remember? ... But, and this is good. There are good omens for a long and happy life."

"What about... didn't you say something about a happy marriage?" Marianne worried at her fingernail with her teeth.

"Yes, right there, at the bottom of the cup... the acorn and the oak tree... it stands for long life and happy marriage."

"Just... not... with me?" Marianne whispered.

Simon leapt to his feet knocking his chair over. "Marianne... What? No! Why would you think that? Of course it's you... it's always you... it has to be..."

"But it was at the bottom of the cup... in your future..."

They both looked at Bella. This was only tea leaves... not real... old wives tales... who believed in things like this these days? But then... they were in Eleanor's house where strange things happened.

"Maybe it's all part of the change or one of the decisions you have to make," Bella said with a shrug. The she looked up sadly at Marianne and then a smile spread across her face. "I don't think you need to worry about your marriage. What's that you are wearing around your neck?"

Marianne's hand went to the delicate gold chain to her throat and around her neck... and the tiny gold acorn Alsea had given her. It was a talisman; something to bring Simon back to her the first time he had visited Aldamar.

"Of course it's you. That decision was made many moons ago an' I don't see it changing. Whatever the change is, it's sumfin new and it's comin' soon... I see some danger, but it'll all work out happily in the end." And with Bella's final nod, Eleanor felt the magic click into place.

Chapter 11

"The Queen's jewels?" Ambrosius repeated. "That rings a bell but I'm not sure why." He scratched his head which made his white hair stand up in tufts.

"Could you check all your archives for any mention of the Queen's jewels please?"

"Any mention at all? From all the archives?" Ambrosius's eyebrows did a little dance as he tried to make sure that he understood what Thanir was asking him. He was not sure Thanir understood the enormity of the task but he agreed "Very well." He closed his eyes and said. "We wish to find any mention of the Queen's jewels, from every source within all of the Brotherhood's archives."

For a while, nothing happened and Thanir was beginning to wonder if this had been a fool's quest but very slowly, one by one, books, scrolls and odd pieces of parchment began to materialise on the table before them. It started slowly with neat piles of books and bundles of scrolls but very soon, they found themselves darting around the table trying to intercept the ever growing heaps of documentary evidence before they slid to the floor in an avalanche of paper.

"Can't you make it stop?" Thanir shouted from the other side of the table.

"You told me to ask for all mentions from every source. If we stop now we might miss something important," Ambrosius grunted as he heaved yet another pile of books back onto the table.

It was nearly two hours later that the last of the documents finally arrived. The two men were exhausted.

"I had no idea there would be quite so much," Thanir said as they surveyed the muddled mess. "Lady Aurelia seemed to be the only person aware of them, so I rather assumed that there would not be very much..." he gazed at the confusion around them.

"There is a reason why people say be careful what you wish for…" Ambrosius said from behind yet another teetering pile of books. "Oh I do wish these books would…" He began to complain but stopped himself before he accidently said the wrong thing, especially after his words to Thanir only moments before. He paused for thought and said. "I wish these documents would sort themselves in an orderly, tidy and logical manner."

No sooner had he spoken than there was an almighty thunder clap, like a great flock of birds taking flight. Books, scrolls, pieces of paper and parchment flew through the air with such speed and confusion that Thanir and Ambrosius had to take shelter beneath the table.

"I'm sorry old friend," Thanir apologised.

"Sorry for what? Giving us both a little more excitement than we're used to?"

At Ambrosius's words, a strange little shiver shimmied through Thanir as the inexplicable image of the Lady Sylvestri popped into his head. This was neither the time nor the place to be thinking about her, he told himself.

"Are you going to explain what this is that we've started here?" Ambrosius asked.

For a long moment, Thanir did not answer. He was still caught up with the images in his head.

"Thanir?"

Ambrosius finally got a response. "Sorry… what?"

"A little explanation might be helpful about now."

"Do you think it has stopped?" Thanir blinked, crawled to the edge of the table and peered out.

"It has gone very quiet," Ambrosius agreed.

Thanir slowly edged his way forward. Nothing fell on him, nothing flapped around his head so he carried on cautiously until he could stand.

"Oof!" Ambrosius grumbled as he

followed his friend. "I really am getting too old for this..." Ambrosius muttered as he accepted Thanir's assistance in getting back to his feet. He stretched and straightened up with much huffing and puffing.

"You don't have to do that for my benefit," Thanir said. He knew very well that his friend was probably stronger and fitter than most men a fraction of his age, but that was another story. "Well, you did ask for order and logic," Thanir said as they both looked at the table where the magic had sorted everything, putting multiple copies of the same text together. "This should speed up our search. At least we won't have to look through twenty copies of the same book."

"Ah! Possibly true but..." Ambrosius rubbed his chin, deep in thought. "I think we might still have to look through every book, even if they look the same on the outside. There may be annotated copies or... remember Queen Orlagh's book within a book? She hid her secret story within the mundane text of a household journal."

Thanir sighed and nodded, feeling slightly defeated. "I hadn't thought of that and I have a feeling that this story is going to take us back further than Queen Orlagh."

The two men slumped into chairs and stared at the mountain of documents. Even with the piles sorted and tidy, they had no idea where to start.

"You are going to have to tell me a bit more about these jewels. It might help to sort the wheat from the chaff." Ambrosius was no more eager to search through page by page than Thanir was.

"You recall His Majesty's foreign cousins?"

"The Lady Eleanor and Prince James, the ones who freed the Elven magic and brought it back to Faerie? Aye, I remember..."

"Recently, His Majesty had a brief visit from friends of theirs. They came to return property that rightly belonged to the Crown which had been stolen more than... well...

possibly millennia ago."

"Ah! A bit before my time then," Ambrosius said with a chuckle.

"Quite so," Thanir nodded seriously. "This... property came in three black velvet bags. His Majesty is eager to find out anything he can before he feels safe allowing the Queen to wear any of it. One of the bags held a pair of arm bands." He patted at his upper arm. "She tried those on very briefly, without any harmful effects. And, I believe the other two bags held a large torc and a finely wrought circlet or small crown with blue stones which are probably sapphires."

"I see... do you have any idea what metal these pieces are made from?"

"A white metal, shiny... There is no iron in the construction because Their Majesties were both able to handle them.

"So... silver most likely..." Ambrosius did that chin rub again. His thought processes were turning over ideas almost too rapidly. "Do you know if there are any crests or engravings?"

"I heard mention of moonstones and bloodstones but I don't know for certain." Thanir blushed slightly at having admitted to eavesdropping on Their Majesties.

"And what about the people who delivered these pieces, do you know anything more about them?"

"As I said, they are friends of Lady Eleanor. I believe the four ladies called themselves witches which is something akin to our Maení. There was also a group of men in the party. They carried themselves like warriors, guardians to the ladies, I think. They all appeared to be known to the Lady Sylvestri and I am certain she could tell you more about them."

"The Lady Sylvestri…" Ambrosius delved into his vast memory but could not put a face to the name. "I am not sure I know this person. Is she new to Faerie?"

"Oh my no… she has been…" Thanir's voice became a little tight and his cheeks turned a delicate shade of red.

"Are you all right?" Ambrosius had never seen his friend so out of sorts.

"Oh... yes... The Lady is also known as the Queen of the Four Winds. She is the Elemental of the Air."

"An Elemental... now that is something new... I should very much like to meet this lady. You look a little pale old friend. Are you ill or is there something amiss with the Lady Sylvestri?"

"Oh, no... not at all... she's very um... very..."

"Very what? Why are you squeaking?"

"I do not squeak," he said indignantly. "It's just... I um..."

"There you go, squeaking again. Spit it out man."

Thanir took a deep breath so that he could get all the words out. "She is very beautiful and whenever she is around I seem to trip over my own tongue."

Ambrosius was tempted to continue teasing his friend... only gently... but it would be unkind. So he cleared his throat.

"Well, I should like to meet this lady that has you so out of sorts but maybe we should pick a text each and see what we may discover before someone comes looking for me." He would return to the topic of the Lady - at a later date.

Chapter 12

Kesia lay very still in the straw that had been strewn over the floor as though she was little better than an animal. The holes in the wagon were so small that they let in very little light but by the time the wagon came to a stop there was no light at all in her little cell. The darkness was suffocating and she had lost track of time. It took her a moment to realise that the voices were getting louder which meant they were coming closer. Maybe they were going to let her out now.

The door opened and a man stood holding a flaming torch.

"Come on, out you get. You're home." The smile he gave her was not friendly and her heart sank as she discovered that although they were now in her home village, they had not taken her to her home. They had pulled up outside a large, two storey house that stood on the outer edge of the village. When she had last been there, this had been an open field with sheep grazing on it.

"My house is just over there. My father will be there. He'll be worrying about me," she said.

"You should've thought of that before you went off running about the countryside and getting yourself into trouble."

"What do you mean trouble?" Did these people know about the demon? She shuddered at the thought.

"Please, could I see my father?"

"It's too late now. He'll most likely be abed. It's time all good citizens were tucked up nice and cosy. Come on, this way." He grabbed her arm and dragged her around the side of the building.

In the light of the torch, she could see that the fancy brickwork had been reserved for the front of the building. The rest of it was a ramshackle mess of timber and wattle. Most of the walls had been plastered with daub, but not all. It looked rougher than even the most run-down of the village hovels. It was odd to notice all these things she thought as the man dragged her along.

They came to a door at the back of the building. It was tucked in between two single storey lean-tos that had been added on. The door opened into a hallway that led straight to the front door. Why had they not come in that way? That was where the wagon still stood.

"People come in the front door, goods come in the back," the man said in answer to her question.

"Goods?"

"Things... food, furniture, goods to be bought and sold," he chuckled and squeezed her arm a little harder. "This way."

He gave her a shove towards a dark staircase and she stumbled.

"Watch it," he grumbled. "We don't want damaged goods... gotta get the best price we can."

Kesia was holding her breath so that she did not let out the sob that wanted to escape.

It would only open her up to more ridicule. This was surely a nightmare and she would wake up soon. This could not really be happening. People did not buy and sell other people.

Fyr visited Barras every day for a week. He milked the cow and the goats and collected the eggs. He accompanied Barras to the local market and helped him to sell his meagre wares. While they were at the market, Barras put on quite a show, coughing as though his lungs were failing and complaining about the need to rest, all the while praising Fyr.

"Don't know what I'd do without 'im right now..." he told any one that would listen. "Prob'ly be dead an' me poor cow gone un-milked. I couldn't 'ave got to market wi'out 'im."

The next day Fyr took Barras's goods to the market, alone.

"What's up with Old Barras?" a few people asked.

"Where's the old bugger today?"

someone else asked.

"Is he not feeling any better then?" others said.

One or two people gave Fyr sidelong glances and muttered behind their hands. They were probably wondering if he had done the old man in so he could steal his pitch at the market. But by the end of the week, Fyr had been accepted in Barras's place.

It was the last day of the week and Barras had already warned Fyr that the Market Official always did his rounds on Saturn's day. They had a story ready; Barras was an old friend of the family and had been ill. Fyr was running the stall as a favour, just to help him out. It was not a lie but a massaged truth. Barras and Fenyo had been Town Elders together for many years. Sadly though, Fyr knew that Barras's illness was real. The old man was beginning to look frailer by the day.

On Sun's day, there was no market but the animals still needed tending and so Fyr arrived at Barras's house at the usual time. The old man was still up on his sleeping platform. He could not manage to get down his ladder. Halfway through the milking, the old man stopped talking and started snoring. He had obviously gone back to sleep but Fyr did not like the rattle he could hear in his breathing.

"Are you sure he's eating properly?" Frea asked later, while they ate their evening meal.

"Maybe we should invite him to eat with us," Fenyo suggested.

"I don't think he would come," Fyr told them. He liked the curmudgeonly old man. "He thinks if he leaves his house for too long someone will steal it out from under him, steal his animals or worse burn it all to the ground. He's beginning to talk about not going to market."

"Surely not," Frea said.

Fenyo reached out to hold his wife's hand with a sad look. "It's not just an old man's fears these days. It's already happened to a few who got on the wrong side of…"

Frea knew who he meant. It was not a good idea to say the man's name out loud.

"Only two days ago, I heard about a family over in the next village evicted from the house their family had built and lived in for generations, for non-payment of tithes that they didn't even know they had to pay."

"Tithes? Since when did people start paying tithes?" Fyr demanded in a hoarse whisper.

Fenyo gave a shrug. "Quite a while now. It crept in while we were looking elsewhere, apparently. We have been given notice to move out of this house." Fenyo's firm hand on his brother's arm stopped him from launching himself out of his seat. "This house was built as an Elder House. We Elders no longer have a function within society apparently, so the house will be put up for sale. We could try to buy it back but I doubt we'll be able to afford it."

Fyr looked from his brother to his sister-in-law. Her expression told him that she already knew and, like her husband, was resigned to their fate.

"But where will you go? What will you do? You've two small children."

"I know..." Fenyo sighed. "I am expecting to be called very soon. Frea and the children will stay with her parents for a while..."

"Wait... called for what?" Fyr demanded. He did not like where this conversation was going.

"Most of the men in the town will be called soon... you'll get the call too... to train."

"Train for what... you're a farmer, I'm a carpenter... what are we training for?"

"To fight. Everyone has to be prepared to defend the land for their local Knight or follow him into battle." Fenyo said as Frea hid her face in her hands. "All men of sixteen years and above are to be trained in the art of battle," Fenyo quoted.

"Art of battle..." Fyr gasped. "Who are we going to fight, each other?"

"Possibly. I thank the Powers that be that

Bor isn't yet old enough," Fenyo said. "Married women, children, the old and the sick will not be called upon to fight but unmarried women are being called too, to work the fields and in the Noble houses."

"Yes," Frea said when Fyr looked aghast. "And we married women are expected to take over and do all the jobs our men used to do in addition to our own work. It's completely ridiculous of course," Frea whispered.

"Are they really going to expect the Blacksmith's wife to take over at the forge? Have you see the size of him? And she's so tiny, most of his hammers are bigger than she is," Fenyo said.

"I saw her at the market the other day. She said they're not going to take him away but she said he's not happy about it. They have him making strange things; small rings that link together and metal plates that make protective garments. He used to make plough blades, kitchen knives and cooking pots but now they have him making blades whose only purpose is to maim and kill people. We used to be able to take things for him to repair but his new assistants, more like guards, are so rude and turn people away. He's too busy, they say. Everything is changing. I almost wish we'd never been rescued." Tears ran down her face.

"You don't mean that, my love." Fenyo wrapped and arm around her shoulder.

"No... I don't... not really," she sniffed.

"According to the old man," Fyr was loath to use Barras's name for fear of being overheard. "All of this began long before the Forest Mage came and saved us. He said most of the older Elders were persuaded to retire to the hills and pass their houses and land onto these others... these Knights. It seems as though these Knights are all friends of the same man. These are the same people that want to turn you out now I don't doubt." Fyr said.

"I still don't know what they want all this training for. Or why the smith is making weapons and metal clothes," Frea said. "Did you know the tanner and the cobbler are both working with the smith too? They're making heavy boots that would be no good to a farmer, far too heavy... and other straps and contraptions to go with the metal garments and weapons. But there's children having to go barefoot because they say there's not enough leather to make shoes. I don't understand."

"Armour, weapons, boots... training all the men to fight and kill. I don't understand this either," Fyr said. "Who are we supposed to be fighting? We've always been peaceful... farmers, shepherds, helping our neighbours. If there's a dispute, it's discussed and debated."

"There are whispers that some people refuse to believe in a world beyond our borders, never mind other worlds... and there are those who do believe but fear what might be coming from outside," Fenyo explained.

"But of course there's an outside and there are whole other worlds outside. Why would anyone think they would be hostile?" Fyr said.

"This is the fear that he is using to stoke the embers... that someone might come here and try to take over our lives... to change the way we've done things for years," Fenyo told him.

Fyr could not help it. He just had to laugh. "Are these people so blind that they can't see what is right in front of them? This is precisely what is happening? Only, it's happening from the inside."

Chapter 13

Marianne had made a note of everything Bella had said and then read through it several times but she could not make any sense of it. Now Eleanor was going to use her magic to help Simon. He needed to get some sleep before he could face whatever danger or challenge Bella had seen in the tea leaves. She knew he needed to make certain those magical batteries or his psychic fuel tank or whatever analogy she could think of was recharged.

"Are you sure you don't mind us staying over?" Marianne asked.

"Of course it's fine," Eleanor assured her. "And it's not as though we haven't got enough rooms. Come and take your pick."

"Shame you can't just plug me into the mains and charge me up like a phone," Simon said with small chuckle.

"Don't tempt me," Marianne smiled.

"That reminds me..." She held her hand out. "Come on, hand it over."

With a quick roll of his eyes, Simon reached into his pocket and took out his phone. She turned it off and handed it to Bella. "Please hide it somewhere safe, sweetie." She turned back to Simon. "Anyone needing their hedge trimming or a lawn mowing or tree pruning will just have to leave you a message and wait until you're feeling better."

"I don't want to lose customers or business," he protested. "They might decide to go to someone else."

"Don't be daft. They all know how good you are. Why would they go to someone else?"

Simon shrugged and followed the women up the stairs.

The room he chose was on the first floor overlooking the garden. They had slept there before, so it was familiar.

Eleanor set out the things she had brought up from the kitchen. "After we've performed the spell you should use some of this." Eleanor handed Marianne a small piece of paper, two small, dark brown bottles and a larger bottle of clear liquid.

"What is all that?" Simon wanted to know as he tried to read over Marianne's shoulder. "More potions?"

"No, this one's a lotion," Marianne said.

"It's one of Emma's recipes," Eleanor said.

"Oh no, not one of her teas?" Simon made a gagging noise. "I saw what happened to Dee after they gave him some."

"No," Eleanor laughed. "It's just a body lotion. The small bottles are lavender and chamomile oils. Marianne can add what she needs and the massage will help you relax."

"That sounds okay," Simon conceded. "Come on then, let's get this over with."

Eleanor cast a protective circle on the bedroom floor and once they were seated inside, placed the lavender scented candle between them and lit it. She took a deep, cleansing breath and began the spell to help Simon sleep and dream.

"I light this candle to aid my sight,

My will doth seek a restful night.

Set free the mind that's unknowingly bound,

And find the path to sleep unwound."

Eleanor then handed Simon the white candle.

"In passing through this circle round,

Your dreams, unseen, shall soon be found.

Betwixt the worlds and lost in thought,

Dreaming and drowsing, the power is sought."

Eleanor stood and held the hoop of willow over his head.

"With this circle the barriers will fall,

To sleep, to dream, heed my call.

Audio, Speculor Dormio et Somnio.

(Hear, see, sleep and dream)

As I will, so mote it be."

Simon stood, slowly within the hoop and

stepped out as Eleanor ended the spell.

"I'll leave you now. Don't forget to use the calming lotion. Sweet dreams." She smiled at them both and left. There was a charge in the air as Marianne cast her own spell for silence. She was not going to let anything distract Simon.

After Eleanor had left Simon followed the instructions and hung the willow hoop above the bed like a giant dream catcher... maybe that's what it is, he thought. He bent down and removed his shoes and socks and dug his toes into the deep carpet pile. It was not quite the same as grass or soil under his feet but it was always a relief to walk around barefoot.

"Come and lay here," Marianne said as she plumped the pillows. It was not that they needed plumping but it gave her something to do.

"Are you sure the door's locked?" Simon waited for her nod and then stripped down to his bare skin.

"Don't you be looking at me like that woman. I'm supposed to be getting some sleep." Marianne knew his quip was to cover his growing sense of unease.

What if the spell doesn't work? What if it does? Will I dream… or have nightmares? His thoughts bombarded her.

Hush, my love. It will be fine, she assured him and joined in with the gentle self-mockery. "I can look at my man." She tried for a pout but she could not help grinning. "Okay, look," she swept her hands down her body. "See? Fully clothed and intending to stay that way."

"Spoil-sport," he returned her mock-pout.

"Behave. Come and lie down." She peeled the covers back and Simon climbed onto the bed. Marianne sat on the bed at his side. "Turn over."

Simon wriggled and stretched to get as comfortable as he could on his stomach. Marianne poured some of the now lavender and chamomile scented oil into her hand and rubbed them together before spreading it across his shoulders and down his back. He closed his eyes and felt himself sinking into the bed as a feeling of deep relaxation and peace settled over him.

"That smells nice." His words were beginning to slur as he drifted off.

Marianne continued to massage his back until she was sure that he was fast asleep. She pulled the covers over him and then she walked around to the other side of the bed and, still fully clothed, climbed up beside him. She was certain he was fast asleep when he turned onto his side and spooned himself around her.

"Sn...mr...crs..." he murmured against her neck. Not real words but Marianne understood and smiled at the image she received from his drowsing mind... something to do with her having too many clothes on.

"Down boy." She sent back. "Go to sleep my darling. I'll still be here when you wake."

Downstairs, Eleanor was curled up in her old wing-backed chair with her shawl draped around her. She knew the spell was working because she could feel the draw on her power. It was more than she was used to all in one go. The cold set in first. She pulled the shawl tighter about her and tried to tuck her cold feet up under it. The drain began as a tingle that started in her fingertips, weakness creeping up her arms until her mind felt woolly and confused. The spell continued to draw on her power reserves and she knew she should be doing something to counter it but she could not move; her limbs felt like wet spaghetti. It was an odd sensation, she was aware of her body shutting down to conserve energy. She needed to move now, before she passed out.

As she tried to uncurl her body and lever herself out of the chair, a wave of dizziness and nausea washed over her knocking her back. She closed her eyes and breathed deeply until the feeling began to subside but now she could not move at all. Maybe if she just leaned her head here and kept her eyes closed...

... Need to go to sleep... no, mustn't... not a good idea...

"Eleanor... Eleanor... can you hear me? Wake up darling... Eleanor".

"Miss Eleanor..."

"Come on darling... open your eyes for me... time to wake up now..."

"Goway..." She managed to get her mouth to move but the sound barely registered, and she was not sure whether she had spoken them aloud or just thought them. She just wanted the dream voices to go away and leave her alone but they would not go away.

"Miss Eleanor... you need to wake up..." Oh, did that sound like Bella?

"Come on darling... open your eyes for me..." a man's voice... James? They were getting repetitive.

Why wouldn't they go away and let her sleep?

"Here drink some of this..." Maybe she

wasn't dreaming after all. Something cold touched her lips... a glass... cold liquid... She managed to move her tongue just enough to taste the sweet fruit juice. That was good... she hadn't realised how thirsty she was. She managed a tiny sip, then another until she was able to lift her hand and hold the glass herself.

"That's it Miss Eleanor... Drink it all up." That was Bella... and the other voice? Her fuzzy brain registered that it really was James. But what was he doing here? He was at work. What time was it? Had he come home early? Had she been asleep all afternoon?

She managed to open her eyes just a little and moved her mouth into a smile for him. It took energy.

"I had to come home. I felt you... you were fading... slipping away from me..." he told her. He picked her up out of the chair, turned and sat down with her cradled in his arms.

"I'll just pop to the kitchen and make you both a nice cup of tea...and some sandwiches. Might even be able to find you a bit of cake... Bit o' sugar, it's good for shock they do say." Bella's voice grew further away as she left the room on her errand.

"What were you doing?" he asked quietly.

"A spell... to help Simon and Marianne... didn't know it was going to be this big though..." she managed to whisper.

"As soon as you've had something to eat, you'll feel better. Is the spell still active?" he asked. Eleanor nodded. "I know you're strong my love but this isn't Faerie or Aldamar. There isn't enough background magic left in this world for you to draw on for such a big spell." He spoke gently, not wanting to scold.

"I know but I thought being here in the house, it would be enough. I didn't realise it would need so much... it's only a sleep spell... to aid his dreams."

"Ah I see... that might be the problem. A sleep spell on its own would stop drawing once it had done its job and sent the person to sleep. But this is going to continue to draw on your power with every dream he has. I'm here with you now. I can help."

"Okay," she agreed.

"But first... you eat," James said as Bella appeared with an enormous tray of sandwiches, scones and jam. "And then we go to bed," he whispered as Bella left the room.

Chapter 14

Thanir and Ambrosius spent the rest of the night reading through almost as many different versions of the story as there were books. So far, every single one had been written as a children's story. There was no evidence of fact or historical accuracy as far as they could see. Some were written with simple language and large print for children to read. Other versions were obviously meant to be read as bedtime stories by an adult or older child. Some of the texts even had pictures, but none bore any resemblance to the real jewels. So, thus far, they had found nothing. Of course that was not to say they would not eventually find a historical document. There was so much more material to wade through yet.

"Maybe you could try another spell to weed out the stories and concentrate on historical accuracy," Thanir suggested.

"Possibly so, but even that could be

biased depending on who wrote it and for what reason," Ambrosius sighed. "Besides, I'm not sure I could take another paper storm like the last time."

Both men looked up in surprise as a large, sonorous bell tolled in the distance.

"Oh my, can that really be the time?" Ambrosius put a ribbon in the book he had been reading and placed it carefully on the table. "I must leave at once. If I don't appear at morning devotions, they'll think I've died in my sleep and send someone to check. Please, stay if you wish but it can get very lonely down here on your own."

"I had no idea… we've been here all night? I must leave too and attend upon His Majesty."

Ambrosius stretched and yawned loud and long.

"Will you be able to stay awake for your devotions?" Thanir asked.

"Doesn't matter. They already think I'm a doddery old fool. They won't be terribly surprised if I fall asleep. I often do and someone will nudge me if I snore too loudly." Ambrosius managed to hold off another yawn.

When Thanir arrived back at the castle, the Great Hall was filled with people and noise: talking, rattling cutlery and the clatter of crockery. The King sat up on the dais with his family and their guests, breaking their fast while his people were seated at the long tables that ranged down the length of the hall. This was not the time to bother Their Majesties with his current frustration at finding nothing in the archives. There were other duties to attend to. He would revisit Brother Ambrosius later.

Thanir realised there was someone missing from the long table up on the dais. Just as the thought crossed his mind, a warm breath caressed the back of his neck.

"Hello darling," the voice purred and he almost tripped over his own feet as he spun on his heel. Sylvestri grabbed him by the arm to stop him falling.

"Beg pardon, mi' lady," he did his best

not to stammer.

"There's no need to beg my pardon, darling." She smiled at him, partly because she wanted to but mostly because she was still holding on to his arm and he hadn't noticed or pulled away. "Have you been up all night?" she asked him. She had watched him go into the old historian's house and had kept watch until he had re-appeared a short while ago.

"Yes ma'am."

"Did you find what you were looking for?"

"No ma'am."

"You should get some sleep. You look tired. Let me explain to His Majesty. And by the way, I am not a ma'am, nor a mi lady, far from it," Sylvestri said with a sad smile.

Thanir eyes grew round as he wracked his brain to see if there was another title that he might have forgotten. She was known as the Queen of the Four winds so… Your Majesty? Your Highness? Your Grace?

"Thanir?"

"Yes m..."

She stopped him with a finger to his lips. He did not move. "People may call me the Queen of the Four Winds but it is merely a pretension left over from my predecessor. Yes, I have the honour to be the Air Elemental," she said before he could interrupt. "But, underneath all that, really I am no one, just a woman."

"Yes Miss," he said against her finger. She smiled at him and moved her hand. She could see he did not believe her and the sudden urge to tell her story came from nowhere.

"The realm into which I was born was not pleasant. They called it a city but it was little more than a ramshackle collection of worm-eaten, rat-infested wooden houses all leaning one upon another. If one had fallen, all the others would have followed. Houses loomed over streets which rarely saw sunlight and ran thick with mud and ... worse. They politely called it night soil as they threw it out of their upstairs windows or their front door, but if it looks like shit and it smells like shit... it is shit. You really had to watch your head and where you put your feet. In my case, bare feet."

Thanir looked shocked. She was not sure whether it had been her language or the idea of her running around barefoot, but he held his tongue and nodded for her to continue. Sylvestri took a deep breath.

"Why don't we go and sit somewhere quiet? This could take a while," she smiled. This was it. She was going to do something she had never done before and tell someone her truth... all of it.

"I was the youngest of nine children and I was named Nonus. Not much of a name at all, it just means number nine. I was just another mouth to feed, another body to clothe and a girl so... surplus to requirements. At six, they said I had become too difficult because I asked too many questions that they could not answer. My parents were not bad people, just very poor and uneducated.

"There was an Abbey just outside the city. It was dedicated to some saint or other, I don't really remember, but the Abbey offered a school with board and lodgings. Every year someone from the Abbey would come to the city and round up all the unwanted children, the ones living on the streets and the ones their families could no longer cope with, like me.

"We were expected to work to earn our keep, just small tasks they told my parents. They were quite happy with that and it got rid of an uncomfortable problem for them all in one go."

Thanir wanted to say something to take the pain away but there was nothing he could say so he kept quiet and waited for her to continue when she was ready.

"So there I was, six years old I think; a scrawny, ragged creature, used to doing what I pleased, as and when I pleased. I was taken to the Great Abbey along with four other children. The school, such as it was, was in a row of rickety old sheds at the back of the main Abbey building, far from the city and well away from the pious Abbess and the Holy Sisters. To the people of the city, the Abbey was a fine and holy place... the Holy Sisters made sure they were seen working in the fields and orchards; they grew their own food, husbanded animals, spun and wove the wool to make their habits... only they didn't. They did just enough for show but they were far too pious and conceited to get their hands dirty. Not very holy at all really. This is where we – me and the other children came in; it was work or suffer humiliation, starvation and punishment. We were slaves. Oh, they did educate us to a point. We had lessons in reading, writing and numbers, but it was a grudging sort of education. If we did not learn well, or quickly enough, we were beaten. Or if they thought we learned too well and too quickly... well, they still beat us.

They punished us in as many ways as you could think for every tiny infraction; like falling asleep over our books after working all night in the laundry, making one tiny mistake at the weaving loom, having dirty hands or face or feet after mucking out the animals. Our clothes were the rags on our backs that we came with. I don't think I was ever given anything else to wear. I had no shoes when I arrived and none were forthcoming at the school, but that didn't worry me, I was used to bare feet.

"We were given food once a day and it was usually the slops that the Holy Sisters had finished with... but when you're hungry you'll eat almost anything... woe betide anyone found stealing food that was meant for the Holy Ones."

Thanir could not help himself. "What did your parents say when they saw you?"

"Once I was taken into the Abbey I never saw them again. Visits were discouraged. One child's mother came once and she cried. She was later beaten so badly that she could not walk for days. It didn't stop them making her work though." She looked down and realised that he had taken a hold of her hand.

"Then, one day a group of travellers arrived and asked the Abbess for hospitality. It didn't happen often but there were rooms for guests and if requested they had to put travellers up. The only time we were allowed anywhere near these rooms, was to clean up after visitors had left. We were supposed to be unseen and unheard.

On this particular day, I had been sent to make up five more of the rooms. They usually only kept one ready. Each room had two beds which had to be made up and I had already spent the night working in the laundry; washing the bed linens of the previous visitors. I was almost asleep on my feet so I did not work fast enough to finish the task and disappear back into the woodwork. The Abbess's Housekeeper found me when she brought the visitors in. I was still making the last bed in the last room.

She demanded to know what I was

doing there and why I hadn't completed my task. She shouted at me, cuffed me around the ear then grabbed my arm, digging her fingernails in, before I fell. I knew better than to cry, that would only make my punishment worse. She shoved me towards the door and told me to wait outside. I suppose I could have run, but where to? I heard her apologising to the visitors for having to look upon one of the 'dim-witted gutter-snipes' that the Abbey took in off the streets.

When she came out, she was alone. She dragged me off to the school room where some of the younger children were chanting their numbers. There, in front of them, she made an example of me. I was beaten, for any and all transgressions that she could think of and probably a few that she couldn't..."

Sylvestri looked down to where Thanir still held onto her hands. She expected him to pull in disgust away any minute, but he did not. She had intended to tell him part of her story but not all of this. Once she had begun it all came pouring out and she realised she had never spoken of this to anyone before, not even her predecessor. Now the flood gates had opened and she couldn't keep it in. His thumb stroked gently across the back of her hand and it made her want to cry... no, crying was bad... She looked up into his face expecting him to flinch at their eye contact – not a flicker, nor did he let go of her hand.

"After she had beaten me so bloody that I could no longer stand, I was put into The Room. It was really a cupboard. Not enough room to stand or stretch out, all I could do was lie there, curled into a ball. It was dark in The Room. While in there, there was to be no light, no warmth, no food, no drink and no contact with anyone. There was no way to tell the passage of time. I tried counting but I was too busy concentrating on not crying, or at least crying as silently as I could. My only relief in there was a row of small holes at the bottom of the door. After all, they didn't want us to suffocate." Her smile was tight - gallows humour. "I could feel a breeze through the holes and most of the time it chilled me to the bone. My rags were barely enough to cover me as I had recently grown taller, and they did nothing to keep me warm but that didn't seem to matter. As long as I could feel the breeze moving, I knew I was still alive… although sometimes I wished… Sometimes the breeze tormented in other ways, bringing sounds and smells. I admit, while in there, I often thought it might have been better to die… at least there would've been no more pain."

Thanir squeezed her hand gently and moved a little closer to her so their shoulders were touching. He was in her personal space now and that gave her some comfort.

"I suppose I must've slept or passed out while I was in there. There was never enough to eat so I was used to being hungry but I was so thirsty that I barely had enough spit to swallow. She'd been so angry with me when she threw me in there that I didn't know if I'd ever be let out. I was just one of many… expendable…

and a feral one at that. No one would miss me, just another ragged, dirty, barefoot urchin. I came from nothing, brought nothing, was given nothing and would leave with nothing." There were no tears while Sylvestri told her story. She had cried them all out so long ago, now she had none left. She blinked at him once and carried on.

"I don't know how long I had been there and I was probably semi-conscious. I thought I heard raised voices but I wasn't sure if they were real or a hallucination because the breeze through the holes was, for once, warm and I could smell flowers. Right at that moment, I made a wish - I wanted to be like the breeze, to roam free and unseen. That felt like the most fabulous dream but... I was certain that this was death coming for me. The voices sounded as though they were coming closer. I couldn't make out any words, only angry sounds. A moment later, the door was pulled open so hard it came off its hinges. I curled myself up to be as small as I could and tucked myself into the far corner of The Room. I waited for the cruel hand that would drag me out as it always did but it never came.

A dark shape blocked the doorway. Someone crouched there, peering in at me. The light behind them hurt my eyes. I waited for the inevitable blow but it didn't come. The dark shape spoke. The voice was deep and hard to tell if it was male or female at that point. All I knew was that the voice sounded calm and kind as they asked me to come out but I couldn't move. I was too frightened and in too much pain. I had not known much kindness in my short life and didn't trust it.

The voice asked me my name... soft, quiet, speaking just for me. Even when I didn't answer straight away, they didn't shout or reach in to grab or slap me. They just sat on the floor a little way from the door and waited – for a long time.

Finally, it took almost more energy than I had to uncurl my battered body and move to the edge of the doorway. I still didn't attempt to leave the Room. I'd been deceived by their cruel tricks before. Then another voice came from behind the shadow, loud and strident – I recognised the Housekeeper – she swore loudly and said something along the line of 'she won't be worth your time and money. But take her if you must.'

The person kneeling by the door spoke again, not to me this time. It was over their shoulder, to the Housekeeper. The voice was strong, firm and, I realised then, female. She said 'I'll pay whatever you ask, but be warned; it is an ill wind that blows nobody any good.' I remember thinking that was an odd thing to say.

I heard the Housekeeper stomp out of the room and the speaker turned back to me. She was still quiet and calm, and promised I would be safe if I came out. I still did not trust her but something in the tone of her voice made me want to believe. I managed to shuffle forward slowly and painfully and held my grubby little hand out to her. For a long while, we just sat there, my hand resting on hers. She didn't hold it but waiting for me to come to her. I moved at a snail's pace which was all I could manage but still she showed no impatience. And that was how I first came face to face with the Queen of the Four Winds.

I have no idea why she chose me. Maybe she just felt sorry for me knowing that I was punished because she had turned up earlier than expected and I didn't have the room ready. Or, maybe she had come looking for me. I never really knew for sure, and never thought to question, I was so grateful to her for taking me away from that hellish life.

She took me away from the Abbey, away from the city, from everything I had known and feared. I think I was probably about ten, or eleven by then. We travelled constantly for many years, wherever the whim took her. I had no real idea who or what she really was in the beginning. She was my teacher and my friend. Understanding came later. She was more than kind to me. There were no more beatings. It didn't matter if I didn't learn something quickly and she encouraged me to ask questions, even silly ones. She didn't lock me up or put me in small, dark places if I fell asleep over my books. She made sure I was never hungry, thirsty or too cold. She cleaned me up, clothed me and educated me through kindness and patience.

When I was old enough, I suggested to her that I might get a job and repay her but she kept saying there would be time enough for that. It was not until many years later, when she was very old and tired, that she explained who she was. Even though it sounded ridiculous, I believed her because she was the one person who had never lied to me.

When she told me it was time for her to pass on the mantle of Air Elemental, I was only too grateful to her and willingly agreed so that she might rest in her old age. As she held my hand and explained it to me, a feeling of déjà vu swept over me... I was in that pitiful creature, in the Room feeling the breeze blow through the holes and wishing I could be that breeze, free to roam at will, unseen. My given name had been Nonus, but she had given me a new name many years before. She called me Sylvestri, named for a sylph or spirit of the air. Although I hadn't known that at the time. It was her little joke." Sylvestri smiled at the memory. "Sylvestri is such a mouthful, don't you think? My friends call me Ves."

"Ves?" Thanir whispered as though trying out the feel of the name on his tongue.

Chapter 15

Fyr was finding it hard to reconcile the situation. He had grown up here. They were his people and yet, right now, he felt like a stranger. He was on the outside looking in.

Surely, someone must have been aware of what was going on. How had they allowed it to go on for so long? He wondered.

Fyr took Barras to the inn to get something to eat. It was not healthy for the old man to stay cooped up in that byre of his all day every day. His health was not improving.

"Mind your tongue, lad. You never know who might be listening," Barras had warned but Fyr just needed to get the signal to Thorn and Gould. Luckily, there were no soldiers at the inn right then, but that did not mean there would not be someone watching or listening.

"Gentlemen, what can I get for you?" Thorn asked as Barras perched himself on a stool at the end of the bar.

"Pint o' best," Barras grumbled. He was putting on his best bad-tempered, irritable old man face. It was useful for keeping people at arm's length.

"Make that two pints please," Fyr said with more civility. He gave his nose a rub as he sat next to Barras, which Thorn recognised as their signal.

"Can I get you any food?" Thorn added as he placed the foaming mugs of beer on the bar.

"Bread'n cheese," Barras grunted. "That'll do me." He could keep up his grumpy old git act all day if necessary.

Fyr rolled his eyes at Thorn in an exaggerated 'what can you do? He's a crotchety old fool,' way.

"Could we have some bread and cheese with ham and pickles please?" he said.

"Be right with you," Thorn said and turned to go through the kitchen door behind the bar where Gould could be found, working as a cook.

Kedros had been in earlier, delivering the bread order for the inn. Thorn and Gould had outlined Fyr's plan while helping the carry the baskets in. At first, he said he did not approve of them running off in all directions but then bemoaned the fact that he would not be able to help them without putting his business at risk.

"Both my boys have been called up for this ridiculous training thing. I tried to appeal for some sense because a baker's lot is a long and heavy one. I can't do it on my own any more but that fell on deaf ears. I was told to be grateful that I was being allowed to stay and there were plenty of women, children or old folk who could replace my sons... as if!"

"Keep your chin up, old man," Gould slapped him on the back.

"Less o' the old," Kedros muttered. He gave them a smile as he left. "Be safe."

As Thorn entered the kitchen, he gave his nose a rub. Gould knew the signal. It meant the plan was about to begin. Without giving

Thorn any acknowledgement, he took off his apron and called out to the kitchen in general, "I'm just popping out for some fresh air before the rush starts." He disappeared out the door while Thorn bustled about gathering up the bread, cheese and ham for Fyr and Barras. He took the plates back out to the bar and placed them before the two men with a small nod.

"Where's me pickles?" Barras demanded with a scowl.

"My apologies. I won't be a moment." That was his cue. He went back through the door to the kitchen and, following in Gould's footsteps, continued on, through the pantry and out into the yard. He stopped to tie his boot lace while he checked there was no one watching him. He did not see anyone about but that did not mean there was no one lurking, ready to report any suspicious activity to the authorities. However, Thorn knew that, with the exception of those taught by the dryads in Aldamar, no one could follow where

he was going. Not all the Boroviche were
driadi - dryads from this land. It meant those
who dwelt near the forest. However, when
Thorn was a boy, driadi was a derogatory term,
used to mean those considered in-bred, dim-
witted and slow. How little they knew. Thorn
could not help but smile as he stepped around
the large tree trunk and disappeared inside,
just as the dryads of Aldamar had taught him.
He found Gould waiting for him. While, back at
the inn, Fyr and Barras ate their meal quickly
and left before anyone noticed that one of
the bar tenders had vanished into thin air

    The Aldamar dryads must have known
their countryside exceptionally well because
they had been able to cover vast distances
very quickly. Into a tree in this place and out of
another tree far away. Fyr, Thorn and the
others were still novices. They had to be able to
see the tree they wanted to move to. The
journey, for them, meant many short hops from
tree to tree. It was quite tiring and the two men
had to stop several times to rest.

Initially, they travelled north to the lower slopes of the mountains, deliberately in the wrong direction. They laid a false trail should anyone attempt to follow them. It also kept them well away from the larger estates, the heavily guarded roads and Hedeon's fortress.

Once they crossed over the so-called border and into Faerie, they headed for the wide swathe of dense forest that ran below the steep escarpment. At the fringes of the forest, there was a greater distance between the trees and they were able to move quickly but once they were further in, they were into the remains of the ancient forest. Here, the trees were huge, ancient and surprisingly sentient. A great many strange and terrible creatures populated the ancient forest; things they had never seen before, and hoped never to see again. Especially the great lumbering beasts covered with tufts of dark bristling hair. They mostly shuffled around dragging their knuckles along the ground but once they scented food and went on the hunt, they did not give up.

They watched as the creatures climbed into the boughs of the trees to drop onto their prey from above, causing damage to the trees as they went. Thorn and Gould soon became aware that trees did not like these creatures, but the two driadi men were welcomed.

It was night by the time Thorn and Gould reached the outer edge of the forest where it bordered a wide, paved road. Beyond the road, the land was open fields and meadows. Trees large enough to support them were few and far between. Although aided by the light of an almost full moon, it was difficult to tell where their next step would take them. They would get a better view in daylight but there were several hours to go before the sun was due to rise again. Not being able to fix their sight on a tree meant no more jumps for the time being.

Standing at the edge of the forest and listening to the sounds from within made then feel very exposed and vulnerable. They had brought nothing with them but the clothes they stood up in and a small pocket knife. It was not enough to protect them against one of those great beasts.

It took conscious effort for them to remain inside a tree but they needed to sleep. Dozing off would mean they would fall out of the tree and become prey to the creatures. Thorn offered to let Gould sleep for a couple of hours while he kept watch and then they could swap. Behind them one of the trees rustled. The men jumped and spun around expecting to see one of the shambling creatures but there was nothing but the large trees. The tree rustled again and they had the distinct impression it was trying to get their attention. Two steps forward and they were inside the tree. Immediately they felt welcomed with open arms and the tree offered to keep watch over them and hold them safely should they wish to become dormant.

"Dormant? Does that mean asleep?" Gould wondered.

"Yes, I think so," Thorn nodded and they both settled down to sleep.

While Thorn and Gould were travelling towards the King's castle, Fyr and Barras were also travelling. Fyr had been unwilling for Barras to become embroiled in the deception any further than he already had but somehow, the old man had managed to procure two travel permits for the market in the next town.

Barras's hand cart was laden with milk from his cow and his goats and eggs from his hens as they set out before the sun had risen the next morning. Barras knew the best spot for them at the market and they had to be early to make sure they got it. All day long Fyr and the old man had stood by the cart, selling and bartering Barras's wares. They last of the eggs had been sold and they began packing everything away ready for the return journey. Now came the difficult bit. They were just manoeuvring the cart down the rutted road when there was a loud crack and the wheel came off spilling the empty pails and baskets all over the road. With the help from some of the other stall-holders they man-handled the broken cart into a nearby barn. In all the confusion, no one saw Fyr leave.

"Where's the lad you 'ad wiv yer?" the roadside guard demanded to know as he checked Barras off his list.

"Poor bugger has to spend the night in't barn wi'me ol' cart. S'a good job 'e was wi'me though, axle's gone and the bloody wheel came off. I offered to stay wi'it... can't leave good cart lying about or some bugger'll nick it... but truth be told lad, the cold gets into me old bones tha' knows..." Barras wheezed. He was on a roll. He was telling the truth, but it was a carefully tailored truth. He could keep it up for hours with so many twists and turn to the story that the guard would not know what day of the week it was. However, the guard got bored very quickly and waved him on with a grunt.

"Get yourself home old man. It'll be dark soon. Wouldn't want you caught out after curfew."

"Curfew... when did that happen?" Barras asked, but the guard had moved on to someone else. Yet another new rule to keep people under the thumb of the tyrant. Barras did not take telling twice and made his way home.

Chapter 16

The stairs were not well lit and Kesia stumbled a second time.

"Watch it... they don't like it when the bruises are places that can be seen," the guard chuckled and grabbed her arm again.

The stairs led to a long gallery on the first floor. Opposite the head of the stairs was a door and there was another at the other end of the gallery. It was to this farther door that he pushed her. He took down a key that was hanging on the wall beside the door and unlocked it. It soon became obvious that a large room had been partitioned into small rooms or cells. The doors all had bolts on the outside. He opened the nearest door. Inside the cell, two narrow beds took up most of the space. There was a narrow walkway between the two and a bucket at the end.

"This is where you'll be sleepin'. Put this on." He took a shapeless grey dress from a peg on the wall and handed it to her. "Take off everything and put this on." He said with a nasty glint in his eye. Kesia stood and stared at him. Was he intending to watch her? Her eyes stung as she held a tight rein on her tears.

"You, guard? What are you doing?" It was a woman's voice. Maybe this was someone who could help her.

Then again...

Built along the same lines as the guards, the woman was big and muscular as though used to heavy manual labour. She almost had more whiskers on her chin than the male guard.

"You," she poked the guard in the chest. "Leave. And you," she rounded on Kesia. "Strip!"

The male guard grunted his displeasure and sloped off.

"Please..." Kesia begged. "I don't understand why this is happening."

"Everything off," the woman barked. She stood, feet apart and her arms folded under her ample bosom. "Got to check you over; make sure there are no marks or sores or fleas. Who knows what you might have picked up."

"But..."

"We can do this one of two ways. You can strip or I can do it for you." She took a large knife from a leather sheath on her hip.

Kesia realised that she had no option but to comply with the order and very slowly began to remove her clothes. The woman watched her but there was nothing in her blank stare. She may as well have been waiting for her horse to be shod, that was how Kesia felt, no more than an animal.

The female guard stepped around behind Kesia and looked over every part of her. She bent Kesia's head towards her and began to pick through her hair looking for lice; there were none.

"Arms out to the sides, feet apart," she barked.

Kesia did as she was told, feeling more

exposed than ever. The woman ran her hands along each arm and inspected her armpits.

"No lice or lumps... good for you girl." She turned Kesia to face her. "Tell me true girl, are you still a maiden? We have ways to check that you're not lying to us," she added as Kesia nodded. "What about that boy you were with? You telling me you and him never...?"

"No ma'am. I wanted to wait. He was going to ask my father for my hand..." Kesia bit her bottom lip to stop it quivering.

"Oh, how very sweet!" the female guard said, not meaning a word of it. "But that's good for you and good for us, might just bump your price up. Right, put that on." She grabbed the grey dress and tossed it to Kesia. The material was rough and scratchy on her bare skin and it was huge and shapeless like an old flour sack. "This way!"

The female guard led the way back out into the long gallery and back towards the door opposite the stairs. Pulling open the door the guard revealed a small ante room with three male guards sitting around sharpening blades. They all looked up. Kesia could feel her face heat up. The way they were looking at her meant they knew she was naked under that baggy dress. They could not see anything but that did not matter to how it made her feel. The female guard took a brass key from a hook beside the door and unlocked it. It was dark inside.

"Time to meet your new sisters," she was told then, a hand shoved her between the shoulder blades, propelling her into the room. The door slammed behind her and she heard the lock click into place. Kesia thought the room was in total darkness at first but her eyes soon became used to the dim candlelight and she could make out the shapes of six women. They were all dressed in the same shapeless garment as her. It must be some sort of uniform.

For a moment no one spoke.

"Hello new girl," a voice whispered at her side. She had not heard anyone approach her, but there was a girl with mousy hair tied back off her face smiling shyly at her. "I'm Hebe," she said.

Hebe took Kesia's hand, drew her further into the room and introduced her to the others. "This is Rosa…"

Rosa was the oldest of the six women in the room.

"I was the only surviving child and my parents had been quite old when they had me," she told Kesia. "I looked after them for as long as I can remember… all my life. My father died a couple of years ago and my mother was ill for a long time but she died too, only a month ago." Rosa stared at the floor as she tried not to break down. It was all still too raw.

In the not so distant past, Rosa would have inherited her parent's house and contents but the new laws had changed everything and now it was illegal for a single woman to own property. The house and everything that she had ever known was sold. She had nothing left and no rights to anything.

She had come to this house because she was homeless. They had told her she would go to a hiring fair to get a job but she soon learned the truth of it. She sat back down and picked up her needlework. Kesia wondered how she could see what she was doing in this dim light. Why did they not open the shutters?

"They've been nailed shut, to stop us trying to escape," Hebe said when she saw where Kesia was looking. She took Kesia's hand and they moved to the next person.

"Hello, I'm Lobelia."

Kesia knew that the lobelia plant had blue flowers that were small and delicate and she could not help but think that poor Lobelia had been miss-named. She was over six feet tall with broad shoulders and huge hands, yet she did not look masculine like the female guard had. She was a gentle giant and gave Kesia a very careful hug of welcome.

Floria was next - a tall, red-haired woman. She gave Kesia a small smile but said nothing.

"She's not very friendly," Hebe whispered. "She thinks she's better than us. She was married but her husband ran off with their neighbour."

In the far corner of the room, Hebe took her to meet two young women who were identical twins.

"This is Posey and Petal," Hebe said. "We can't tell'm apart... an' they ain't tellin' neither."

The two women grinned at her and nodded.

"Even our parents couldn't tell us apart most of the time," one of them said.

"So sometimes I'm Posey and sometimes I'm Petal," said the other. The way they spoke, it was almost as though they were one person.

"And then there's me," Hebe said. At a mere nineteen, she was the youngest of the women. "Like Rosa I used to look after my family. I barely remember my mother. I've cooked, cleaned, and kept house for my father and three brothers for this past seven or eight years but they were all sent away to train. They were told they would have to pay for my services now and they can't afford to do that, so I have to be put up for auction. So, what about you?"

"My name is Kesia, my father is the local chandler and he doesn't even know I'm here."

Chapter 17

Eleanor felt better just having James there. They had eaten the sandwiches and scones Bella had brought up and the tea made her feel more human. Of course, the 'afternoon nap' that James persuaded her to have might have had something to do with her sense of well-being too. She and James had created a buffer zone around the spare bedroom. A feedback loop of magic inside the room now powered Simon's dreams ridding her of the constant drain on her power. It just needed a tweak every few hours until it had played out and Simon was feeling better.

"Oh, with all this fuss… I quite forgot," she said. "When Alsea came, she asked me to scry for Hob. I'd almost reached him when we got thrown out."

"He obviously didn't want to be found," James suggested.

"Anyway, almost as soon as Hob

disappeared Branchir came through. He needs to talk to the sisters about those jewels they found in Daphne's old nest... and about John Dee."

"What does he want with him? Nothing good I hope."

"Well, no," she chuckled. "He thinks we should consider some sort of... punishment or at least, he should face some consequences for his actions."

"And so he should," James agreed.

"Trouble is... we can't really use magic to force the issue because of the rule of three fold return. It would all rebound on us."

"So how come it hasn't affected him after all these years?" James had a point.

"Maybe it will now. His machinations took so long to come to fruition but now they've played out, he's probably got it all coming at once. He's been losing power for years. It's why he tried to steal mine. And didn't I hear that he lost Ivy as his familiar? Mind you, I can't help but think that we were thrown back in time to help Lily for a reason. It was meant to happen... it's why the magic was here waiting for me when I first stepped into the house."

"Ugh!" James groaned. "Don't mention time travel. All that paradox stuff gives me a headache."

"Anyway, I promised Branchir I would contact Dorcas. She'll get a message to the others."

"Okay, but you've got to let me help."

"Scrying doesn't take much power these days, but I'll be glad to have you holding my hand."

They sat opposite one another, on the hearth rug in their bedroom, with the bowl of water on the floor between them. James took hold of her hands.

"Try and picture Dorcas in your mind," she told him as she did the same. She gazed into the water until it started to swirl with a myriad of colours. The maelstrom cleared to form an image, a bright blue sky with small white clouds drifting lazily across it.

"Dorcas?" Eleanor called. "Hello Dorcas, are you there?"

Dorcas's slightly red face appeared in the bowl. She looked a little... ruffled.

"Hello dear, I had a feeling that you would be getting in touch. Apollo and I were just playing backgammon while we waited."

"Is that what they're calling it now?" James chuckled under his breath.

"What's that dear?" Dorcas asked.

"Oh, nothing," he grinned.

Dorcas gave James a little frown. "Have you seen Emma recently?"

"No dear, but I shall be seeing her very soon," Dorcas smiled when Eleanor explained Branchir's request. "She will definitely want to know about this."

"It would be so much easier if they all had mobile phones," James said after Dorcas had disappeared from the scrying bowl.

"I've suggested that a couple of times but Dorcas said 'where's the fun in that?' To be honest I think they are all a little technophobic.

Besides, phones wouldn't work between worlds, not like scrying can. I'd better keep this bowl handy for when Dorcas gets back to me."

As it happened, it was less than ten minutes later that Dorcas's face reappeared in the bowl.

"They've just arrived. We'll be leaving here soon," Dorcas confirmed. "So we should be with you tomorrow morning to use your gate."

"Lovely, we'll see you tomorrow," Eleanor smiled down into the bowl and with a wave of her hand the image rippled and vanished.

In the room next door, cocooned by layers of spells, Simon and Marianne slept. Snippets of his dreams drifted in and out of her subconscious but the images were so fleeting that they disappeared before she had a chance to wonder what they were. And then, Simon slipped away from her, deeper into a dream.

Simon knew this was a dream right from the outset. He was in a place that he had never seen before and yet it felt strangely familiar.

A young boy played with a ball, all alone in a garden.

Somehow, as it is with dreams, Simon knew that this child would grow up to be Salamander, but that was not his name, not yet. He had yet to earn it. As far as he could see this child looked nothing like the Salamander that he knew. His hair was slightly too long and a little wild but it was a mousy brown colour and looked like ordinary hair. Where were the flames? There was not even a spark.

Somewhere close by, two men were arguing. They always argued. The boy did his best to ignore them but he always felt the arguments were his fault even though they were not. He could not hear the actual words but the tone and volume told him all he needed to know.

Time leapt forward. The boy was a little older.

In a small, dark bedroom, he sat at a desk hunched over his book, studying hard. With his head down and his hands clamped over his ears, the tension in the air was hot and suffocating.

Simon tried to see what the boy was studying but it looked like an unintelligible jumble of marks on the paper; a language and script he did not recognise.

Despite his best efforts, the distant angry voices filtered through. They were coming this way and the boy flinched, withdrawing into himself.

"I blame your mother for this…" a deep voice growled.

"Don't bring her into this," a second voice yelled. "How can she be at fault? She died so long ago I barely even remember her."

"If I had known the truth of her…" the first voice went on as though the other had not spoken.

The boy's eyes flitted around the room anxiously, wondering whether there was a suitable place to hide. His shoulders slumped. Wherever he tried to hide, they would find him.

The voices were getting closer and he held his breath, praying they would pass him by.

Not this time.

The door burst open and two men stood blocking the doorway.

"Now is not the time, father," the younger of the two said, stepping into the room and positioning himself between the old man and the boy. The old man, the boy's grandfather, had oddly glowing eyes that always frightened the boy. He tried to shrink into the shadows but all the shadows had disappeared. The old man's eyes lit up the room like the beam from a search-light.

"You spend too long in here on your own," he said to the boy.

"Yes, Grandfather," the boy whispered.

The grandfather's eyes shone even brighter.

"Father, this is not the time or the place." He tried to shield his son but the grandfather pushed him out of the way and held his hand out to the boy.

"Come here boy," he ordered.

"Leave him alone, this is nothing to do with him," the boy's father begged.

"You've already made your position quite clear Zjarr," the old man said. "Your refusal to take on the gift has done this. It must be passed on and the boy is the next in line."

Suddenly Simon saw the whole of the young boy's story.

His grandfather was the clan chief and the local blacksmith. He was a big, brawny fellow, used to working with his hands – and his fists when necessary, but he was getting old.

His father was a quiet, thoughtful man. He was an artist, a sculptor and glass blower. He made delicate drinking vessels and ornaments. There was no way he would take on the forge. The two men might both work with heat and flames but their jobs and their temperaments were chalk and cheese.

Surely, grandfather did not expect him to take over the forge. He was too small and not strong enough to lift the hammers. Besides, he had his heart set on becoming a doctor. He had been studying hard for the last few years, mostly in secret. Neither of the older men understood his quiet, bookish nature.

Simon looked at the boy again and saw that the boy was now a young man.

The grandfather's name was Draak. He was the head of the Tarakona clan, descendants of the Great Dragons. The clan was predominantly male and the women, few and far between, hid in their own homes so that they could not be stolen away by others. Men had to venture beyond clan lands to find wives and mothers for their children and Draak had been no different. He travelled far and wide and returned with a wife, just as he should. He had been certain that she, like him, had been born of the blood of the Great Dragons. She had shifted into a dragon just as he had asked. But she had not understood, had not been of the blood. In truth, she was skin-walker, able to take on the shape of any creature she chose, including a dragon. Her kind needed physical contact or they became touch-starved and weakened. It was difficult for her to hide away from all physical and emotional contact, inside Draak's house as was proper. Those women she tried to connect with feared her for her foreign nature and her different ways.

Finally, weakened by lack of contact, she died, leaving her young son, Zjarr, who did not fit in the clan any more than his mother had. He was part skin-walker, part dragon and more like her than his father. His delicate hands were good at shaping and sculpting delicate glass objects. His work was exquisite and everyone wanted to own pieces made by Zjarr. It was through his work that he eventually gained acceptance within the clan. But his father never forgave him for being his mother's son.

Zjarr should have followed in the clan's footsteps when the time came to take a wife but he had no need to travel. He had fallen in love with a girl he had met at the markets. She was from the Yangjin clan and his father had not approved of her. The Yangjin clan were not born of the blood of the Great Dragons but were wyverns and as such were of a lower order. Her name was Vatra. The boy remembered his mother as a beautiful woman, slim and delicate like him. He remembered the smell of her perfume and the way she would kiss his hurts and sing him to sleep at night. She gave him the name Vurr, after her father. It was just another thing to berate and belittle her for. His grandfather made her life a misery.

By the time Vurr was twelve years old, Vatra had had enough of Draak's constant ridicule and abuse and Zjarr's spineless lack of support or defence. She promised Vurr that she would take him with her when she left but Draak stepped in and refused to let him go. Finally, she could take no more and left. Once gone, Vurr took her place as the target for Draak's vitriol. He would never be dragon enough.

"What are you doing cowering in the corner

boy?" Draak roared. "Look at you. There's nothing of you… like your mother… all skin and bone. And no muscle, like your father." He pushed at Vurr, trying to provoke his anger but he refused to take the bait. He decided to force the boy's hand.

"Here boy, catch."

The boy did not see what his Grandfather had thrown but instinctively put up his hands to catch whatever it was.

"No!" Zjarr's voice seemed to come from far away.

It hit the palms of his hands, bounced off, and hit the desk.

Vurr screamed and dropped to the floor as white hot pain bloomed, burning through his skin and deep into his bones. Flames ate greedily at the books, the papers and the desk.

Zjarr ran to his son but stood over the writhing boy with no idea how to help him. Draak growled and turned to the desk. He held out his hand and pulled the flames back into himself leaving nothing but scorch marks on the wooden surface and ash floating in the air.

"Show me your hands boy," Draak demanded.

Vurr could not move. He curled his body around

his hands and shook with the pain. His mouth was open but he could not make a sound or cry out. Black and white spots danced before his eyes as he gritted his teeth. Feeling sick and light-headed, he knew he was going into shock. This was it. His grandfather had finally got what he wanted and he was about to die.

"Look what you've done… I told you he wasn't ready… you might have killed him."

Zjarr lifted Vurr into his arms but the boy did not respond, not even a whimper.

Vurr lay on his bed, covered by a cool, white sheet. He lifted his hands. Swathed in bandages, they felt too heavy. Zjarr sat, dozing, in a chair at his bedside. He awoke with a start as he sensed Vurr wake.

The tight bandages made movement in his fingers impossible but he had to try, had to know that he still had fingers. The pain was indescribable and even though he tried to hold the sound in, he could not help but cry out. He wanted to weep… wanted his mother's calm presence to hold him and soothe him and tell him it would be all right. But all he had were his father and grandfather. Neither of them knew how to give comfort. Openly weeping was not an option with those two. Vurr stared at his bandaged hands through pain blurred eyes and wondered what his grandfather had thrown.

Although Zjarr still thought of Vurr as a child, he had to admit that he was almost grown. He had become a man without him even noticing.

"Father, what happened? What did he do to me?"

"It wasn't supposed to be like this. It should have been me. I should have stepped up and shouldered the responsibility but... I'm sorry son... I couldn't do it. He wants to pass his gift on to you."

"What gift father... what does he want to give me?"

His father took a deep breath and turned his face away as he began to explain. Ashamed of his own weakness, he could not give his son eye contact.

"Your grandfather is head of our clan and we are descendants of the Great Dragons..."

"This I know, father..."

"Once, many generations ago, we had the power to shift and become the dragon but we became too proud... but that's another story. It is partly because your grandfather is the blacksmith and the strongest of the clan, but mostly because of our blood line that he inherited the gift from his father. This gift means that he has certain… obligations… and needs a successor to train before he is too old."

"And he wanted that to be you but you refused?"

Zjarr nodded.

"And now he wants that to be me?"

Zjarr nodded again, still not able to look at his son.

"But I can't even pick up the smallest of his great hammers… I'm going to be a doctor…" Vurr said the last in a very quiet voice. His father nodded as though he knew but said nothing for a long moment. Eventually he had to turn and face Vurr. He put a hand on his shoulder.

"It's not the forge he wants to train you for."

"Then what?"

"Your grandfather's gift is a great responsibility. It feeds from the magic still hidden within us. Your grandfather is the Elemental that represents fire and he wants you to take over from him."

"He's the… what?"

"Let me check your hands," Zjarr deflected. He very gently took one of his son's bandaged hands. Unwrapping the linen carefully, he kept going until he reached the final layer of gauze. Vurr squeezed his eyes shut and held his breath from the pain. He did not want to see what had become of his hands. With his delicate touch, Vurr did not feel his father lift a corner of the gauze and peel it back but he was aware when he stopped moving. Vurr opened his eyes and stared at his hand. He had expected the skin to be blackened or at the very least red raw, and his fingers little more than stumps. He was surprised and relieved to see they were still whole and almost healed although the whole of his palm and all the way up his fingers and thumb was covered in huge blisters with dead-looking white flesh between.

"It hurts…" he could not keep the quaver from his voice.

"I know it hurts Vurr… I've had many a burn in my time…" It was the first time in a long time that his father had used his name. His heart sank as he glanced up at the shadow that had appeared in the doorway.

"Can I see? … Your hands…" his grandfather asked. He sounded so unlike himself. He was hesitant and uncertain. Vurr had never seen the old man like that before.

Vurr held his hand as still as he could. He did not want his grandfather to see him tremble and have to face yet more ridicule. He was surprised when his grandfather came in and sat on the side of the bed. Just as Zjarr had done, Draak took Vurr's other hand and unwound the bandages. It was just as blistered as the first. Vurr frowned at the odd, almost ticklish prickle in his hands. The dead and blistered skin was rapidly drying out without the moisture from the gauze. His grandfather was surprisingly gentle as Vurr's hand rested on his huge calloused one.

"Try and straighten your fingers," Draak said. He did not demand or shout he just sat looking at the damage to Vurr's hand.

A cold shiver passed through Vurr as he tried to do what his grandfather asked. He looked at his hands. They felt tight and his fingers were curling into his palm. He had to use the side of his left hand to try and push the fingers of his right hand and straighten them. He tried not to whimper.

"That's it… a little more…" His grandfather still sounded calm.

Vurr was about to say that it hurt too much but the pain was beginning to diminish. He chanced a glance at his grandfather's face. There were white, tension lines around his mouth, as though he was in pain.

"Keep going, a little straighter…" He still did not shout or bully but waited for Vurr to do it in his own time. "That's it, you're doing well… look at me Vurr, not your hands."

Eye contact from Draak was unknown. He could not remember when his grandfather had ever looked at him with anything other than scorn. He was sure he had never used his name before. The pain had almost gone but now his palms felt strange, cold and as though he wore gloves that were too tight.

"That's it stretch your fingers," Draak encouraged.

The tickling, prickling sensation got worse and he could not help but look down at his hands. As he stretched and flexed his hand, the dead skin cracked and flaked. It began to peel away in a papery sheet.

"No, look at me, not at them." It was a command but delivered with rare compassion. He felt his grandfather put his hand over the top of his and it felt strangely cool. As he took it away again, he said,

"You can look now."

Vurr looked down at his hands and all the dead skin was gone leaving new skin that was soft and pink and completely healed.

"Vurr… the speed with which you healed shows me that you truly are my heir. I shall teach you how to use the magic of the fire drake within you so that you need never fear the flame. When I am gone, you will become the Fire Elemental in my place. I give you a new name. From this day forth you shall be known as Salamander but… you will have to earn this name…"

Vurr gasped at his grandfather's words and slapped a healed hand to the side of his neck. When he removed his hand there was a mark. Looking in the mirror, he could see that it was identical to the one his grandfather carried on his upper arm.

Simon felt the dream slipping from his grasp. He hoped that he would be able to remember it when he woke. He had to tell Marianne and Eleanor about this. Then he wanted to talk to Salamander and find out if it had really happened.

Chapter 18

Hundreds of copies of the same story surrounded Thanir and Ambrosius and, without exception, every one they picked up was a children's story.

"Pick another one at random," Thanir suggested. "Maybe we should look more closely at the story."

Ambrosius reached out, picked up the nearest book. It was small and non-descript, with a white paper cover. He began to read aloud.

"The Queen's Jewels Or How The King Found His Bride. We might have something here."

The Queen's Jewels Or How The King Found His Bride.

There was once a young and handsome King by the name of Aradon. He was a good and fair King beloved of all the people in the land. The young King was sad because there was just one thing missing. His people knew, that to make his life complete, he was in want of a wife, a Queen to share his throne and his life.

There were many fine Ladies in the King's court and any one of them would have been glad to be his Queen. Unfortunately, they were too young, too old or already married. The King's most trusted advisor had a suggestion.

"Sire, send your most loyal and faithful Knights on a quest. They will each search out and bring back a potential bride. Then you may judge their worth."

Once all the loyal, faithful Knights returned to the castle there was to be a Grand Ball the like of which the Kingdom had never seen before and there the King would dance with each one of the Ladies in turn and at the end of the ball, he would announce his choice.

The eight most loyal and faithful Knights rode out from the castle and within a week, the first returned.

The first Knight bowed to the King.

"Your Majesty, May I present Lady Polyphagia."

"Welcome Lady Polyphagia." The King smiled but the Lady Polyphagia said nothing. She was busy looking at the table laden with food and before the King could speak again, she fell upon the feast with great gusto.

When the second Knight returned he bowed to the King.

"Your Majesty, May I present Lady Inertia."

"Welcome Lady Inertia," the King smiled but the Lady Inertia ignored him and gave a huge yawn. She lay on a litter carried by six strong slaves.

"I'm tired, take me to my room," the Lady said with a bored wave of her hand.

When the third Knight returned he bowed to the King.

"Your Majesty, May I present Lady Envia"

"Welcome Lady Envia," the King smiled but the Lady was gazing around at all the other Ladies in the court.

"Send a dressmaker to me at once. I must be better dressed than each one of them."

When the fourth Knight returned he bowed to the King.

"Your Majesty, May I present Lady Narcissia."

"Welcome Lady Narcissia," the King smiled but she turned to the court saying,

"I am Narcissia, fairest Lady in all the lands. I have the best hair, don't you think?"

When the fifth Knight returned he bowed to the King.

"Your Majesty, May I present Lady Avaricia."

"Welcome Lady Avaricia," the King smiled but she stamped her foot.

"Where are the gifts and the gold I am due?"

When the sixth Knight returned he bowed to the King.

"Your Majesty, May I present Lady Acrimonia."

"Welcome Lady Acrimonia," the King smiled but she scowled, angry at everyone and about everything.

"Can we get this over with? I object to this cattle market."

When the seventh Knight returned he bowed to the King.

"Your Majesty, May I present Lady Aphrodisia."

"Welcome Lady Aphrodisia," the King smiled but she made comments about the King's person which were so rude they left him red-faced.

When the eighth Knight returned he bowed to the King.

"My apologies your Majesty," he said. "The lady you are expecting has been delayed by bad weather. Her party have travelled across the sea from the land of Athanar. They will arrive on the morrow."

"Very well," the King nodded. "I shall wait upon the morrow."

With only one more Lady to arrive preparations for the ball could begin. The King looked around the hall at the candidates who had already arrived and gave a deep sigh. He was not looking forward to having to choose between these candidates.

Firstly, there was Lady Polyphagia. She was so greedy. She ate so much that the poor dressmaker had to let out her dresses not once, not twice but three times.

Then there was Lady Inertia. She was so lazy that she rarely got out of bed before noon and then only if someone came to get her up. She only bathed if someone came and bathed her. She only dressed if someone came and dressed her. She only ate if someone came and fed her and she never walked anywhere, but reclined on her litter and was carried about.

Then there was Lady Envia. She was very demanding and jealous of everyone around her. She only had to see someone in a fine dress or with delicate slippers or an intricate hairstyle than she wanted one that was bigger or better or shinier.

Then there was Lady Narcissia. She was so vain and would stop people in the hallways and demand they tell her how beautiful she was. More than anything, she was proud of her flowing golden locks.

Then there was Lady Avaricia. She was so greedy for jewels and trinkets that her room was almost full to bursting.

Then there was Lady Acrimonia. She was so angry all the time, with everyone and everything. After a particularly bad tantrum, the King began to fear for his best dinner service and fine crystal goblets.

And then there was Lady Aphrodisia. The King's advisor told him that he should not be left alone in her company lest she attempt to kiss him or climb into his bed uninvited.

The King feared the last candidate would be just as awful as all the others were. Not one of them would he wish upon his people for their Queen. Not one of them would he wish upon himself for his bride. But he had made a promise to his people and the King always kept his promises. He was a man of his word.

The following day, the hall was crowded with people. Some were afraid and others were excited, but they were all eager to see what a foreign Lady from across the sea looked like. The crowd began to murmur and mutter. Would she have three arms… or one eye in the middle of her forehead… or be bald… or old… or too tall… or ugly?

Each of the potential brides sat and smiled smugly, confident that they would be the one he would chose.

The great doors opened and the eighth Knight began the long walk down the hall to the King sitting upon his throne. Following along behind him was a raggle-taggle party of oddly assorted people. As they neared the throne, most of the group stopped and the Knight and a small, cloaked and hooded figure came forward.

The eighth Knight once again bowed to the King.

"Your Majesty, May I present Princess Eloiny?"

"Welcome Princess Eloiny," the King smiled but before the Princess could speak, the Knight knelt before the King.

"Sire, my humblest apologies for the delay but the bad weather that held us up caused a member of the Princess's party to become unwell. The Princess begged for a little time to allow the lady to recover. If there is a fault, then it is mine for allowing it."

"Should have thrown the old dear overboard and saved time and money," Lady Acrimonia was heard to say.

The cloaked figure dipped into a formal curtsey. Then, as she stood, delicate hands appeared from within the folds of her cloak, reached up and lowered the hood. Moments later a beautiful, raven-haired young woman with dazzling blue eyes was revealed.

There were oohs and ahhs from the crowd. Amongst the many murmurs of approval, there were a few mutters of disappointment that she did not have three arms or two heads.

Scornful sneers and contemptuous comments came from the direction of the other candidates.

"Your Majesty," the Princess's voice was as soft and light as a summer breeze. It sent a sense of calm through the King. "I humbly thank you for this invitation to visit your court and your fair lands. My father, King Balaur of Athanar sends you his very best wishes."

The King returned her curtsey with a formal bow.

"Thank you for your kind words Your Highness and those of your father. Is there anything you require after your arduous journey?"

He was prepared for almost any demand now.

But the Princess said, "There is nothing I require for myself."

The she turned to look at the raggle-taggle group and said, "But I would be grateful for some sustenance for my friends and a place for them to rest."

She turned and gave the King a shy smile.

"Please," the King told them. "Come and eat your fill, rest your weary bones and partake of our hospitality."

Platters and trays of food and flagons of ale were placed on the High table and the visitors were made welcome.

The King heard a voice behind him.

"This food is far too good for the likes of these dirty, old wretches. They should know their place and be grateful for a dry crust and a mug of water. Make way there," Lady Polyphagia elbowed her way to the table and began to grab food and pile her plate high with meat and pies and fish and cheese.

One of the travellers was a very frail looking old woman. The Princess rushed to her side and politely requested a chair be brought that the old woman might rest her weary body. The chair appeared quickly but before the old woman could sit down Lady Inertia insinuated herself between the old woman and the chair and took the seat.

"You should know your place, old woman," she yawned loudly.

"It is no matter, Princess," the old woman said but the Princess smiled and went to fetch the old woman another chair and helped her to sit.

Lady Envia sidled up to Princess Eloiny and picked up the pendant she wore about her neck. "I like your necklace. Will you give it to me?"

"I am very sorry but I cannot give you this necklace as it was a gift from my father."

"I want one, only bigger," Lady Envia demanded loudly.

Lady Narcissia approached Princess Eloiny from the other side and stroked her hair. "I like your hair. It is so dark and shiny, but you must admit mine is more beautiful. My hair is the most beautiful in all the land."

Another member of the Princess's party was an old and wrinkled man, bent with age and leaning heavily on his stick. With one hand on his stick to steady himself, he used his other hand to slowly and shakily reach out and select a small piece of fruit from a platter on the table. Before his gnarled fingers touched the fruit, he gave a pained cry and he fell to the floor. Lady Acrimonia did not even look at him as she stepped over him and took the fruit for herself.

"You should know your place, old man. If I was at home, I would have had you beaten for coming near my person."

Princess Eloiny rushed to kneel at the old man's side. The King appeared at his other side. He held the old man's walking stick, which Lady Acrimonia had kicked out of his hand.

The King made sure that the two old people were given seats at the head of the table and then he and the Princess sat with them and made sure they were served with food and drink.

Lady Inertia's servants lowered her into

another seat closer to the King. She gave the person nearest her a poke.

"You, get me some meat."

The man held out the platter so she could make her selection but she looked aghast.

"Put it on the plate and cut it up small. I don't like to chew too much."

He did as she asked and placed the plate on the table before her.

"Well?" she demanded. "Feed me."

At that point, the man stood up and left.

"She is rather small and skinny... those are not child-bearing hips... and she consorts with paupers. Where does she think she is? Who does she think she is... calling herself Princess and acting like a servant," Lady Aphrodisia poured scorn and contempt into the King's ear. "No, you need someone like me to take you in hand, someone with plenty of curves in all the right places and plenty of experience." She reached over and placed her hand just above the King's knee. He managed to move out of her grasp before her hand could move any further.

Eventually, the sun went down and it was

time for the Ball. Musicians played quietly while the guests entered the Great Hall where hundreds of candles and mirrors lit the hall with a warm glow.

The King had promised to dance with each of the candidates in turn, and the King always kept his promises. He was a man of his word.

The first dance was with Lady Polyphagia but he found that she had grown so large that he could barely get his arms around her. She did not last the whole dance because she needed to sit down halfway through.

The second dance was with Lady Inertia but she hung limply on his arm. Dancing with her was rather unpleasant because she smelled so bad. After all, she said, why go to all the fuss and bother of bathing when one could use a whole bottle of perfume. The King did his best not to gag.

The third dance was with Lady Envia who talked all the way through and made it difficult to hear the music. It was not so much a conversation though, more a running commentary on the clothes and shoes and jewellery of the other guests and how she wanted one like it but bigger or better, or maybe two.

The fourth dance was with Lady Narcissia. She danced with excessive vigour and wild expression, making sure that everyone was looking at her. She boasted that she was by far the best dancer in the whole Kingdom. The King's toes said that was a lie.

The fifth dance was with Lady Avaricia. She boasted and gloated about everything she had collected. The King knew he would have to return most of it to its rightful owners before she left.

The sixth dance was with Lady Acrimonia, but she refused to dance, at first. She was angry that she had had to wait so long for her turn. The King bowed and began to move away but she grasped him rather roughly and danced as angrily and aggressively as she did everything else.

The seventh dance was with Lady Aphrodisia. Throughout the dance she had her body pressed so very, very close to the King's that he was finding it difficult to breathe. She whispered naughty things in his ear and made the King feel rather uncomfortable.

The eighth dance was with Princess Eloiny.

She smiled sweetly and dipped into a small curtsey as she accepted his hand and they twirled out onto the floor. Suddenly the King felt as though he was dancing on air. Her steps were light and her conversation was bright. The King felt as though he could dance all night.

"Your Majesty, I do believe the music has stopped," Princess Eloiny whispered when the King carried on whirling her around the floor.

"So it has," he said as they came to a graceful stop. He smiled and gave her a bow.

And then, as the bell sounded to announce the end of the ball, the King realised the time had come to announce his decision. The musicians struck up a fanfare as he made his way to the throne.

"I had thought this would be a difficult decision to make but I must thank you all ladies for making it so much easier."

All but Princess Eloiny smiled with arrogance and self-assurance that they would be chosen.

"Lady Polyphagia," the King said. "I am sorry. I cannot marry you for you are too gluttonous. There would not be enough food left to feed my people."

The Lady would have replied but her mouth was full of food.

"Lady Inertia," he said. "I am sorry. I cannot marry you for you are too lazy and full of sloth. My Queen will need to work alongside me to support my people."

The Lady yawned and could not even be bothered to reply.

"Lady Envia," he said. "I am sorry. I cannot marry you for you are too jealous and covetous."

"Well I…" she began to bluster but he cut her off.

"Lady Nar…" he began.

"Lady Narcissia," she interrupted. "Yes, that's me, of course I'll…"

"I am sorry. I cannot marry you for you are far too proud."

"But I am perfect to be your Queen… just look at my beautiful hair…" but no one was listening. All eyes were on the King.

"Lady Avaricia," he said. "I am sorry. I cannot marry you for you are too greedy and quite frankly, I could not marry a kleptomaniac."

"Lady Acrimonia," he said. "I am sorry. I cannot marry you for you are too angry and full of wrath."

"Lady Aphrodisia," he said. "I am sorry. I cannot marry you for you are too bawdy and rude."

"Princess Eloiny," he said. "I am sorry."

There was a gasp from all of the King's people as he walked down the steps of the dais and took the Princess's hand. "I am sorry but I do not wish for you to return home. You are my choice… if you will have me. You have shown everything that I could wish for in a Queen. You are kind and compassionate to those less fortunate. You show humility rather than pride and calm where others show only anger. You are kind and generous of spirit to all those around you. Your very presence makes people feel joyful and light. You make feel joyful and light. Princess Eloiny, will you consent to marry me?"

As she gave him her answer, everyone cheered, clapped their hands and stamped their feet in pleasure - everyone that is, except the other candidates who were all in a state of shock at not being chosen.

The people began to celebrate and pushed, elbowed and generally manhandled all the other candidates out of the court.

And that is the story of how King Aradon found his Queen Eloiny…

The End…

Well almost…

For this is also the story of the Queen's Jewels.

To express his love and devotion to his Queen, the King had some extra special jewels made for her. He had them imbued with all the magic and love that they shared and set with gems that, while not precious, were able to enhance Queen Eloiny's natural talents of wisdom, love and empathy that calmed and healed all those in need.

In celebration of their marriage, the King had a crown made. It was a delicate silver circlet set with cornflower blue sapphires, to match her eyes. It was said that the crown was a symbol of the King's love for his Queen, for a circle has no beginning and no end.

The sapphire crown enriched her essential wisdom and she became known as the wisest of Queens – caring for all the people of the land.

On the first anniversary of their marriage, the King presented her with another jewel made especially for her. Golden circlets for her arms were set with dark green bloodstones, which heightened her instinctive empathy and protective nature. When she wore them, she was able to heal all but the direst of physical wounds and ailments.

And then on the birth of their first child, a beloved son and heir whom they named Daechir, the King had another jewel made for her. A golden torc to be worn about her neck set with opalescent moonstones. It was said that when she wore it, the magic within these stones could calm the raging beasts and lighten the darkest of moods.

Throughout their long lives, King Aradon gave everything that he was to his Queen and she gave everything that she was to her King. They ruled long and wisely together until the end of their days."

Thanir listened carefully for anything that

might give them some clue as to what the jewels were all about but there was no mention of them until the end of the story. Ambrosius was quiet for a moment.

"Hmm, I was beginning to wonder when the jewels were going to get a mention."

"There appears to be something written on the back of the pamphlet," Thanir pointed out. Ambrosius turned the book over to a comment written in another hand. The ink was faded but he was just able to make out the words.

No one knows what happened to the jewels after the King and Queen died. When King Daechir came to the throne, he wished to bestow his mother's jewels upon his own Queen but they could not be found. The King's treasure house had been cleared of all treasures and no one knows who took them. We must hope that one day they will be found and returned to their rightful owner.

"Is the footnote dated?" Thanir asked.

"Not that I can see but I think I might have a theory. I need to think about it for a while. Why don't you come back tomorrow and I should have… yes… I should have…" Ambrosius got up and wandered back to the secret door. He was muttering to himself and seemed to have forgotten that Thanir was there.

    Thanir picked up the little booklet and followed Ambrosius out.

Chapter 19

Fyr's journey was slow as he was not sure where he was going exactly, just the general direction. He was only able to move to a tree in his line of sight and the density of trees made that painfully slow. It would probably have been quicker to walk but it was getting dark and from the sounds around him, things lived in this forest that he would rather not meet in the daylight, never mind the dark. He climbed higher into the branches and tried to settle into the crook between the trunk and a wide branch. It was not very comfortable but he had no intention to sleep, only to rest his body and his eyes for a while, but before he knew it, he was fast asleep. The tree curled its branches around him to make sure he would not fall and covered him with leaves so that he could not be seen. It cradled him and kept him safe throughout the rest of the night.

Fyr woke with a start, totally

disorientated. He opened his eyes and for a moment could not work out where he was. The leaves around him shivered and shifted slightly, then twigs and branches slowly uncurled and moved out of his way. He gave the trunk a pat.

"Thank you for keeping me safe, friend. I am very much obliged to you."

The leaves gave another shiver that almost sounded like a giggle. As soon as his feet hit the ground, the leaves began to shift again. He watched in fascination as they curled together until they had made a small bowl. With a twisting and turning of its leaves, the tree gathered all the rain and dew that had collected on it during the night and funnelled it into the bowl. The tree was offering him a drink.

"Thank you again, dear friend," Fyr said after drinking his fill. "I hope we shall meet again."

Fyr decided to continue on foot, he decided. Should he come across one of the shambling creatures he had heard lumbering about, he knew he could step into a tree and wait until it had moved on. The forest floor was densely packed with ferns and brambles that could have made the going difficult, but luckily, he could follow the narrow trackways created by various small animals. Although as Fyr walked on, he was unaware that the pathways were closing up behind him. Anyone following him would find their way barred.

Around midday, Fyr arrived at a river and he knew that Kesia's village had to be somewhere on the other side. He needed to find a place to cross. Any bridges would be heavily guarded, he assumed. He set off, walking downstream until the river bank became too steep and slippery. He turned and retraced his steps until he found himself at the confluence of two rivers. He knew he was getting close but, frustratingly, there was nowhere to cross this river. He briefly contemplated trying to swim but a broken branch came swirling along at a great rate of knots, being thrown about by the current. It rather put a dampener on his idea of swimming.

Somewhere close by, Fyr felt, rather than heard, a tree fall. He took off and followed the river upstream this time and it was not long before he found the fallen tree. The fast flowing water must have undermined its roots and caused the huge tree to topple. Fortuitously, it had fallen so that it spanned the river from one bank to the other. He gave the trunk an experimental shove; it was not going anywhere. He climbed up through the roots and crossed the fast flowing water. Climbing down through the branches on the other side, he stopped long enough to send the tree his thanks and show his sorrow for its untimely end. As he continued his journey, he was unaware of the tree curling its roots, digging them back into the soil and levering itself upright once more. No one else would be crossing the river here.

The rest of the way to the village was a series of easy jumps from tree to tree until he came to the edge of the forest and then his luck ran out. There were no more trees in his line of sight. There must be other trees around the village but from this vantage point, they were not visible to him. He climbed higher into the upper branches to get a better view. It did not help but it gave him better view over the village green.

Arranged around the common, the village was small, there was not a lot to see. A few animals grazed on the green and there was a large, muddy-looking pond on the far side. To his left, the largest building was an inn or some sort of hostelry, beyond which there were stables and what looked and sounded like a forge. The hollow ring of hammer on anvil carried on the breeze. To his right the ground sloped steeply up to a ridge of high ground where a small chapel sat, serenely surveying the whole of the village. If he could get up there without being seen...

Everywhere, except the common, was surrounded by hedges and hurdles so he would have to keep to the lanes but there were far too many people about for him to just wander around. They probably did not get many visitors these days and a stranger would stick out like a sore thumb. Someone was bound to want to see his non-existent travel permit.

A noise from the inn caught Fyr's attention. Three men in chain mail came dragging a fourth man who was yelling and struggling to get away. His captors just laughed as all the other people in the vicinity turned away, deliberately not seeing or hearing anything as they went about their business. The prisoner continued his struggle, swearing loudly enough for Fyr to hear almost every word as he protested his innocence. The soldiers hauled him across the lane to the common, to a set of stocks and a pillory beside the pond. One of the soldiers cuffed the man about the head and he slumped in their grasp. They almost dropped him and with his waning strength, he tried to take them by surprise and make a run for it but he was soon caught and overpowered again. They man-handled him into the stocks and locked him in. Fyr wondered what the man had done to warrant such treatment.

One of the soldiers looked as though he was in charge. He turned towards the stables waved his hand and shouted at someone. A small boy, the stable lad, came running. Something the main man said had them laughing uproariously and slapping each other on the back. The stable lad's body language showed his reluctance to comply but the soldier gave him no choice and he narrowly missed a clip around the ear before he ran back to the stable. Moments later, he reappeared with a barrow full of manure.

The soldiers began to gather people around them. They too were clearly unwilling participants. Once a small crowd had gathered, they began to pick on people and made them throw dung and filth at the poor fellow in the stocks. They began half-heartedly but were soon bullied and intimidated to throw harder and hit the target almost every time. Fyr gritted his teeth. He wished he could stop them but he was one man, a stranger with no papers and would most likely end up joining the poor man, locked up quicker than he could spit. He had no choice but to stay put, hidden within the trees until he could decide what to do next.

He began to think that maybe…just maybe… he had been a little too hasty. He should have had a better plan. He had not thought beyond getting here. He had to be here for Kesia, if only he knew where she was. Maybe he should find out where her father lived. He did his best to wrack his brains. On their travels, they had talked about her father, where he lived and what he did but for the life of him, right at that moment, his mind had gone blank and he could not remember a word she had said.

Chapter 20

Kesia had met all the other women, none of whom she recognised as coming from her village, and they all seemed far too calm, quiet and accepting of what was happening. Most of them seemed to be on their own for one reason or another but she was not. Her father lived in this village. He was only a few minutes' walk away. They had to let her see him and then they would have to let her go. This was a ridiculous situation.

A noise just outside the dark room had all the other women rushing to find seats and busying themselves. Kesia still stood in the centre of the room as the door opened. There was a gasp from behind her - Posey? Petal? or maybe both.

"Come on out new girl. It's time for you to learn the rules," the guard stood at the door but did not come in.

"He's not allowed in," Hebe whispered.

"This is a women only space."

Their relief was short lived as the female guard pushed her way in and grabbed Kesia's arm. "First lesson, do as you're told." The other women were silent as she hauled Kesia out into the guardroom and slammed the door behind them.

The male guards all leered at Kesia as she was thrust into the middle of the small room.

"So," the female guard looked down her nose at Kesia. "What makes you so special, I wonder?" It was obviously a rhetorical question because she continued without waiting for an answer. "The rules are quite simple. One," she began to count them off on her fingers. "Do as you're told. Two, don't ask questions. Three, know your place. You are no one and should endeavour to be unobtrusive unless your new master wishes otherwise. And four, you will do whatever is asked of you. Do you understand me?"

Kesia could only nod.

"The Auctioneer is on his way to assess your suitability for sale. Come this way." The female guard turned without waiting for Kesia to follow and walked out into the long gallery.

"Well go on..." One of the male guards laughed and slapped her on the bottom.

Kesia ran. The female guard was waiting down by the bedroom cells, tapping her foot.

"There are punishments for not following orders." There was a nasty look in the female guard's eye. She was just waiting for Kesia to step out of line. "When the honourable gentleman comes in, you will follow his orders to the letter. Do not speak unless he asks a direct question."

She could do nothing but comply. She had no idea what the punishments could be and was not eager to find out.

The female guard stiffened to attention as footsteps were heard coming up the stairs.

"Remember, don't speak and keep your eyes down," the woman whispered.

Booted feet walked slowly across the

wooden floorboards and Kesia dared not turn around.

"Well, who do we have here? Ahh yes... our travelling lass, the chandler's daughter. Stand easy, Maud," he said to the guard. He walked around Kesia and looked her up and down. As he came around to the front, she did as she was told and kept her eyes down. All she could make out was a long dark robe and the toes of his polished boots. His voice sounded severe, strict and forbidding.

"Has she been bathed yet?"

"Not yet sir, only just arrived. It should be ready now," Maud said. The name did not suit her.

"Well, let's get to it." His voice had an edge to it that made Kesia shudder.

"Very good, sir." Maud grabbed Kesia's arm and dragged her back towards the stairs. They went down to a room off the central corridor. The door led into a large open kitchen. A black-leaded range filled the hearth, a water pump stood in one corner and a large dresser stood against the wall opposite the range. Kesia thought there should have been a table in the centre of the floor but it was tucked under the window out of the way. To the right of the hearth was another door. The laundry was a small room in comparison to the kitchen and it was much warmer. The fire had been lit under the copper and the water steamed ready.

The bath was a wide, shallow wooden tub, lined with linen. It was good to know they did not want her to get splinters. Posey and Petal were hustled in by one of the other guards. They gave Kesia no more than a quick glance as they passed by to fill the tub with cold water from the pump and hot water from the copper boiler. The Auctioneer leaned down and tested the water.

"A little more hot water if you please," he spoke to the guard rather than the girl actually doing the work. Kesia felt as though she and the other women were being dehumanised by this experience and standing there, in nothing but a scratchy linen shift, there was nothing she could do. He tested the water once more and waved the guard – and Posey and Petal – away. That left Kesia alone with the Auctioneer and the female guard, Maud. She knew what was coming next.

The Auctioneer walked slowly around her, studying her with an impassive face. He might have been looking to buy a cow… or a cart… or… he was not looking at her as though she was a person. He took a step back.

"Strip!"

Kesia stared at him. He was going to stand and watch while she took a bath. Kesia stood, frozen to the spot.

"I take it you have explained the punishments for non-compliance," he said the Maud.

"Not yet sir. She's been told the rules but hasn't been here long enough for that yet."

"Very well, explain it to her."

"If you don't follow the rules, you will be punished," Maud said, coming to stand in front of Kesia without blocking the Auctioneer's view of her. "Food will be withheld and you will be put on rationed bread and water. If you speak out of turn and question your betters, you will wear a scold's bridle and paraded around the town. If you do not learn your place, you'll be shown it. You'll be locked up, in solitary, in the cells below us, on bread and water. For not complying with orders, there are various punishments as the Masters see fit: pillory or stocks, chained up here," she pointed up to a hook embedded in the heavy beam that crossed the ceiling. "Or, you could be beaten."

"We would rather not beat you because that tends to lower the value, depending on who wants to buy you of course. Do you understand?"

"No! How can people be for sale? It's not right." Kesia could not keep the words in.

"Oh dear, what a shame. You had to go and spoil it," he said. She could not help but look up at his face. His smile said he thought it was anything but a shame. He turned to Maud. "Get the cuffs."

"Yes sir." She went over to a small cupboard in the corner. From her position, Kesia could not see what Maud had found. The Auctioneer grabbed her arm and strapped the leather cuff around her wrist. A short chain joined it to a second cuff that went around her other wrist. A rope attached to the short chain ran up through a wooden block and from there to the hook in the beam. The other item Maud took from the cupboard was a wooden bar with more straps that went around the head and acted as a gag. All Kesia could do was watch as the ropes were pulled and secured.

"I asked nicely but you refused, so now..." The Auctioneer grasped the front of her dress and tore it from her body. Before Kesia could move her arms to cover herself, the rope pulled taut and her dragging her arms up over her head. He walked around her again. His face was anything but impassive now. Kesia shook her head and groaned around the gag. She wanted to tell him not to touch her but she knew he would not have taken any notice. He did not take his eyes off her but spoke to Maud.

"You can leave. I'll make sure she's nice and clean."

Chapter 21

As promised, the sisters and their familiars arrived at Eleanor's house the next morning.

"I'm glad to see you looking so much better," Eleanor greeted Daphne.

"Thanks, it's taken a while." She had a tight grasp of Belus's hand.

Marianne had come downstairs to join them but she was on her own.

"You look a little distracted, darling," Addie said to her.

"Simon is still asleep. He's still got a bit of catching up to do," she joked. Eleanor and Addie looked at one another. They had both noticed the strain in her voice. Addie took hold of Marianne's hand and sent some of her healing power through their familial bond.

Eleanor turned to Emma. "So where's... you know... your father?" It would not have surprised Eleanor to discover that he had absconded.

"Never fear dear," Emma smiled. "I think the magic took a leaf out of your book. Remember when you turned that Ivy creature into a rat?" She gave Hermes a nod and he produced a small wooden box with a fine mesh set into the lid. Eleanor peered in to see a very disgruntled mouse. She had no idea that a mouse could sit up and fold its arms.

"It was entirely his own doing," Emma said. "We were having a 'conversation'…" She did the air quotes. "…about his exploits and to be honest, the way he was trying to wriggle out of taking any responsibility, he was lucky not to turn into a worm. It would have been more appropriate."

"So the mouse is John Dee?" Eleanor peered into the box again.

"Emma merely asked if he was a man or a mouse," Hermes commented, "and as you can see… We assumed it was a little of the magical backlash catching up with him at last." He let his cat's eyes and teeth show as he growled down at the mouse/Dee.

"Yes, thank you Hermes." Emma patted him on the arm. "We don't want him to die of fright before he can be properly brought to justice." She winked at Eleanor as the mouse gave a squeak and scrabbled furiously at the inside of his box.

"Just so you know. The box is bespelled so he won't be getting out of there until we're ready to let him out," Daphne added.

They sat around the table in the kitchen while Bella, who had decided to remain visible most of the time, bustled around preparing lunch for the group. She popped up here and there, muttering to herself that upstairs people should stay upstairs and not get in her way downstairs.

"Don't let her fool you," Eleanor smiled. "She's in her element... and enjoying every minute of it."

Addie leaned in to Marianne. "Are you sure Simon's okay? Want me to take a look?"

"Thanks for the offer, Aunt Addie,"

Marianne said. "But I think this spell is a bit like magical antibiotics and has to run its course."

"Did you get any sense that he was dreaming at all?" Eleanor asked.

"I'd say he was. I got odd flashes but nothing I could explain," Marianne gave a small chuckle. "He's not sharing."

"Are you sure you don't mind taking us through the gate dear?" Emma asked. "Are you sure you have the time?"

"It's fine. I'll open it this side and Branchir will send someone to meet you on the other side. It'll be just my luck that Edmund and Kitty choose that time to turn up."

"Don't you fret, Miss Eleanor, me an' Jack'll look after Mr Simon and Lady Marianne. An' if Mr and Mrs 'arrington arrive, we'll take care of them too," Bella said.

"Anyone would think you're trying to get rid of us," Eleanor laughed.

"Not you Miss Eleanor, just everyone else…"

"Thanks," Daphne grumbled good-naturedly.

"Besides, Mr James'll be 'ome soon. 'E knows where to find you."

Upstairs, Simon slept on. He was unaware of events elsewhere in the house. Deep in his dream, he saw a little girl called No one... no, her name was Nonus – odd name.

The child was all skin and bone and dressed in rags. She was covered in welts and bruises. The Holy Women who should be caring for her blamed her for every little misdemeanour whether she was at fault or not. When they were not beating her, they were locking her in a small, dark cupboard and starving her.

A woman arrived at the Abbey and, horrified by the treatment meted out to the child, decided to come to her rescue. She took the child away from the Abbey and together, they travelled across many worlds. The girl grew stronger and happier. She was no longer beaten or locked up and she was properly fed and clothed. For the first time in her life, she had someone who cared for her. Her rescuer became her mentor and her friend. After many years, they returned to her mentor's home. The girl had grown into a tall ethereal beauty and her friend had shrunk into old age and frailty.

The young woman sat in a chair at the side of the bed, reading aloud from a favourite book. She had read it so many times that she could quote it without looking at the pages. It meant she could keep her eyes on her old friend who was almost as pale as the sheets upon which she lay.

Outside, the weather was wild; the wind howled and buffeted at the walls of the building. It rattled the glass in the windows and whistled down the chimney raising sparks from the embers in the hearth.

"Try to stay calm, dear heart." Her mentor whispered. "You will soon learn better control."

"But I can't do it without you," the girl began to gasp as though short of breath.

"Calm, remember? Try not to panic." The old woman's voice was quiet and calm – no longer strong and vibrant as it had once been. "You are not going to suffocate. You are the air. Picture a warm, blue, cloudless sky…"

The girl clutched at her throat, her face turning red, until the old woman lifted an almost skeletal hand and gently stroked the girl's cheek. She relaxed at the touch.

"Focus on your breathing now, deep and slow

and steady, in and out." The old woman's voice was soft and coaxing. "There's nothing to fear. I have taught you all I can, child. It is up to you to make the gift your own now."

"No… please…" the girl pleaded quietly. "Not yet! It's too soon. How will I do this without you?" Huge tears ran down her cheeks, matched by the big fat raindrops that hit the window and rolled down the glass pane.

"Do not… fear it… Use it… make it yours…" The old woman was beginning to fade. "Use those tears… they are an emotional release. It is time to let me go. Where there is rain, there will be a rainbow. Look for it; it is a promise of better things to come."

The room became very quiet as the young woman concentrated on her old friend's breathing rather than her own. She held her hand until she took one last breath, and then there was no more. For a moment, everything went very still…

And then the weather went completely haywire.

The room lit up as lightning forked across the sky and thunder exploded simultaneously above the house. The rain slapping at the window became huge hailstones that threatened to break the glass and then silence as snowflakes feathered down to gather softly on the windowsill.

"Focus… focus… focus…" the girl screwed up her eyes and pressed her fingers to her temples while she chanted under her breath. "Blue… blue skies… no clouds… blue sky… sunny day… warm breeze…"

The wind slowly died down and the sky turned from a sickly yellow to a stormy, slate grey gradually paling and brightening into a deep azure. The girl had her eyes closed so she did not see the rainbow but it was there… just as promised.

"Goodbye my teacher… my friend… I think I understand now," the girl said as both she and the old lady vanished.

"Well… this is… awkward," the girl's surprised voice said. The bell rope next to the mantelpiece began to flail and then it was tugged sharply. A smartly dressed man appeared at the door. He stepped in and gazed about the room. When he caught sight of the empty bed, he bowed his head and his shoulders slumped.

"Goodbye my lady," he said quietly.

"Um… Welkin… Can you see me?" the young woman's voice asked.

Shocked, Welkin jumped and then raised an

elegant eyebrow as he looked around the room for the source of the voice.

"Er, no Miss… you appear to be… rather… you don't appear to be… not at all."

"Well, that was as clear as mud, Welkin."

"My apologies Miss. I was rather taken by surprise." He took a deep breath and became his usual efficient and professional self. "Am I given to understand that her Grace has… left us?" Unsure where to address his remark, he stared straight ahead.

"Yes. I was holding her hand when she died. The last thing she said was that I would get my wish."

"Pardon my presumption but… what was your wish?" Welkin asked thin air.

"When she came for me… all those years ago," the girl's voice said. "The Holy Sisters had locked me up in a small, dark cupboard. I remember feeling a warm breeze through holes in the door and wishing I could be free to roam unseen, just like the breeze. Welkin, do you think I'm dead too?" she asked in a small voice. "Do you think I have become a ghost?"

"I do not believe so, Miss Sylvestri. The Queen of the Four Winds is dead. Long live the new Queen."

"Oh, Welkin. I can't even see myself," she

complained and thunder rumbled in the distance.

"I am sure you will acclimatise very soon, my lady."

"Was that a joke, Welkin?"

"Yes, I believe so, my lady," he said in his deadpan voice.

Chapter 22

Thorn and Gould came to a stretch of road familiar from their previous visit. They could follow it directly to the Elven King's castle and had to hope that he would see them and listen to what they had to say. Initially, they followed the road using the trees growing alongside and were relieved when they eventually came to a place where they could see the castle in the distance. It sat proudly on a hill surrounded by a small town. A few more tree to tree jumps and they had arrived at the town gates, which stood open to allow a steady stream of people in and out. Once inside, they discovered that all roads within the town eventually led up to the castle.

"Should we just go up there and knock on the front door?" Gould asked.

"Do castles have a front door?" Thorn wondered.

"Well, how else would they get in?"

Gould said.

They walked around the castle mount looking for the entrance. Between them and the hill were a series of ditches, some of which were full of water with no obvious way across until they rounded the next tower and came to the gate house. It was hard to miss; a huge imposing structure with a portcullis within and a drawbridge without. The drawbridge was down and the portcullis was up so they probably could have walked right in but that seemed a bit rude.

Thorn noticed people moving about high up on the parapet of the gate house, patrolling back and forth.

"I say... hello!" Gould shouted up at them.

"I say... hello? What kind of greeting is that?" Thorn muttered.

"First thing that came into my head," Gould whispered back.

"State your name and the purpose of your visit." A man had appeared at the far side of the drawbridge. It did not escape the two men's notice that all the guards up on the gatehouse roof were now looking down at them with bows and arrows poised.

"I'm Gould and this is Thorn. We are Driadi Boroviche and we'd like to speak to His Majesty, King Branchir."

"Or General Sardo," Thorn added.

"You would, would you?" said the man on the drawbridge. "Well, you'd better come in then."

The two Boroviche men crossed the wooden bridge and through the gate house, intimidated by the sheer size of the place - which was, no doubt, the intention. The guard led them along alley after alley, round one corner then another, in the maze-like structure, until they had no idea where they were going. Thoroughly confused, they arrived at yet another archway. It opened into a wide courtyard with buildings on all sides and realised they were at the foot of a round, central tower. A set of steep steps led up into a huge hallway.

Everything about this place was enormous and rather overwhelming; the floor was a wide expanse of black and white tiles and an intricately carved staircase wound its way around the walls, up towards the high ceiling. Across the hallway, a blast of sound assaulted their ears as a huge door opened just wide enough to yield a man in a long dark robe.

"You were asked to bring them straight here," the man said, speaking to their guard. Then he turned to Gould and Thorn with a slight bow. "My apologies gentlemen, I am Thanir, the King's Chamberlain and should have been the one to greet you on His Majesty's behalf. I have no idea why you were taken the long way round." He turned back to their guard and waved him away muttering, "Ridiculous man ..." he shook his head and turned his attention to the two Boroviche men again. "If you would follow me, I will escort you to the library."

As they passed through the huge doors, Thanir stroked the surface of the wood and said, "I believe this was your home for many years."

Thorn frowned. "But we've never been here before."

"Pardon me," Thanir gave a slight bow in apology. "I was not referring to the castle but to the doors."

"You mean it really was true?" Gould gasped.

"Oh my, yes... indeed." Thanir confirmed.

Walking between the doors made the hair on the back of Thorn's neck stand up.

The noise level rose again as they entered the Great Hall. They had never seen so many people gathered in one space. They were sitting and eating and talking... and talking and eating. Despite the size of the place, it felt surprisingly ordinary: bare stone walls, a flagstone floor and row after row of long tables and it was filled with very ordinary looking people.

"Is the King here?" Gould asked. He could not see anyone who looked like either of the men they had met.

"His Majesty will meet with you in the library. It is much quieter in there," A small door at the back of the hall led them to a long corridor lined with doors. Thanir opened one of the doors and showed them into a surprisingly small room, in comparison to what they had seen so far. The furnishings here had the opulence that had been missing from the Great Hall. Shelves lined most of the wall.

"I've never seen so many books in one place before," Gould whispered. "How could one person ever hope to read this many?"

Arranged around a low table set before a roaring fire, were three long, well-padded sofas. Thanir held out a hand to indicate that they should sit.

"His Majesty will be with you directly." He gave them a small bow and left the room.

The crackle of the fire was the only

sound as the two men sat perched on the edge of their seat, feeling quite out of place and shabby. Their eyes were drawn to a painting hanging above the fire. They recognised the King. He was holding hands with the most beautiful woman either of them had ever seen and both the King and Queen were smiling down at the two beautiful children playing with a puppy at their feet.

"It really doesn't do my wife justice."

Thorn and Gould leapt to their feet, at the sound of the voice behind them. They had not heard anyone enter the room. Branchir smiled at them. "Come gentlemen, let us sit a while and chat."

The two Boroviche men had met the King before but it had been on the road and much less formal. He had been very easy to talk to then but this was his castle and they were unsure how to behave.

Branchir sat back on one of the other sofas and crossed one leg over the other, looking calm and relaxed. "Will you take tea with me?"

The two men nodded, dumbstruck as a tiny woman with dark, beady eyes came in carrying a tray that was almost as big as she was. Thorn was about to get up and offer help but Branchir raised an elegant eyebrow and gave an almost imperceptible shake of his head. Thorn could not help but think this was somehow wrong for such a small person to be carrying such a large burden while three grown men sat by and did nothing.

The tiny woman placed the tray on the table between them.

"Thank you Finch," Branchir said.

"All is being goods, Majesty," she said as she bustled about giving out plates and pouring dark brown liquid from a round, spouted pot. General Sardo came into the room and she poured him a cup too.

"Ah, Finch, my favourite little lady," he grinned.

"Oh, nows... Be goings on with yous ..." her little face flushed with pleasure and she hid her grin as she pretended not to approve of him. Sardo sat and accepted the plate of sandwiches Finch handed to him.

"What's this Finch? No cake?" he grinned at her.

She gave him her best fierce look. "You be waitings for cake… Eatings saminds first… greedy boy. New lads is in needings of food." She gave all the appearance of scolding him but he roared with laughter.

"Drinkings tea now," she scolded. "It is gettings wretchedly not too hot soon. "

"Sardo, please don't tease poor Finch," the King said good-naturedly.

Finch gave the King a smile and patted Sardo on the knee. Then the two Boroviche men found themselves under the scrutiny of those dark, beady eyes again. She waved her hands at them and nodded encouragingly.

"Good, eatings up… nice, polites boys." Having decided that they had everything they needed she gave a nod to the King and left.

"That's a relief," Sardo grinned. "Finch

has decided to like you both."

"What if she hadn't?" Gould asked.

"Probably would have put poison in your tea," Sardo chuckled. The horrified looks on Thorn and Gould's faces said they were not sure whether to believe him.

"Finch has been looking after my family for many years now," Branchir said. "She can get a little... over-protective. Oh, don't worry. She is far stronger than she looks. Probably stronger than all of us. Yes, even you my friend," he said to Sardo who was about to contest the statement.

Thorn had eaten the food, drunk the warm brown liquid and had begun to get a little fidgety. "I wonder if we might explain why we've come..." he began.

"But, of course," Branchir nodded at him. "Please enlighten us as to the reason for your visit." Branchir was no longer smiling. He was ready for business.

Sardo sat forward with his forearms resting on his thighs with his hands held loosely between them. He looked relaxed but he was far from it. "Somehow, I have a feeling we're not going to like what you're going to tell us," he said.

"No sir," Thorn shook his head. "Do you recall, Your Majesty, when you accompanied us to the gate to Aldamar and we were stopped by some men guarding a toll gate?"

"Indeed I do," Branchir said.

"And I'm pretty sure that you sorted that out and sent them on their way with a flea in their ear," Sardo added.

"Am I to understand that this was not an isolated incident?" Branchir asked.

"It was not, Your Majesty. When we got home, everything had changed," Gould said.

"In what way changed?" Branchir asked.

"It feels like everything," Thorn said. "Our whole way of life has been turned upside down. We don't know when or how this happened but there's a man of the Boroviche calling himself Hedeon – we don't think it's his real name – he's built himself an army and intends to set himself up as... as a king, I suppose."

"Go on," Sardo encouraged. His face had darkened and he frowned, his eyes almost disappearing beneath his heavy brows.

"Our people have lived off the land for as long as anyone can remember. We grow what we need to feed our families and we barter with our neighbours for goods and services. But now, they're putting folks out of their homes so that this Hedeon can move his own people in to rule over the rest of us. He calls them his Knights. There are so many new laws and rules that our people have had no say in... It's not our way. We have... or had... Elders. They're chosen from the wisest of us, to make the laws according to the good of the people. These new rules seek only to serve Hedeon and his men. Most of the Elders have gone... moved away... or, more likely, been moved. Those who remain are too few to make a difference without putting themselves and their families at risk. Everyone now lives in fear, not knowing who to trust anymore."

"And don't forget the training," Gould added.

"Training for what?" Branchir asked.

"Fighting. It took us a while to find out what was going on. People are too afraid to talk in case we're spies for Hedeon," Gould said.

"We soon found out though. We too were called upon. They are taking every able-bodied man away from their family, from their trade, their farm or workshop to make them swear a loyalty oath to Hedeon. They say we could be called up at any time, to fight for the Knight or Hedeon. We're farmers, tanners, dyers, millers and what-have-you, but that is no longer good enough for them," Thorn said.

"Who are you expected to fight?" Branchir asked.

"We don't know. No one does," Gould said.

"So who does all the work that the men

are no longer able to do? Presumably these Knights still need food and supplies," Sardo asked.

"The women, the children, the sick and the old... Oh, apart from blacksmithing, men still do that job," Thorn said.

"Yes, but in the old days, smiths used to make and mend tools, pots and pans, cartwheels. No one is making useful things or mending anything now. Guards stand over them while they make weapons," Gould added.

It all began to pour out in a jumble. First Gould, then Thorn added details as they thought of them.

"There are officials everywhere, overseeing the roads, the markets..."

"... Taxes, travel... oh and whether or not couples are married..."

"... or can prove that they're married."

"If they have no proof the women are taken away, as they can no longer prove that they are... pure... and therefore marriageable to the Knights… Hedeon says only he has the right to say who is allowed to wed and who to…" Thorn's throat was feeling increasingly tight with emotion.

"What happens to the women who are taken away? Where are they taken?" Sardo growled. "And for what purpose?"

"They're put up for auction. Some become servants… or, more likely, slaves to the Knights," Thorn said.

"Or worse," Gould muttered.

Sardo leapt to his feet, his fists clenched.

"And this is why Fyr isn't here with us," Gould added, looking wide-eyed before the General could speak.

Thorn looked fearfully between the King and Sardo. "When we got home and crossed the border… well, Fyr and Kizzy had become close but of course they weren't married yet. They said they'd send her to her home village… to be auctioned off… to the highest bidder because she had become a fallen woman, traipsing about the countryside and the like... Then we were all split up and sent on our way without being able to see her, or Farris's wife, again."

"This is monstrous," Branchir's voice was barely above a whisper as he fought to retain his calm. Standing up, he paced to his desk with its three-dimensional map. Until fairly recently, the top left corner of the map had been a blank space. Now it showed the area the Boroviche called home.

"So, did Fyr travel to her village with her?"

"No, they wouldn't let him. We need permits to travel anywhere now and they don't grant them to anyone - not unless you know whose palm to grease, and even then..." Gould said.

Branchir stood over his map. "I wish to see where Hedeon is right now," he said through gritted teeth. He called the others over to join him as a small area in the north east corner of the island rose up and enlarged. "Show me where this coward is hiding."

A smaller area north of the mountains rose up further. It showed several small settlements ranged along a river. An area of construction showed something being built just outside one of the settlements. Branchir held his hand, palm down, over the area and enlarged it further still. A wooden tower stood on top of an artificial hill, surrounded by palisades, banks and ditches.

"Looks like he's building himself a very small castle," Sardo said grimly.

"And Kesia's village?" Branchir asked. "Do you know where that is?"

Gould and Thorn shook their heads.

"It's somewhere south of where we live, not far from the coast I think," Thorn said.

"I wish to see where Fyr of the Boroviche is right now," Branchir said.

The image moved and showed them a small village surrounded by forest and fields.

"And he's gone to find her... alone?" Sardo asked.

The two men nodded.

"I'll fetch my gear," Sardo said eagerly.

"Not so hasty my friend," Branchir said. "We can no longer justify rushing off into the unknown. Besides, your wife would skin us both." He gave his General a tight smile. "We need more information than we can glean from this map. I will ask the Lady Sylvestri for her assistance."

Chapter 23

Lurking about in the trees was not going to help him find Kizzy, or her father. The chapel on the hill was his best option as it was the highest point and if he could get to the top of the tower, he would be able to see the layout of the village. That was all well and good but getting there unseen was going to be the problem. He had no choice but to wait until dark.

Even after the sun had set, the village continued to bustle with activity for several hours. Luck really was not on his side as a full moon, a big, bright full moon, hung in a cloudless sky, illuminating the landscape. It meant he could see where he was going but unfortunately, it meant he would be far too visible – should anyone be looking.

From his perch in the tree, he watched as one by one the lights in the buildings around the village green went out; the mill sails stopped turning first then the shops on the far side of the pond closed down their shutters. The forge fell silent and finally the inn's lights went out. He turned back to study the row of shops: there were five and from this distance, they all looked alike. He was too far away to see the paintings on their hanging signs but he was certain one of them belonged to Kesia's father.

The time between the moon setting and the sun rising would be very short, so there was nothing for it, he had to make his move and try for the chapel now. Climbing down the tree, he crept to the edge of the forest. He stood as still as the trees and studied the area around him. Everything was still and quiet. To his left the narrow lane ran off into fields of a low growing crop; no hiding place there. To his right, the lane broadened out into the village. A narrow strip of dense shadow ran up the lane, tight against the hedge that bordered the fields. It gave him a little cover so he took a deep breath and moved out. He crept along in the semi-darkness until he came to a wooden road sign. The moonlight was bright enough to read the sign.

Carved into the right arm were the words Chapel and Tithe Barn while the other arm indicated The Sea, Mayor's House and New Place. Hoping that no one saw him, he set off up the lane towards the chapel.

The end of the lane was a dead end and a lych gate, which offered him temporary cover as he crouched on the ledge. Heart banging in his chest, he could see the main door of the chapel clearly in the moonlight. It was a small building with white-washed plaster walls, a red tiled roof and a squat tower with an equally squat spire at one end. Moonlight silvered the grass surrounding the chapel showing up several darker patches, which were most likely recent burials. The more he looked the more he saw and there did seem to be rather a lot of them. He had to hope that this had not become a plague village.

Fyr shuddered as he hopped down from

the ledge and vaulted over the five-bar gate. He landed on the grass in a crouch, making himself as small as possible, and scanned the area. He held his breath until he was sure that nothing moved and there was no other sound beyond the pounding of his heart. Staying low, he crawled to the chapel door only to discover his way barred by a locked door covered by a locked metal grille. He crept around to the west end of the building. There was a round window high up on the gable end but, even if he had been able to reach it, it was too small. The windows on the north side were lower but, like the door, they too were barred. Continuing around the building to the far end, he came to a small annex, added to the main chapel at some time in the distant past. Concealing himself behind a large bush to give him time to think, he was surprised to discover a small wooden door. It was rotten along the bottom edge and some of the joints were loose. It would take very little effort to break it open. Hidden by the shrubbery as it was, it had apparently been forgotten when the metal grilles had been added to the other doors and windows. There was no evidence of a lock either. Holding his breath, he took hold of the handle and pushed the door. There was a little resistance but it opened with the barest of squeaks. The weight on the door was from a heavy tapestry that covered the wall and concealed the door from the inside too. Maybe his luck had not run out completely.

Despite the brightness of the moon outside, inside the building was dark and shadowy. He had just enough light to see the piles of chairs stacked in the main body of the chapel. He managed to pick his way around them without tripping or knocking them over. He found his way to the inside of the main doorway and found a ladder propped up against the wall. Glancing up he could make out the dark lines of a trapdoor set into the ceiling. This had to be the entrance to the tower. Testing his weight on the first couple of rungs, he found it sturdy enough and climbed up. Pushing up the trap door, he could see that it opened into a small square room. This was obviously a storage area but from the layer of dust on the floor, it was evident that no one had been up there recently.

Cobwebs hung in tattered curtains from the rafters and cross-braces of the short spire. Dust rose up in a choking cloud as he walked across to the nearest louvered window. He held his breath, now was not the time to cough or sneeze. The sound would probably carry across the village. The air was a little clearer by the window. There was one set into each wall. The louvres were wide enough that, from here, he had a good view out over the village and surrounding countryside. He could see the mill, a granary and, just below it, the bakery. Forest and fields disappeared into the distance in all directions. The broad expanse of roof below him had to be the tithe barn and just beyond that, in the same grounds, the Mayor's house, as signposted.

Further out, beyond the Mayor's house,

on the edge of the village, was another large house standing in its own grounds. He had to move around to the next window to get a better view. It was larger than the Mayor's House and a much newer building. This was no farm house. The grounds around the house were set out as an ornamental garden: an intricate knot-work of paths, low hedges and flowerbeds. Farther away, down the hill, he could see a few newly planted trees - placed here and there for effect. This had to belong to Hedeon or one of his followers. With its fancy carved plasterwork on walls painted a dusky shade of dark pink, it looked out of place in this small village.

Fyr suddenly realised it was much later than he had thought. His attention caught by the bright sparkle of early morning sunlight on the sea on the horizon.

As the sun rose, far below him, people began to emerge from their homes to go about their business. He heard the creak and grind of the mill as the miller started the sails.

Smoke rose from the bakery's chimney and the resonant ring of hammer on anvil could be heard clear across the village.

Fyr stiffened. Voices were coming his way. Two men walked up the lane towards the chapel, their voices carried by the early morning air. Fyr hoped they were heading to the tithe barn but they passed it by and continued up towards the chapel. He doubted that they would come up into the tower but he was not going to chance it. He needed to find something to erase his footprints. An old flour sack from a pile in the corner would do. He draped a few more of the sacks over some packing crates to make himself a small crawl space to hide. He managed to shuffle inside just in time as he heard the jangle of keys from below.

Listening to the sounds, he heard the key rattle in the metal grille, heard it unlock and open. Then there was the deeper clunk of the lock in the wooden door. The heavy door creaked slowly as though the hinges were rarely used.

This was going to be another waiting game. He had no idea how long these men would be there or why they were there, but maybe he would hear something that might be to his advantage.

Kesia lay on the bed in her tiny cell of a room. She had endured the humiliation as the Auctioneer made her stand in the bath and then he washed her. His movements were rough and rapid as though he did not enjoy the task but the look on his face and the sound of his breathing gave lie to that. His hands stayed too long in some places.

"Have to make sure you are clean," he muttered to himself. Then he began to ask her questions, some that he had already asked. Although she did not see anyone else, she had the feeling that there was someone watching and the questions were for this other person's benefit. However, she could only answer with a nod or a shake of her head because he did not remove the gag.

Now, alone in this tiny dark room, she wanted to cry but the pain inside her was so fierce that it felt as though letting go enough to allow the tears would somehow make her disappear. Maybe that would be for the best. A slight scratching at the door startled her. There was no light but she was aware of the door opening slowly and a small voice whispered her name.

"Hello?" she whispered back.

There was a sigh of relief and the sound of bare feet on the floorboards. A slight bump to the bed frame told her where the person was.

"Who is it?" Kesia whispered.

"It's me, Hebe. I'm not supposed to be out of bed, but I had to come and make sure you were all right. Did they hurt you? Posey or Petal said they had you tied up before your bath."

"Yes," was all Kesia could say without the choking feeling coming back.

"Don't worry. I heard them say you were all good. Lobelia wanted to come and check on you but it's easier for me – I'm the smallest. I can't stay long, just needed to check that you were safe... you are all right, aren't you?"

Kesia felt Hebe's hands reach out for her and she allowed the girl to hug her before she disappeared back the way she had come.

The one thing that Kesia had to hang on to now was that they were going to let her see her father tomorrow. Then all this nonsense would be sorted out.

Chapter 24

Simon was aware of Marianne as she moved quietly around the room. She had spoken to him once or twice and he was sure that he had answered her but then, he might have dreamt it. His dreams were weird. He managed to rouse himself when Marianne answered a quiet knock on the door and a smell tickled his nose making him aware that he was hungry and very thirsty.

"Can you sit up?" Marianne fussed about, plumping up the pillows and making him comfortable. He was not an invalid but a little fussing now and then was nice. She straightened the quilt around him and handed him a plate… and there was that smell again.

"Bacon sandwich, mmm…" He closed his eyes as he took a bite, chewed and appreciated the savoury, salty goodness. "Thank you, I needed that." He felt as though he had inhaled the sandwich without it even touching the sides. He took the glass of water and gulped it down in three mouthfuls.

"Slow down… you'll choke yourself." Marianne was only half joking as he coughed. "How are you feeling now?"

"Like I'm only half-way here," he said. "My head is muzzy and I can't seem to wake myself up properly." He gave a long yawn. "I think I need to go back to sleep… just for a little while longer." Another yawn and he shoved his pillow under his head to get comfortable as he lay down again. Marianne cleared away the plate and glass then sat in the chair at the side of the bed with a book. She propped her feet up on the bed and settled in to read. She had only read a couple of pages before her eyes felt heavy and her head began to nod. She was not even aware that she had fallen asleep until she saw Simon standing on the opposite side of a mill stream. He looked over at her and gave her a smile but then his attention shifted and he focussed on the small house beside the stream. He glanced back but, as is the way with dreams, Marianne had disappeared.

Two children ran out of the mill building.

"Miro, keep an eye on your sister… and keep away from the water," a woman's voice called from the dark interior. The boy was probably about ten years old. He wore a rough woollen shirt with a dark waistcoat and ragged britches that barely covered his knees. His bare feet were filthy.

The boy pushed floppy hair out of his eyes as he turned and frowned and watched his younger sister run towards him.

"Ma!" he complained. "Does she really have to come?"

His harassed looking mother appeared in the doorway. She wore an apron tied over her long skirts and her sleeves were rolled up beyond her elbows. A hand, red and raw-looking, pushed a stray lock of hair out of her eyes.

"You know it's washing day," she sighed." I can't have you two under my feet while I've got the water boiling. Just keep an eye on her for me… and keep out of old Manzi's orchard." Then she called to the little girl. "Milara?"

"Yes mama?" the six year old's long, pale blue, woollen dress tangled around her bare feet, almost tripping her as she turned.

"Don't forget your cap and pinafore, and do try to keep them clean today. And Miro, you need your cap too."

The two children trudged back to their mother where she helped Milara into a white pinafore and pulled a mob cap over the child's unruly curls. Then, before he could get away, she plopped an over-large, floppy, flat cap onto Miro's head. From a distance they could have graced a twee Victorian painting but close up, the dust and dirt of poverty was too deeply ingrained.

Milara followed Miro through the garden gate and out onto a deeply rutted, dusty lane. It was dry and dusty now but when it rained, the lane became an impassable river of mud. Today though, the sun shone in a cloudless blue sky, with the promise of heat later.

The children were a fair way down the lane when they ducked left and disappeared through a gap in the hedgerow. Moments later, Miro was halfway up an apple tree picking the biggest and best of the apples and dropping them down to his sister who caught them in her pinafore with a practised ease. She carefully placed each apple on the growing pile under the tree. So much for listening to their mother and staying out of the orchard.

"Oy!" An angry male voice shouted from a distance. Miro quickly shinned down the tree and grabbed Milara by the hand.

"Run Lara!" he gasped as they dodged between the low trees, giggling, while the angry man thundered after them.

"You wait 'til I catch you… little beggars… I'll tan your hides… think you can steal from me do you?"

They may have been picking the apples but they had not actually stolen anything. The little girl had taken great care with each apple, shining it on her pinafore before placing it gently on the pile.

Miro let go of his sister's hand as they ran around a large bush. The angry man was getting closer. Suddenly a scream pierced the air followed by panicked shouting. Miro dashed around the bush expecting to see the angry man had caught Milara but the angry man was not there, nor was Milara. He was closer to the water's edge than expected and there was no sign of his sister. There was only one place she could be; a small depression showed where the bank had given way.

Miro ran up and down, scanning the water for

movement but he could not find his little sister. He had not seen her fall and the water was neither deep nor fast-flowing near the edge but she was not there. His blood was pounding in his ears and his heart was trying to force its way out of his chest.

Several metres downstream a dark shadow moved beneath the surface of the deeper water in the middle of the river. The boy was unaware of it as he ran in a blind panic, screaming his sister's name. Beneath the surface, the dark shape turned against the flow and sped towards a patch of shadow below the overhanging branches of a weeping willow. The small body was sinking fast, dragged down by the heavy water-logged material of her dress. Suddenly she was out of the water and on the bank, gasping for air.

"Stupid child. Didn't your mother tell you not to play near the water?" The voice came from the shadowy figure looming over her - a deep male voice but not the angry man.

"Thank you sir," Milara rasped, in between coughing up a lung-full of water.

"Don't thank me yet. I saved you from drowning and no good deed goes unpunished."

She had no idea what he meant.

"How old are you child?"

"Six and a half, sir."

"Too young…" he sighed. "Well, you owe me your life and now you are indebted to me. When the time is right, I will return for you and you will come to me. Sleep now and recover." There was a faint swish of the willow in the water and the shadowy man disappeared back into the water.

Miro kept on screaming until his voice was hoarse with the effort. The angry man stomped into view.

"Where's your sister, boy?"

"She fell.. In the water…. I can't see her. She can't swim."

"Right, calm yourself now. Show me where she went in," the man's voice was rough, brusque but no longer angry.

Miro ran and pointed to the spot where the edge of the bank had collapsed. The man scanned the area and, noting the way the water flowed, made his way along the river towards the willow. Holding the branches back like a curtain, he called out over his shoulder.

"Here boy, come here." He dropped to his knees beside what at first had appeared to be a pile of soaking rags. Leaning in close, he checked to see if she was breathing and then turned her over to search for a heartbeat.

"Is she…?" Miro choked out.

"No, she's fine, just sleeping. She was lucky. Her dress was nearly the death of her. All that wet wool was almost too heavy for her. I'm surprised she managed to get herself out of the water."

"Come on, show me where you live boy," the man said as he scooped the small, sodden figure up off the ground and set off across the orchard without waiting for Miro.

The weather or the season or possibly the year changed in the blink of an eye. The lane was a quagmire, impassable to anything other than foot traffic. It was time that had moved on. As the mill came into view it clear that it was in a shocking state of disrepair, almost derelict. The mill race had long since silted up and the sluggish water had barely enough power left to turn the water-weed draped wheel, which was also missing several of its paddles. Chunks of plaster and daub missing from the walls had exposed the wattle skeleton beneath and one of the window shutters hung by a single hinge, creaking gently as it swung in the breeze. Surely, no one could still be living there. Quiet voices drifted from inside.

"I'm so glad you came back, my darling girl," the woman's voice sounded old and frail.

"I'm here, as promised," the other voice, a young woman, sounded sad and weary. "I said I would come."

"Milara," the old woman sounded a little brighter. "You will stay a while, won't you? Your brother will be along soon."

"No, he won't Mama. Miro can't come. Don't you remember? He died in the war. Ten years ago."

"Don't you worry my darling girl. Your Papa will bring him home to me."

"Oh Mama, Papa has been gone a long time… even longer than Miro…"

Inside the house, the mill gears and grinding stones took up most of the space. The other half was split by a table with long benches on either side beyond which, against the end wall, was a narrow bed. The woman lying in the bed was barely recognisable as the same one who had scolded her children on laundry day. She was a frail, sunken creature with yellowed, papery skin. The young woman was Milara, now grown up. She held her mother's fragile hand until long after the sun had gone down. Eventually she gave a huge sigh and crossed her mother's hands over her chest and covered her over with the sheet. She had slipped away between one blink and the next.

Without a backward glance, Milara turned, left the house for the last time and took a slow walk down passed the mill pond, towards the overgrown orchard. Putting one foot in front of the other, she trudged through the sticky mud through the orchard and to the river beyond. She was not really looking where she was going and was surprised to find herself standing by a weeping willow. She crumpled to her knees, only now letting the tears come in great wracking sobs.

A faint splash in the river made her look up and wipe her face on her sleeve. A shadowy shape stepped up out of the water behind the willow branches.

"I'm here, as promised," she whispered. She had said the same words to her mother but this time they did not have the same feeling behind them.

"So I see," the deep voice said.

"I have nothing… and no one left…"

"Then the time has come. It is time to pay your debt."

"I cannot pay you, I have no money. I have nothing left to pay with; the mill doesn't belong to me and…"

"I have no need of money or things. You are all that I require. My time is almost up and I must train a replacement. By allowing me to save your life, you incurred a debt. Becoming my replacement is your payment."

Milara had no idea what the man was talking about.

"Come, it is time to go," he said, holding out a shadowy arm.

Milara did not move. "Go where?"

"You must come with me, now." He reached though the willow branches and grabbed her arm. It must have been a trick of the light or her frazzled and bereaved mind because his hand on her arm looked as though it was made of water. Before she could protest, he dragged her into the water.

She fought against him as he pulled her towards him and plunged them both beneath the surface. She came up for air, coughing and spluttering hard.

"Be calm girl. I'm not going to hurt you," he said. The soothing tone belied by his actions.

She obviously did not believe him and almost managed to twist out of his grasp but he pulled her close and they went under again.

"Relax… feel the water flow over you… through you." They were under water and yet, she could still hear his voice clearly. It was strangely calm and comforting although a little strained as he struggled to hold on to the woman thrashing about in his arms. "Stop fighting. You cannot drown. You did that already, years ago, remember?"

Despite the man's assurances, it felt very much as though he was trying to drown her. Why bother saving her life as a child only to kill her now.

"Stop struggling. This is inevitable and has been since I pulled you out of the water. You are about to be reborn, to become something other than what you were. We shall wash away your old life of hardship and pain so that you may begin anew. I shall teach you everything you need to know so that you may immerse yourself in your new element."

The man was obviously a psychopath or religious maniac or both. He seemed to think that this was some sort of baptism.

Milara continued to struggle but she was tiring.

Eventually she could no longer hold her breath. She had no choice; she had to stop fighting and give up. Her struggles slowed and then ceased altogether as the last few bubbles rose to the surface and then, nothing moved.

"There… all done… it wasn't that bad was it?" he said with a smile.

A sudden spasm… a gasp and… "What did you do to me?" she demanded to know as she realised she was actually breathing under water… and still alive.

"I told you. You have been reborn. You are like me now, but you have a lot to learn about this new power."

But she was not exactly like him. Under water, he looked as though he was made of glass – transparent. She on the other hand had become a pale green version of herself, with flowing green hair the colour of the pond weed that floated in the mill stream. She dragged herself out of the water and onto the riverbank. Turning, she gave him a scowl and then let out a shriek as a spout of water shot high into the air.

"Water is now your element. That mark on your arm is proof."

She looked down at her forearm to see a strange triangular mark embedded in her skin.

"I will teach you to control it. As befits your new life, I gift you a new name. From this moment forth you shall be known as Undine."

Simon woke with a start, surprised to find himself still in bed and Marianne asleep, slumped in the chair at his bed side.

Chapter 25

"These people need help," Sardo argued.

"Yes they do my love but..." Aurelia was doing her best to stay calm but he had a point. They both knew he had the itch to go and fight for what was right and it was a feeling he had not had for a long time now. These two men of the Boroviche had come begging for assistance to ease the plight of their people. Sardo knew he wanted to help but beyond his fighting skills, he was just not sure what sort of help he could give. He knew in his heart that Branchir wanted to support these people too but he had to think with his King's head on not his soldier's heart.

Logically, Sardo knew that to go racing into an unknown situation without all the information or a properly thought out plan was beyond stupid so he paced the room while his mind mulled over their options. Every time he passed the map, he stopped momentarily, to search for a route that would lead them to the Boroviche homelands. Each time it was different: the shortest route, the quickest route, the safest route. They needed to be ready when the call came.

"Sardo, my love, please come and sit down. Your pacing is making me anxious," Aurelia appealed to him. "From what Thorn and Gould told us, there are plenty of crops in the fields. They won't go hungry."

"But they will," he said. "There aren't enough people to complete the harvest. It will all go to waste. And the animals are suffering too. The people left to manage the farms are trying to the jobs of two or three people. They do everything and then to have to give up a tenth of their produce to these people who have set themselves up to rule… this Hedeon character needs to be taken down…" Sardo tried to explain to her again.

"I have an awful feeling of deja vu," Aurelia said quietly to her husband as she took his hand. She did not need to say more, he knew she was talking about her brother.

"You must promise me to be careful," Daewen said to Branchir. "We have no idea what this man really wants. Will he be satisfied with the Boroviche lands or has he set his sights on something more?"

The door opened and Sylvestri breezed in.

"My Lady," Branchir and Sardo both stood and bowed as Thanir announced her.

"A little bird tells me you have a small job for me," she said. Thanir had shuffled to her side to offer his support. Hidden by his robes, he held onto her hand. Branchir asked the two Boroviche men to explain the details once more as he indicated certain areas on his map.

"I'm very good at listening to the whispers on the breeze. I hear all sorts of interesting little secrets." Sylvestri gave Thanir's hand a grateful squeeze and let it go to sit on the sofa beside Daewen. "I shall investigate this Hedeon person for you and find out what he wants. I'll discover his plans without him even knowing I'm there.

"You will be careful, won't you?" Daewen said to Sylvestri with concern. As much as she had no wish for her husband and Sardo to go riding off into the unknown, it would be even more dangerous for this woman to be wandering abroad, alone.

"Don't worry, Your Majesty. No one will ever see me. Without doubt I am the perfect spy." She was there one moment…

… And gone the next. A faint breeze tickled the back of Daewen's neck, tugged at a lock of Sardo's hair. Moving on to each person in turn, she whirled around Thanir with a stiff breeze that rustled his robes.

"Ves, please," he murmured as she giggled in his ear.

"Of course darling," she whispered and sinuously wrapped him in a warm breeze before becoming visible once more.

"How long will it take you to get there?"

Branchir asked, bringing the conversation back to business.

"I can be there as fast as lightning, literally. Although, they may experience some stormy weather for a while."

"Very good, let us consider where this Hedeon might be found," Branchir said as they went to the map again. Twenty minutes later an invisible Sylvestri had flashed away and all they could do was wait.

Sylvestri had not been gone long when Branchir received a message through his mirror.

"I thought you'd like to know, the sisters are on their way," Eleanor said. "Would you be able to send someone to meet them?"

"Thank you, I look forward to meeting them again."

An hour later Thanir showed four elderly ladies and four men into the library. Now that Branchir had the time to study them, the four women looked nothing alike. Nothing about them said they could be related. The four men had a feline bearing, not their physical appearance as such but in the way they held themselves and moved about the room. Sardo recognised them as the warriors that they were.

"Ladies and Gentlemen, may I offer you a proper welcome to Faerie this time," Branchir said. "Thank you all for coming so promptly."

"It is our pleasure, Your Majesties," Emma smiled at Daewen then at Branchir. "How exactly can we be of help to you?"

"Firstly, we must thank you once again for the return of the missing jewels. They are obviously very powerful but we are still unsure as to just how powerful. The only evidence we have discovered so far is a children's story, which may or may not be truthful. I need to be sure that they are not dangerous before allowing any experimentation." Then he looked a little embarrassed. "And secondly, well you can tell me to mind my own business. I know he is your father but..."

Emma smiled. "I have never been close

to my blood family. These people with me are my chosen family. We are what might loosely be called coven sisters, and I include young Eleanor and Marianne in this family. These men are our familiars... our protectors. They anchor our magic and sometimes boost our power when needed. As for John Dee or Zeus or Jupiter or Odin or Merlin or whatever name he chooses to go by - and there have been so many - father is the least of his names." Emma's voice was calm and measured but her flashing eyes said that she was having difficulty keeping her emotions in check. Branchir was interested to see that when Hermes placed his hand on her shoulder she visibly relaxed.

"Besides, this is just as much your business as it is ours," Daphne added.

Branchir nodded. "He is not with you, I see. Do you know of his current whereabouts?"

"Oh yes, we know exactly where he is," Belus said. His grin showing a pair of wickedly sharp canine teeth – or possibly, Branchir thought, feline fangs. Belus produced the small wooden box with the indignant mouse and placed it in the middle of the low table. Sardo leaned over the box and peered in.

"Are you telling me that this tiny creature is the Great Zeus?" his guffaw nearly knocked the mouse over.

"Belus dear," Emma said, "Put the lid back on. We wouldn't want him to escape, not with so many cats about."

One by one, the familiars dropped to all fours. The small cats sat and stared at the box with a studied focus that only cats could achieve.

"Oh, well that's different. I wasn't expecting that," Aurelia said and then slapped a hand over her mouth. "Sorry, that was very rude of me."

"They won't mind," Daphne assured her.

"Maybe we should sit and discuss this over light refreshments," Daewen suggested.

Thanir and Finch brought in tea and coffee with several platters of small savoury and sweet morsels.

"Finch, you do love me after all," Sardo grinned as he swept her up off her feet. "Look at all this cake you've brought me."

"Be puttings me down now! Big brute!" She frowned at him and batted at his chest and although she tried, she could not keep up the pretence of being angry with him. He put her back down, gently and she turned to the room in general. "Making sures he is not eatings all of cake," Then she wagged her finger at Sardo. "You be sharings nicely. Naughty boy!"

He gave her a little pout and tried to look contrite as he nodded at her and then grinned as she flounced out of the room with Thanir.

"Where should we begin?" Emma asked.

"Well, probably with the jewels," Branchir said. "Thanir and Brother Ambrosius of the Guild of Historians have combed the archives and found the story. It may be based on true events but... The good Brother has a theory."

Chapter 26

Hiding out in the loft above the chapel gave Fyr time to think and to worry. As the day wore on the temperature in the tower room rose. It was stiflingly hot and airless. Dust hung in the still air, drifting about with every tiny movement. He tried to move as little as possible lest the people in the chapel below should hear something and decide to investigate.

Infuriatingly, he could tell from the low hum that there were two or possibly three voices in conversation below him yet, even with his ear pressed against the floorboards, he could not hear their actual words. He did not know what they could be doing down there, with no way to tell if they were friend or foe.

Fyr woke with a start. He had not meant to go to sleep but he had not slept the night before and with the heat and the forced inaction, it had been inevitable. It was a noise from below that had woken him, he was sure of it. He needed to stretch his cramped limbs but dared not move. His heart was thumping through his body as he wondered if he had moved or made a noise in his sleep and someone was coming up to investigate? He held his breath until he realised the sound he had heard had been the heavy front door closing. Now all he could hear was the pounding of his own blood. He let out a small sigh of relief when he heard the clunk of the lock and then the clang of the metal grille. He lay very still, counting silently to himself, waiting and listening.

The silence weighed heavily and was almost as oppressive as the heat but at least he could move around now and massage out the pins and needles in his arms and legs. He crept over to squint through the slatted window. From the height of the sun, he guessed it had to be around mid-day. He watched as the shops closed their shutters and people headed, in unison, towards the inn.

Were they all going for their midday meal at the same time? That was a little odd – or maybe it was a town meeting. At the thought of food, his stomach gave a loud grumble of protest. He had to make his move now. This might be his only opportunity.

Whilst curled up in his hidey hole he had replayed his conversations with Kizzy. Some of it had come back to him. Her father's name was Ori, he made and sold candles and honey and he had a shop; one of the five he could see from here? But from this position, he could not tell which one. He had to get closer. Right at this moment, the village appeared to be deserted. It was now or never.

Fyr raised the trapdoor just enough to peer through the crack and listened. Although he had heard them leave and lock up, it could have been a ruse, but the chapel appeared to be empty. He climbed down the ladder, erasing all signs of himself as best he could and crept out through the hidden door behind the tapestry at the back. He made his way to the corner of the building, constantly checking. There was no sign of any activity beyond the animals grazing on the common.

A dense hedgerow ran down the lane to the road. It had the look of an ancient boundary line and there should have been trees but they had been cut back hard, very recently, sending them into shock. It was not possible for him to travel that way so he crept along keeping as close to the shadows as possible. He came to a gap just large enough for him to squeeze through and emerged close to the lane that ran along the back of the gardens behind the shops.

His luck was holding for the moment. Most of the gardens still had some fruit trees: apple, pear, plum, medlar, walnut. None of them were very large but they had not suffered the harsh pruning of the others, and they all welcomed his presence, apart from the walnut, which was rather grumpy and ill-tempered. Still, it allowed him to move freely and he went from garden to garden until he arrived at the last of the five. It was the only one with the bee hives, or skeps; conical baskets, lined up around the edges of the garden and around the feet of the fruit trees. This had to be the place. An old apple tree was the closest to the building and it willingly offered up some of its fruit to him when his stomach growled again.

A workshop area took up the rear of the building. This was the place Kesia had told him her father spent most of his time. He processed the bees' wax to make his candles and bottled the honey that Kesia sold in the shop. He remembered her describing her home and telling him that the shop took up the front third of the building, the middle used for storage and then the workroom was at the back and upstairs there were two bedrooms.

The apple tree told him he would not have to wait long, but Fyr was beginning to realise that trees had a strange notion of time. When the three, white haired, old men returned after their lunch and began working, he had no idea which one was Kesia's father, Ori, or whether he could trust any of them. Fyr was at a loss. Should he wait or just step out and announce his presence. The apple tree came to his rescue again and persuaded him to wait until the end of the working day.

"Wait.... Wait...others go... Ori stay... Ori good..."

The three old men worked non-stop, without a word said between them. They continued throughout the afternoon and into the evening - until the sun began to go down and it became too dark to see what they were doing. Two of the men packed up their tools and tidied their work areas while the third continued to work at his bench in the corner. He dipped frames hung with thin candles into a bath of molten wax, building them up layer by layer. Rather than use one of his own candles, the old man lit a foul smelling oil lamp. It did not give off much light but it was enough. He waved off his co-workers with a gruff 'night' but did not bother turning to see them leave, still busy with his candles. After a few minutes, Fyr wondered if the coast was clear.

"You can come out now lad," the old man said without looking up. "I know you're there, the bees told me."

Fyr stepped out of the apple tree. "Good evening sir, are you Kesia Lukash's father?"

That made the old man turn. He stopped long enough to hang his frame up to drip and dry over the wax bath.

"And you must be Fyr."

"You know of me?" he asked in surprise. "I've come to find out where Kesia is. I need to know she's safe, we got split up on the way home."

"Aye, I know some of the story. I've only been allowed to see her once." The lamp light may have been dim but Fyr could see the unshed tears shining in the old man's eyes. "Why don't you come on inside and have a bite to eat while we talk? It's not much, soup and a bit of bread, but you're more than welcome. A young chap like you can't survive on a couple of apples. Besides, we have some stories to share." He held up his hand to forestall Fyr's offer of payment. "Don't you worry, the bees told me the old apple tree offered them up willingly... and you looked after my girl." The last few words came out choked.

Fyr followed Ori Lukash into the building where a small round table sat beside a hearth in the corner.

"Have a seat, lad," Ori said as he added a small log to the glowing embers in the hearth and swung the arm supporting the pot over the resulting flames.

Fyr cast his eyes about the place where Kesia had grown up. It smelled of honey and hot wax and was somehow comforting. Ori took the lid off the pot and gave it a stir. Fyr's stomach gave the loudest growl yet. The old man chuckled as he picked up a wooden ladle and bowl, carved by him many years ago. He served a grateful Fyr with the soup, which was thick and delicious, and a chunk of bread.

While they ate, the old man asked many questions, which Fyr did his best to answer as truthfully possible. He wanted to know about the trip, who they had met and what they had seen. There were a few things about their journey that would have distressed the old man so he kept those to himself for now. Fyr had questions of his own but felt compelled to answer the old man first. Eventually though, he had to ask.

"You said they let you see her once, where are they holding her?"

Ori's face fell and he was very quiet. Fyr did not think he was going to tell him at first.

"When I knew you were all on your way home... the bees, you know..." he smiled sadly. "I eagerly awaited her return. I was looking forward to seeing her and hearing all her stories but instead of my sweet girl, there was this puffed-up, sweaty little man in my shop. He said that I had been without her all this time and proved that I could manage without her so she was going to have to go into service for the Lord of the Manor. Then he gave me a nasty smile and said, however, as she was unmarried but had been allowed to wander away from home, unchaperoned, her services could and would be auctioned off to the highest bidder at the up-coming hiring fair." He went quiet for a moment.

"You should know... there were chaperones..." Fyr said quietly.

"I know my girl, and I trust her," Ori blinked. "I offered to pay but the odious little... he laughed at me and said I would never have enough money to pay her worth. I demanded to see her. I had to make sure she was safe and unharmed. The nasty little man said of course she was unharmed because no one would pay for damaged goods." Ori's face was white with anger. "They said I had to go to New Place... the big house that they've been building over the way... They took me around the back to a little room with a carved wooden screen set into one wall. I couldn't really see her very well but we were able to speak, briefly." The tears that had gathered in the corner of his eyes ran unchecked down his wrinkled cheeks. "I'm lucky I have my bees to keep me informed."

"Was she alone? Is she scared?" Fyr wanted to ask so many more questions but could see it was taking a toll on the old man.

"There may have been someone on the other side of the screen with her because she was very careful what she said but the bees have told me that there are at least six other girls and older women with her."

Fyr sat forward in his seat to catch the old man's words. He was not sure if the old man's voice was quiet due to the weight of emotion hanging around him or because he did not want to be overheard.

Chapter 27

Thanir was accustomed to his friend being at once controlled and enigmatic but he had never seen him quite so disconcerted and anxious. Brother Ambrosius was no stranger to magic but he had always considered shape-shifters to be mythical creatures. So it might have been something to do with three of the four cats suddenly standing upright and becoming men.

On the other hand, it was quite likely that the four ladies were the cause of his bewilderment. Thanir noticed Ambrosius had that same look on his face that he himself often wore when Ves was around: slightly shell-shocked, but obviously not for the same reason.

Ambrosius leaned in close to Thanir and hoped no one could hear.

"These ladies, they are... different. They wear two faces; the old hides behind the young, which hides the old. How can that be?"

Thanir shrugged his shoulders and hoped he was not really expecting an answer.

"Brother Ambrosius?" the Queen's quiet voice brought him back to the present.

"Sorry…" He shook his head, making his white hair stand out like a dandelion clock.

"Why don't you come and have a seat?" Daewen suggested.

"Yes, thank you Your Majesty." He sank slowly onto one end of a sofa and blinked a few times while he gathered his thoughts, then he took a deep breath and launched into his theory. "We have found no documented history from the period of the jewellery's supposed manufacture. History of that age has to rely on the oral tradition of passing information on in the form of stories."

He stopped speaking and looked from face to face to make sure they were still following him. It was difficult to concentrate in this room at the best of times but the way these visitors looked at him, as though they could see through his many, carefully layered lives, well, it was most disconcerting.

"Brother Ambrosius?" Daewen called his attention again.

"Oh, yes... my apologies..." He gave himself a bit of a mental shake. "I wonder, might we refer to your family pedigree upon the wall?" He asked Branchir.

With a small wave of Branchir's hand – a gesture he had picked up from Eleanor – ornate writing appeared and scrolled down the wall between the two windows.

Branchir raised a surprised eyebrow. "This has expanded somewhat since we last referred to it. It has gone further back in time." The original ancestors at the top of the list had been Branchir's great grandparents – King Arcalimon and Queen Callista. Now, three generations back beyond them were the names Nestor, Lorcan and Orlagh.

"They must have been added to the pedigree when the Boroviche were freed from the doors to the Great Hall, Orlagh being the

Boroviche Queen who hid them there in the first place," Ambrosius noted. "But it goes even further back, three more generations."

"Oh my!" Thanir exclaimed. "King Aradon and Queen Eloiny… are the very names… characters from the stories we found."

"Indeed they are," Ambrosius said, distractedly. "So many names… so many generations… so many… centuries…"

"Ambrosius?" Thanir touched his friend's arm.

"Pardon me," and he was back. "There appears to be over a thousand years between King Aradon and King Arcalimon. With such a great time span and events such as the war between Kings Lorcan and Nestor… it is not surprising, really, that things got forgotten. And without wishing to offend Your Majesty, I know King Arvano was your grandfather, but after he killed his twin brother Varyar and his nephew Tallis… magic began to fade away from Faerie. As Arvano lost his power, he outlawed magic use and destroyed or concealed any reference to magic. Hmm... probably why the Queen's jewels became a children's story."

"Sounds plausible," Emma said. Ambrosius blushed at her smile. "However, it is also quite likely that when Zeus stole the contents of the royal treasury and cast his spell of forgetting, which backfired badly, his magic leaked across the barrier between the worlds. That man has a lot to answer for."

Out of ear-shot of the others, Thanir leaned close to Branchir.

"Sire, might I enquire whether you have had any news of the Lady Sylvestri?"

"Not as yet," Branchir answered equally sotto voce. "I have not noticed anything of note on the map either, but that is not a surprise if she is still invisible."

"Indeed Sire." Thanir have a slight bow and moved away from the King.

"Could we see a copy of this story?" Emma asked Ambrosius.

"By all means." He reached into his

habit and drew out several copies of the story which he distributed amongst them.

"My, you have got deep pockets," Addie chuckled.

"Oh, not so, madam. I have created a small portal link between the archive and myself. It saves time and cuts down on the weight I would have to carry." Addie was not sure if he was serious, as his expression remained inscrutable.

Belus once again in his cat form gave a low angry rumble. The box was impossible for him to get out of but that did not stop the mouse / Dee from trying.

Having read the story Emma looked up and said, "I may be reading too much into this but it says King Aradon gave his bride a circlet of silver and sapphires, to match her eyes, as a symbol of his love. Just like a wedding ring, the circlet has no beginning and no end and so also represents eternity... everlasting love."

"Crystals are used to focus magical energy," Dorcas said. "Sapphires are useful for fore-sight, clear-thinking and wisdom."

"If Queen Eloiny was anything like her character in the story, she was a pretty wise lady already," Emma suggested. "Not to mention fair-minded and intelligent."

"Sounds like a sensible lass," Daphne added.

"And then, the lad was very clever, giving her bloodstones," Addie said. "They have been used through the ages to focus healing energy. I've used them many times myself."

"And as Daphne said," Dorcas added. "If her character was recorded truly then she was already empathic and protective of others."

"But what of the last gift," Daewen asked.

"The moonstones?" Addie said. "Apart from bloodstones, it's been a long time since I've used crystal magic. I'm not certain about the calming of raging beasts. I've not heard that one before but I'm sure I've read somewhere that they can be used to help with mediating fraught situations. In the right hands they can be used to induce a peaceful sleep or in the wrong hands, the final sleep."

"I'm not sure I like the sound of that last one," Daewen said.

"Have no fear, my love. You would never do that," Branchir soothed.

"Would you allow us a closer look at the actual items to see how closely they correspond to the story?" Emma asked.

Daewen stood and walked to the fireplace and pressed, seemingly at random, a selection of fruits carved into the front panel of the mantelpiece. With a faint click, a rectangular cartouche flipped open like a door, to reveal a small space behind it.

"I wished for somewhere safe to keep them and this appeared," she told them.

"Until that point, this had been a very old and very solid oak beam," Branchir confirmed.

Daewen reached in and drew out three

shallow boxes. "The magic gave us these cases to store the pieces in too. They fit perfectly." She placed the cases on the table and lifted the lids.

Just as described in the story the silver circlet was set with cornflower blue sapphires.

"I do believe they match your eyes too," Emma smiled at Daewen.

The moonstones sparkled as though lit from inside by a rainbow and the bloodstones, although darker and duller, had been polished to a high shine and the red markings that gave them their name shone, appeared almost liquid.

"The descriptions do appear to be remarkably accurate," Brother Ambrosius said, peering down at them.

"Have you put them on?" Addie asked Daewen.

"Only those, very briefly," she said pointing at the bloodstone armlets.

"And did you feel anything?"

"Yes, but it was… hard to describe."

Daewen frowned as she tried to recall what she had experienced. "There was a sort of... tingle." She wiggled her fingers. "Not like pins and needles, more like... bubbles in sparkling wine... refreshing and... but that's not the right word either. I didn't have them on for long but I felt powerful... in a good way. I think I was able to help Thanir too." She whispered the last comment to Addie. Of course, Thanir heard her.

"You did? I mean... did you, Your Majesty?" Thanir was sounding a little flustered.

"You were a little... high strung... after Lady Sylvestri arrived. I remember telling you that everything would be fine and a strange calm came over you... but... Oh, I was no longer wearing the jewels at that point."

"The magic is not within the jewels, it is within the wearer. The jewels are merely a point of focus for the energy," Dorcas said.

Chapter 28

"It's too dangerous, lad," Ori said. He laid a tremulous hand on Fyr's arm as he tried to dissuade Fyr from going to New Place. "There ain't no one we can trust these days apart from the bees and they don't understand why she can't come home, bein' as she's so close." He gave a sniff and rubbed his nose with the back of his hand.

"I need to see her. I have to try." Fyr sat with his head in his hands. He had come this far and could not give up now, foolhardy and dangerous though it was.

"Look, take this." Ori gave him a small sketch map of the house. He had included as much detail as he could remember from his one, brief visit and from the information the bees had shared. Ori pointed to a small addition at the back of the house.

"This is where I was allowed to speak to Kesia, through a carved screen. Most of the inside is what the bees told me. "

It had taken him a while to interpret their dances but he had drawn the little sketch in the hope of going back to find his daughter.

"The bees told me the girls are being kept on the first floor... here." Ori pointed to the map and a long narrow chamber that ran the whole length of the back of the house. "At one end, a door leads to sleeping cells and at the other, to a room with drones with big stingers and then to another room where they put the girls to work. I'm sure they were telling me that there are guards and the stingers are their weapons. The bees said there was no buzz, it was too quiet. Maybe the women are not allowed to talk to one another. The bees think the best way into the hive... house... is through the... food making cell... they mean the kitchens. They're here," he pointed to the sketch and another extension tacked on to the other end of the building.

Fyr waited until the old man was snoring in his chair then slipped out to the apple tree again. He made his way back through the fruit trees until he reached the ancient pear tree in the last garden. From the top, he could just make out a few small trees in a far corner of New Place's grounds. They were just visible enough that he could make the jump and...

He found himself in an old damson tree. From this position, he had a good view of the front of the building. Whoever owned this place was certainly trying to make a statement. All of the other buildings that Fyr had seen in the village were timber-framed and had either plaster or brick in-fill. This house appeared to be built of stone; glass glinted in the windows rather than wooden shutters. Someone was spending a lot of time and money on this house.

Fyr made his way, via a slender silver birch, to the rear of the house. There were so many people about that he did not dare move from his tree. Stone masons, plasterers, carpenters, labourers and gardeners buzzed around the place like Ori's bees. There was still a lot of work going on at the house and in the gardens. The front of the house turned out to be a façade. The rest of the building was like the rest of the village buildings, mostly timber and plaster-work. It was oddly quiet with none of the usual banter and good-natured mockery that one associated with a group of men working on a building site. It was very subdued.

Just as the day before, there came a point when they all put down their tools and set off around the building, heading for the inn and a meal. This was what he had been waiting for. There was only one door into the kitchen extension. He sidled up to it and put his ear against the wood. No sound came from inside. As far as he could tell, it was as empty as the garden. A ladder, propped up against the side of the building where the plasterers had been working, was a lucky find and he cautiously climbed up onto the kitchen roof. Luck was still with him when he discovered a window still awaiting its glazing and it was just big enough for him to squeeze through. He landed in the long gallery, which was just as the bees had described, and dropped into a crouch behind a tall wooden settle. From his position, he could see the two doors; the one opposite him was closed, but unlocked, the large padlock hanging open from the hasp. According to the bees, this door led to the sleeping cells. He peered inside. He could just make out three narrow, windowless cells, just big enough to hold two beds but they were all empty.

The door at the far end of the long room, stood ajar. Fyr made his way down the long gallery, creeping from one large piece of furniture to the next as he went. He made it to the open door and cautiously squinted inside. The room, illuminated by a window opposite the door, was empty apart from an impressive display of weapons arranged across the wall to the right. The window was barred so was no good as an escape route. To the left, the internal door was padlocked but, very helpfully, an outsized iron key hung on a hook beside the door.

Fyr put his ear to the door and could detect a faint murmur of voices from within. This had to be the place, Kesia had to be here. He took the key down and slid it into the lock. The voices behind the door suddenly ceased. He pulled the door open a crack. Inside it was very dark. All the windows were covered and the only light came from a couple of smoky oil lamps. He could tell there were people inside but it was too dark inside to make out any of the faces. He could not help it and whispered her name.

"Kizzy?"

Her pale face emerged from the depths.

"Fyr! What are you doing here? You shouldn't..." She took a step towards him and then stopped as though she was not sure what she was seeing. "Are you really here?" He heard the catch in her voice.

"Are you alright? I've been so

worried..."

"But you shouldn't be here," she repeated with a sob.

He stepped into the room and took her in his arms.

"No, really... you shouldn't be here," she said, trying to push him away gently. "It's a trap," she whispered. "We heard them... they knew someone was coming... but I didn't know it would be you..."

He felt her body stiffen as the door behind him flew open and rough hands grabbed him pulling them apart.

"We've been waiting for you, sunshine," a rough voice growled in his ear as a sudden pain blossomed in his head and everything went black.

Chapter 29

In the kitchen, Simon and Marianne were drinking tea and eating toast.

"That toast smells good, mind if we join you?" Eleanor asked.

Simon still looked a little hollow-eyed but not so washed out and pale.

"How are you feeling?" James asked him.

"Pretty exhausted still," Simon said. "I seem to have spent the best part of two days and nights asleep and yet, I don't feel any better for it."

"But at least you have been dreaming," Marianne said.

"Yeah! But these are lucid dreams... not like anything I've ever had before. It feels as though I am actually there with these people and yet I know I'm dreaming. It's like... watching past events being replayed but I've no idea if any of it really happened. I need to speak to Salamander or Sylvestri or Undine."

"That's who you've been dreaming about?" Eleanor asked.

"The first dream was about Salamander, but it started out with him as a little boy. He had a different name which I can't recall now. He was afraid of his grandfather who wanted him to take on some sort of responsibility that the boy's father didn't want. It turned out it was all about him taking on the role of Fire Elemental, that's when he became Salamander."

"What about Sylvestri and Undine?" Eleanor asked.

"Sylvestri was the next dream. She was an abused child living in some sort of institution until a woman came and adopted her. I saw her become the Air Elemental. Then there was a little girl called Milara. She was saved from drowning by a shadowy figure and grew up to become Undine. I'm only guessing but if I go back to sleep... am I going to see how Aurora became the Spirit Elemental and what about

Hob? I'm sure it will all be clear sooner or later."

"I'm sure you'll get a better night's sleep when these dreams have played themselves out," Eleanor said.

Simon hid a huge yawn behind his hand.

"And yep... not done yet," Marianne smiled. "We'll say goodnight." She kissed Eleanor and James goodnight and helped Simon back up the stairs.

Simon was asleep again almost before his head hit the pillow.

Up on the screen, in the old cinema, a silent film flickered and stuttered through the gates of the projector. Below the screen, a mighty organ arose through a trapdoor, flamboyantly played with great gusto by a little old lady. Her hands and feet were flying over the keys, pedals and stops as she played along with the film but there was no sound. From the images on the screen, the film appeared to be set in Egypt. The painted backdrop of the pyramids and Sphinx were a bit of a giveaway. The cinema was crowded and the people laughed, cheered and applauded – but in complete silence.

Up on the screen, the figures ran around, fell

down, got up again and the slapstick chase continued. Attention was suddenly on the Sphinx. Its great head turned ponderously until it was looking straight out of the screen and into the audience. Apart from a young girl three rows from the front, no one else in the auditorium had noticed.

"There are many mysteries yet to be solved, but you hold the knowledge within," the sphinx told the girl. "We wait for you to accept the need to act, to do that which you do not wish to do. The strength will be yours when needed but remain vigilant lest the power and wisdom pass you by."

Suddenly the audience had vanished leaving the girl all alone. She sat motionless, watching a blank screen that was nothing more than a bright light while the film flapped rhythmically in its spool.

"Are you sure she's the one?" Two people stood in the aisle a few rows behind the girl. The man wore a long frocked coat, wing-collars and top hat. His pince-nez made his eyes look very small and mean. While the woman beside him stood very stiffly, no doubt the result of her tightly laced corsets and bustle which gave her figure an accentuated S-shape. Her huge, feathered hat shadowed her face as she peered at the child through an ornate lorgnette.

"It is precisely what my granddaughter was born to do. When the time comes she will be ready," the woman said, imperiously.

"Were we in less enlightened times..." the man sighed but did not complete his thought. "It is because she is your granddaughter that she has so far, been thus indulged. There are those who would entreat us to place her in an institution with a straight-jacket and padded cell for her own safety. There are also those who believe in the efficacy of electrical shock therapy to stop her from hurting herself or others."

"Sir! My granddaughter would never hurt... she has far too much empathy towards others, and therein lies the paradox. So far, she has been unable to control the emotions assaulting her and can move from deep anxiety to over-stimulation of the senses within the blink of an eye. She must learn to minimise the impact by strengthening her mental shields. I have been assured that it will become easier in time."

The sphinx was back on screen – seen only by the girl.

"You are yet but a tiny bud... tightly furled... waiting to bloom. You hold great potential within. Have faith child. Do not hide your face. Show them your courage, strength and dignity. Do not allow them to overwhelm you."

The girl looked at the mark on the back of her hand. She knew what it stood for - balance and stability.

She stood up and turned to her grandmother with a bright smile.

"I am ready to go home now, Grand-mère."

"Of course ma fille douce. The carriage awaits us at the back door."

"Merci, Grand-mère." She turned and dropped a little curtsey to the man. "Au Revoir Monsieur Tremblè."

"Bonsoir, little one."

"Come, Aurora," the woman said as she guided the girl down the aisle towards the screen and the emergency exit at the rear.

Becoming the Spirit Elemental was no surprise but she was having difficulty coping with the transition, just as the others had.

And then Simon found himself standing in a garden. It was Eleanor's garden as he had first encountered it: a choked and tangled wilderness waiting for him to tame it. Chaos was about to become order. He moved slowly through the garden and paths revealed themselves, leaves changed colours: green, red, gold then brown as they fell from their branches to create a fertile humus on the soil. Tiny buds grew into new leaves and trees and bushes became shaped by his touch. Flowers bloomed on bare thorny branches that had once appeared dead. Simon knew this was a dream but he also knew that this had happened, to him and to Eleanor's garden, although not at this speed.

Simon looked down at his open palm. An acorn sat there, small and insignificant and an idea began to form. From a tiny acorn, the mighty oak will eventually become huge and ancient. Was this his subconscious cautioning him to patience?

Chapter 30

Belus gave a low growl and patted the top of the mouse's box with his paw – claws extended.

"Hold on my love, we might just have to let him out and… oh!" Daphne blinked as the realisation suddenly hit her. "We can't use our magic here. We can't turn him back and we don't know what might happen if you try to turn him back with your Fae magic… oh blast!" she muttered, arms folded and shoulders hunched in frustration. "After everything he's done, I don't understand how he's managed to escape the backlash of the three-fold return. Why hasn't it leapt up and bitten him on the arse before now?"

"Which is why we need to consider our actions very carefully," Emma added. "Whatever happens to him now, this cannot be a punishment from us. He needs to take responsibility for his actions and live with the consequences of his greed as we have had to."

Before they could take it any further, the door blew open and a strong gust of wind whipped through the room. The fire in the grate flared with the added oxygen and then Sylvestri stood in the centre of the room. She breathed deeply and pushed the palms of her hands down towards the floor as though pushing her temper down.

"Can't speak yet... angry..." Sylvestri seethed. She dropped onto the sofa as thunder crashed overhead and lightning lit up the windows.

"Can we offer you some tea?" Daewen said putting her hand on Sylvestri's arm. "It might help to calm you."

"Calm now, thank you," Sylvestri smiled. "I apologise for my rather dramatic entrance."

"We are eager to hear what you have discovered," Branchir said. "But let us invite the two Boroviche gentlemen to join us again." He turned to his Chamberlain who was standing close to Sylvestri. "Thanir, would you ask Thorn and Gould to return please."

If Thorn and Gould had felt overwhelmed by the King and his library before, now, with all these new people in the room, they were positively intimidated. Four elderly women sat on the sofas, each with a small furry animal draped about their person.

"These ladies are friends of your Great Forest Mage, Simon," Branchir said.

The two men nodded. There was a fifth, much younger woman, with eyes like storm clouds. The King's Chamberlain hovered protectively behind her.

"And this is Lady Sylvestri. She has been gathering information for us with regard to your problem."

Those storm-cloud eyes studied them for a moment as enormous hailstones bombarded the castle.

"This is a very unhappy place you come from," Sylvestri said to the two men. Her voice was flat and emotionless, it had lost its usual sensual purr, Thanir noted. "In all my years I have never come across anything so callous, calculating and cruel. Even your mad cousin whatsisname," she said to Branchir, "was not a patch on this guy. Yes, he was all those things but at least he was upfront in his madness. This Hedeon is sneaky and underhand and it's been going on for a long time. I think this is it, coming to a head. He has squashed and trampled on generations of tradition and your history is being rewritten to suit his agenda and his particular brand of madness." Thunder crashed overhead until Thanir placed a gentle hand on her shoulder.

"We were peaceful... farmers mostly... we were content to share what little we had with our friends and neighbours and to look after those who could no longer look after themselves," Thorn said. "Now it's every man for himself... if you can hang on to it long enough."

"From what I was able to observe... because no one would actually speak to me...

everyone is suspicious of everyone else…" Sylvestri said. "Families have been split up. The old and infirm are being herded into large buildings they call workhouses and are forced to do demeaning and often meaningless tasks just to earn a crust of dry bread to eat, a straw mattress to sleep on or even a simple blanket."

This was far too close to home for Sylvestri. It reminded her too much of her own childhood but she managed to continue. "I followed the men, dragged from their ploughs and forced to march for miles to makeshift camps. They're made to march up and down in formation while abuse is screamed at them. They're made to fight one another to see who can survive the longest. There are beatings for any perceived weakness or minor refusals; these knights like to make examples of people, humiliate those who won't conform."

More rumbles of thunder shook the window frames.

"This Hedeon was a difficult man to track down though. He set his followers up as knights but there's nothing remotely chivalrous about them, they're extremely brutal, ill-educated bullies.

I did eventually find him though, hiding in his fortress. He calls it his castle, although it's nothing like this place... no comparison. It's little more than a wooden tower on a hill surrounded by rings of deep ditches and wooden stakes. But this isn't the worst of it."

Sylvestri's eyes flashed and flooded with angry tears and huge raindrops rolled down the windows.

"They take all the young women from sixteen or seventeen years old away from their families and sequester them in the houses of these so-called knights… unless they can prove they're already married, which is most unlikely as marriages have to be sanctioned by these knights now. Some of the women have been forced into unwanted marriages with Hedeon's followers. Others, sold at auction, have become property, with no rights. They are sold into slavery." A flash of lightning lit up the room and another a gust of wind blew down the chimney causing the embers to spark and spit. "From what I could see, he's been planning this for a long time, gradually putting things into place little by little, possibly even before they left the doors. And... he is calling himself the King of the Boroviche. I believe it is his intention to challenge Your Majesty for the crown of Faerie... though probably not face to face."

"Is that so?" Branchir rubbed at his chin. "Interesting." He turned to Daewen. "Regardless of his intentions... I promise I will not make the first move and be perceived as the aggressor. I give you my word on that."

Daewen smiled but she knew the day would come when he would have to fight, again.

Chapter 31

Fyr's first conscious thought was one of pain. Awareness trickled back slowly. He was sitting on a wooden chair with his hands and feet bound and some sort of hood pulled over his head but he was not in total darkness. A fire pit in the floor a few feet in front of him gave off a ruddy glow.

Fyr's next thought was that the room was empty but as soon as he moved, he became aware that there was someone behind him and they knew he was awake. He picked up the whispers but no actual words. The sound made the hair on the back of his neck stand up.

Heavy footsteps reverberated through the floor as, to either side of him, armoured men marched up to a low platform; the firelight glinted off their burnished leather breastplates and weapons.

The hood was whipped roughly from his

head and he could now see a large, ornate chair on the platform. Painted in a garish pattern of bright reds and greens, the firelight picked out the gilding just visible through the smoky haze. The armoured men stood on guard behind this... throne? Someone obviously thought himself very important. One of the guards placed a shield on the chair and whipped a cover from it just as Fyr blinked in the smoky, sooty atmosphere.

"What do you think of my coat of arms?"

Fyr tried to turn his head to see who had spoken but before he could answer, pain bloomed and his head snapped sideways from a blow to his jaw.

"His Most Excellent Highness asked you a question," a rough voice grated in his ear. Fyr's eyes watered and the pain swelled.

The shield, decorated in even more lurid colours than the chair, was covered in poorly drawn images.

"I'm sure it's ... exceptional," Fyr

managed to say as the fist drew back for another blow.

"Thank you. I am rather pleased with it. I designed it myself." The original speaker said, still behind him. "I am currently considering a suitable motto to go with it... 'Armed and Ready For Battle' or possibly 'Sovereignty, Loyalty, Victory', or how about Loyalty unto Death? What do you think? Personally, I prefer the second."

Fyr glanced at the raised fist poised beside his head unsure if he should answer or not, he was going to be in the wrong whichever way it went.

"Stand down Barda," the voice behind him almost cooed. "A decision such as this should not be rushed or taken lightly."

Barda, the man on the other end of the fist, stepped back with a double stamp and lowered his arm as he stood to attention.

"Borin, shield-bearer," the unseen man called. "Bring my Badge of Office a little closer that our friend might have a better view."

The shield, paraded with some ceremony and placed on a stand, was now at Fyr's eye level a few feet in front of him. A closer view was not necessarily a better view. It was a roughly cut shield shape, not a proper shield at all; no deflective curve or central boss. The background was mostly dark blue with a broad orange stripe across the top and an equally broad diagonal stripe running left to right in purple.

Fyr leaned as far forward as his bonds would allow, to decipher the images crammed onto the surface. At the centre was a crudely painted tree and below that, a clenched, red fist or possibly a gauntlet. To the left of the tree a smudgy black shape looked a little like the head of a black bird - a raven possibly? It was difficult to tell. Likewise, to the right of the tree, the other black smudge might be the head of a dog or a wolf.

The most prominent feature was the gold crown, which appeared to hover above the tree. Fyr was only guessing but he assumed it meant the man was trying to proclaim himself King.

"It just needs a motto. Which should I choose, do you think? Which one best sums this up?"

The man obviously had delusions of grandeur.

"How about 'Sovereignty, Loyalty and Victory'…" Fyr said, trying to sound as though he was giving it serious consideration.

"Good choice," the man said. He strode out from behind Fyr and made his slow and stately way to the chair on the platform. Being quite short of stature, the heavy purple brocade robe hung from his shoulders and trailed along the floor behind him, leaving a wide trail through the dust and dirt. A rather heavy and uncomfortable looking crown of gold was perched on his head, looking as though it might slip off at any moment. Once he reached the platform, it needed two of his guards to help him turn around, regain his balance and rearrange his robes before he could sit. He gave Fyr a condescending smile as his hand idly stroked at the fur edging of his robe. It showed off the bejewelled rings that adorned each of his fingers and both thumbs. They sparkled in the firelight.

"You have given my hounds quite the run around, young man." By hounds, Fyr assumed he meant his soldiers. "We did not expect you to arrive alone however. That was a surprise. Where are your two friends?"

"Two friends?"

"Oh, come now. Please do not underestimate my perceptiveness or my intelligence. You know very well I refer to the two travelling companions you met with several times at the inn in Stonegate. They disappeared just before you did."

Fyr realised he meant Thorn and Gould. He knew where they were going but had no idea if they had actually made it there.

"I'm sorry, I haven't a clue where they are." It was not exactly a lie, just not the whole truth.

"Illustrious Highness…" the one named Barda begged. "Let me work on him a bit… he'll soon give'm up n'tell us where they are."

"Patience Barda. There are other ways first." He turned his attention back to Fyr. "We have been keeping a very careful eye on you and your friends – those of you who went travelling. You did not suppose that your treason would go unnoticed or unpunished did you?" His smile was all teeth and not at all friendly.

"Treason? I don't understand."

"Really… you went out of your way to meet up with enemy agents…" His voice became strident and a little hysterical but he took a deep breath and softened it again. "I take it you know who I am?"

Another one of those questions - whatever Fyr said in answer to this, he knew it was going to end in pain. "Are you the one they call Hedeon?" He flinched, waiting for the blow.

Hedeon held up his hand to halt Barda.

"We must be prepared to show a little leniency. He and his friends have been away from home for a while and are unsure how things work now. Well, you are home now, so it is beholden upon us to enlighten you." He waved his hand again and the blare of a fanfare almost burst Fyr's eardrums.

"Presenting His Most Excellent, Exalted, Gracious, Illustrious Highness, King Hedeon," Barda announced.

"King?" Fyr could not help his surprised outburst.

"Oh yes. King of the Boroviche and soon to be King of this entire realm. There will be no tolerance of usurpers and charlatans."

Hedeon's guards thumped their spears on the ground and gave three loud cheers.

"Now then," Hedeon began again once he had silence. "We know where all but two of your co-conspirators are. We have you all under surveillance but somehow, you and those other two managed to elude my hounds for a while. We had bait for you though... and you took it. Tell me where the other two have gone and it will go easier for you."

"I don't know where..."

"Wrong answer," Hedeon sang.

"Tell me, how did you manage to get here so quickly and without being spotted?"

"I walked."

"Really? And how did you get across the river?"

"A fallen tree..."

"Ah! More proof of your lies. There is no fallen tree across the river for many a mile. Someone must have given you aid. Tell me their names." Hedeon's voice rose higher and higher and then he became very quiet. Ice water flowed through Fyr's veins.

"Take him to the dungeon and show him your toys, Barda."

"Yes, Your Most Excellent..." Barda began excitedly.

"Yes, yes... but Barda... a word of warning... no blood... don't break him... yet!"

Chapter 32

It had been deathly quiet in the women's quarters. They had been hustled down to the small cells and locked in. Then all the guards had left, all but Maud that is. Kesia tried her door to find that it was unlocked. The outer door was padlocked from the outside but the individual cells were open. She made her way back to the others. Hebe and Lobelia were sitting with Posey and Petal. Rosa followed her in. There was enough room for them all to sit on the narrow beds but it was still crowded.

"I asked Floria to join us but she refused," Rosa said.

Hebe threw her arms around Kesia. "I'm so sorry about your young man."

"He shouldn't have come. They've got him now. What will they do to him?"

"I imagine they will torture him," Floria's haughty voice from the doorway caught them all by surprise.

"Shut up!" Posey and Petal said together.

"They'll probably have questions for him…" Rosa tried to soothe Floria's bite.

"You've all heard the stories. She's not a child. She needs to know," Floria sniffed.

"I need to know what?" Kesia had to ask.

"About the torture chamber in the cellars," Floria raised an eyebrow. "Oh, I forgot. You've been away, haven't you?"

"Don't be unkind, Floria," Lobelia said, standing up and towering over the other woman. Floria gave another haughty sniff and went back to her own cell.

"She's only jealous," Posey or Petal said.

"Jealous of what? Of me? Why?" Kesia asked.

"She thinks she is so high and mighty," Hebe said. "She and I came from the same village. Her husband was the Mayor and decided to swap her for a younger model. The house she lived in and everything in it was hers, left to her by her parents when they died but now she has nothing. She's no better than we are. Her husband kept the house and all her money and threw her out without a penny."

"How sad," Kesia said.

"You don't have to feel sorry for her. She's a stuck-up, snotty cow," Hebe said.

"That's not nice, Hebe," Rosa said. "She is in the same boat as us now, but at least we know how to work for our livings, she doesn't have a clue."

"She thinks someone rich will come and buy her and set her up in a nice house again." Hebe could not keep the contempt out of her voice.

"Well, that could happen, but probably not in the way she thinks," Posey said… but it might have been Petal.

"We met a woman like her a while ago," Petal added… but it could have been Posey.

"What happened?" Kesia asked.

"Some rich bloke turned up to the auction house where they first put us. He had another woman with him. Her hair was a funny colour and her face was painted, but it didn't hide the bruises. He wanted to do a swap her because his clients didn't like her because she wouldn't do what they wanted."

"I don't understand," Rosa frowned. "What did they want her to do?"

"Rosa, you have led a very sheltered life," Lobelia said. She took Rosa's hand and sat her down on the bed opposite her. "Posey and Petal told me this story when they first came, and it came as something of a shock to me too. I had no idea things like this went on."

"Things like what?"

"She was a painted lady…" Lobelia said, as though that explained it all.

"Yes, they said her face was painted but…"

"I think what she's trying to tell you," Hebe interrupted. "Is that those of us who know how to cook and clean and have run farms and such... we know how to work for our living... we know what hard work is... we know our place. But some women have never had to work because they were rich or married to rich men. These new rules have changed everything and a man can get rid of a wife he doesn't want by selling her. These high and mighty women, the ones who never got their hands dirty... no one wants to employ them as a house keeper or maid because they wouldn't follow orders or know how to cook or... you know, do stuff like that."

"So what do they do?" Rosa asked.

"They get bought by keepers of Bawdy Houses," Posey / Petal said.

"What's one of those?"

"A place men go to buy a woman for sex... and other stuff."

"Other stuff?" Rosa could not help but ask. She knew that sex was something men and women did when they were married. She had no idea about the actual details and could not imagine what this 'other stuff' could be.

"Really Rosa, you don't need to know," Lobelia told her. "The twins told me all about it and it gave me nightmares for a week."

"So you think Floria will be sent to one of these Bawdy Houses?" Rosa asked.

"Yep, reckon so…" Hebe nodded. "Doubt if she'll last long though."

"Depends if she's got any skills…" one of the twins said.

"I think we should change the subject now," Rosa said. It was making her feel hot and uncomfortable.

The women all leapt to their feet when they heard the key in the padlock. There was a mad dash to get back to their cells before the door opened.

Maud strode in with a lantern held high. She ignored everyone until she came to the last cell where Floria and Rosa sat stiff and upright on the edges of their beds.

"You… Flo… come with me,"

"My name is Floria… where are we

going?"

"You'll find out."

Floria shook off Maud's hand on her arm and walked out with her head held high. She had heard what the others had been talking about and knew she was about to find out if it was true.

"Wait… please…" Kesia called out.

Maud gave an impatient grunt but turned to look at her.

"Well?"

"The man… who was here earlier… is he… is he…?"

"Still alive? Yes, as far as I know. His Glorious Majesty has sent him to Barda's toy room."

"Toy room?"

"Barda likes to play…" she gave Kesia a chilling smile and walked away with Floria.

Chapter 33

Simon was flying...

... Which was not very likely even though this was a dream. Then it dawned on him...

... He was staring down on Branchir's map. He felt rather than saw the hands he was holding but knew it was Marianne and Eleanor.

This dream was another memory - his.

Suddenly his stomach rushed up to his throat as he had the sensation of falling. The ground was rushing up to meet him and he could not stop it.

The fear disappeared. He knew what happened next.

Still, he tensed slightly anticipating the impact but it never came. He was sinking down through the ground. There was no sensation of claustrophobia or suffocation and somehow, he was still able to breathe. There was just the odd feeling of sliding through the earth slowly and smoothly, and a strange calm.

This was a recent memory; he, Marianne and Eleanor had been scrying for Hob;

"What can you see?" Eleanor asked.

"The soil… layers of sands and silts and rock…" He heard his own voice, full of wonder.

"I can see the roots of so many plants and trees… and there are tiny creatures, sleeping peacefully… apart from the worms, they're always busy…," He had forgotten Alsea had been there too.

The next moment he was standing in a tunnel, lit with a pale green phosphorescent glow. He walked through the tunnel and came out in a large cavern. He ignored the shops and the bar and made his way into yet another tunnel, which ended in a pair of heavy doors.

The cavern beyond was much smaller than the first. Light decorated the walls, reflected by the gemstones embedded in it. Hanging from the roof high above, flowing curtains of limestone stalactites sparkled and shimmered. It was quite the spectacle. This time he did not have to look twice to see the diminutive figure sitting on the jewel encrusted throne.

"What kept you lad? I've been waiting ages." Hob leapt down from his seat.

This did not happen last time.

Simon turned to look behind him. Who was Hob speaking to? But there was no one there, only him. He turned back but Hob and the throne room had vanished.

Instead, he was standing on the edge of an abyss. He took a step back and came up against a wall of rock.

"You have to move beyond your own boundaries," Hob's disembodied voice echoed all around him. "You need to be prepared to take risks without knowing the outcome. Can you take that first step?"

"Is this a test?" Simon called out into the darkness. There was no answer but he had not expected one. He leaned forward to peer over the edge, into the deeper darkness and discovered narrow steps cut into the vertical side of the precipice. The way behind him was blocked and the gap was too wide to jump, his only option was to go down. He started counting the steps to give him something to concentrate on but lost count somewhere around the two hundred mark. The steps followed tightly around the curved rock wall until he came to a wide passageway with three arched openings, another choice to make. Above each of the openings, an image was carved into the keystone. The first image was an erupting volcano. He peered through the arch into the dark tunnel. The faint glow in the distance might have been daylight, but the whiff of sulphur made him pull back.

The next keystone was carved with a scene that looked like a rocky landscape with the odd tree and pool of water. Again, he stuck his head through the arch. There was no light this time but an overpowering smell of damp and rotting vegetation. Glancing down, the floor of this tunnel was thick, sticky mud. He did not want to get bogged down there.

That left the final arch. This carving was an acorn and spoke to the part of him that was dryad. He walked on through… and found himself standing in Eleanor's grotto, as it had been that first time; a dark, mysterious place. The walls lined with shells and crystals that glowed a fleshy pink. The magic of the place curled around him sending sparks of pins and needles through his arms and legs. It made moving difficult but he pressed on.

Having crossed the narrow stream, he encountered the small libation altar and yet more doors - each one decorated with a symbol that called to the part of him that was the Forest Mage: an acorn, a leaf, a flower, a tree. He knew he had to keep his mind open and clear before he touched the door handle. He decided to stick with the acorn theme and opened the door.

As he stepped into the small alcove, the door

slammed behind him before he could stop it. He tested the door but could not tell if it was locked or just stuck. He put his shoulder to it but it would not move.

And then...

The ground beneath his feet began to vibrate. A fine lattice of cracks spread across the ceiling and down the walls; dust and fine particles of soil and grit rained down on him as the tiny room began to crumble around him. Earth began to fill the small space. It was up to his knees and rising rapidly.

Still he did not panic. This was a test... in his dream. There had to be a way out. He tried the door again but it would not move. The only thing he could do was dig his way out with his bare hands.

Simon reached out to the wall and his hand disappeared through the soil. He pushed further, remembering the beginning of the dream where he had moved through the earth with ease. He kept moving and found himself standing on the top of a grassy hill with a view out over the Gnome Homes of Faerie.

At the bottom of the hill, two gnomes were in the middle of a heated argument. He could not hear what they were shouting about, nor did he have a clear view of their faces but something told him that, if this was like his other dreams, one of these two was going to be Hob. He made his way down the hill until he was very close to the two gnomes but they did not see him. What would this test be?

"This is what you want father, not what I want," the petulant voice protested.

"You never seem to know what you want. You change your mind like the weather," the father said with a sigh. This was a departure from Simon's previous dreams. Hob was the father not the son.

"Well, I do know this. I am not taking on your Earth mantle," the younger gnome muttered. "I refuse. Besides, there's no need. You've got hundreds of years yet. Give me a few years to find myself."

"Find yourself!" Hob sighed. "You're there Erek, standing in your boots and under your cap, where you always are. Who is it this time? What's her name?" He sighed again. "Which clan is she from?"

"She's not…" Erek huffed a bit and shuffled his feet. "She's not a gnome. Her name is Betula and she's a dryad."

The two men faded away and time wound on but very little time had passed because the two men did not look much different.

""It's good to see you again, Erek."

"And you father," Erek sounded less like a spoiled child now. "Betula said I should come. She thought you would like to know that you are a grandfather." Erek grinned from ear to ear.

"Congratulations lad. Had any more thoughts about being my heir?"

Erek ignored Hob's question. "You have a granddaughter. Her name is Alsea and she takes after her mother's side of the family rather than mine."

"I am pleased for you lad. Now that you have some responsibilities may be…"

"Really father? Not this again…"

The scene faded and the arch reappeared. Simon stepped through into Hob's throne room.

"Glad you made it back in one piece, lad." Hob grinned at him.

"So did I pass your tests?"

"Not my tests. Those tests were your own subconscious working through your options. So, after everything you've seen, do you think you are strong enough to face what is coming?"

"I think I know where this is going. So Erek is your son, which makes him my grandfather?"

"Yes, he was…" Hob looked sad for a moment and then said. "Come and find me when you're ready and we can talk…" and Hob and the throne room faded away into the grey mist.

Simon woke up and rubbed his eyes. He sat up feeling wide awake for the first time in what felt like a very long time.

Chapter 34

The library was eerily quiet considering how many people were crowded into it. Everyone looked pale and shocked after Sylvestri's report. Sardo knew his news was not going to make it any better. He had been called away earlier to investigate the report of an intruder.

"We should probably speak over by the map," Sardo said with a quick glance at Daewen. Branchir followed him across the room and they spoke in lowered voices. It was not so much that they wanted to keep the conversation a secret more that they needed to think carefully about how to share this information with their wives.

"You may as well just tell me," Daewen said with a frown as she joined them. "Surely it cannot be any worse than we have already heard."

Branchir was not so sure. "We should

share this information with everyone."

"Indeed Your Majesty," Sardo bowed in agreement.

Branchir took up a position before the hearth and faced the people in his library. "It would seem that a spy has been discovered in the castle. We know where he came from and although he has been questioned, he is unwilling to give up any further information."

"Maybe we should bring him in here for further questioning. I think we all need to hear what he has to say," Sardo suggested.

At Branchir's nod, two men entered the room with a large birdcage suspended between them on a long pole and covered with a cloth. They placed it on the table and slid the pole out then stepped back to stand guard beside the door. With a flick of Branchir's fingers, the cloth covering slithered to the floor to reveal – not a bird, but… a moth. A large brown and grey speckled moth quivered on the floor of the cage.

"Do not be fooled, dear lady. It is not

what it seems," Branchir said as Emma peered between the bars. "And it's not advisable to venture too close. They have a nasty bite."

The moth's wings fluttered up and folded back to reveal a tiny person. He turned to face Emma and spread his wings again to display the beautiful, iridescent blues and greens of the underside. At Emma's gasp, the tiny fairy turned and grinned at her showing a mouthful of wickedly sharp pointed teeth. He winked and blew her a kiss. She stepped back and looked up at Branchir.

"Are you quite sure he can't get out of there?" she asked.

"Quite sure, dear Lady. The Lesser Fae are repelled by iron. If any part of him touches the metal, it will burn and close proximity will drain him of any power he might have."

"I can hear you, you know," the tiny man said to Emma in a surprising deep voice. He ignored Branchir.

Hermes leaned into her and said, "I do believe he is flirting with you." Although he was no longer in his cat form, he still sported his fangs.

"Who sent you?" Branchir asked the fairy.

The little man turned his back completely to Branchir and continued to ignore him.

"Why don't you let me out and we can get better acquainted? Size isn't everything you know." He was ignoring Hermes too.

"I don't think that would be a good idea," Emma tried to sound calm but something about this tiny creature made her skin crawl.

Daewen appeared at her side and placed her hand on Emma's arm, immediately she felt calmer.

"Oh, hello!" the fairy crooned and focused his attention on Daewen now. "You're her aren't you? You're the one who used to be the Dark Prince's plaything? And look at you now… you're the Queen. Isn't that sweet?"

Emma felt Daewen's fingers tighten on

her arm. It was only a slight pressure change but still noticeable.

"Dark Prince... is that what they're calling that bastard now?" Sardo leaned closer to the cage.

"And hello to you too, General. So nice to see you again, not that you'd remember me." the fairy smiled.

"I don't believe we have ever met," Sardo growled.

"No, you probably wouldn't remember. You were a little distracted at the time," the fairy sighed. "Ah, all that blood and raw flesh and they wouldn't even let me have a little taste. Such a cruel outrage. I'd only have had a tiny nibble and there was so much..." he licked his lips and his face took on a dreamy expression that made Sardo want to shudder at the memory he had all but managed to put behind him. But the fairy was not finished yet.

"And then you went and abused the Dark Prince's hospitality by running away and kidnapping his beloved sister and his sweet, amusing little toy. She was to be his consort you know... very ungracious of you to deliver them both to his enemy."

Sardo stepped towards the cage. He would squash the little bug flat. All he had to do was open the cage and... Daewen touched his arm and he stepped back again with a startled blink. What was he thinking?

"What a thoroughly unpleasant creature," Emma muttered.

"Oh! And there was I, just beginning to like you," the fairy licked his lips lasciviously again. Hermes hissed and bared his teeth.

"Are you going to answer my questions?" Branchir asked.

"Er, nope! I'd rather play with these lovely ladies here," the fairy grinned and grabbed at his crotch suggestively.

"Then you leave me no option. Should you decide to continue with these games, let this be your only warning. I wish the cage would grow smaller with every failure to answer a civil question with the truth and every inappropriate comment," Branchir let just a tiny bit of his magic loose.

"Ha! You might wish for it but... hey!" The iron bars of the cage gave a creak as they shimmered and contracted by a hair's breadth.

"You will answer my question," Branchir said. "Who sent you?"

"What did you do? How did you do that? Ow!" the bars shrank a little more.

"Who sent you?"

The fairy turned back and addressed Daewen. "Doesn't he repeat himself...ow, ow, ow!"

"He gave you fair warning," Daewen said. "It would be better for you if you answered quickly and truthfully."

The fairy raised one tiny eyebrow and opened his mouth to speak but stopped as he thought better of it.

"Please answer our question. Refusal will have the same effect as an untruth," Daewen said. "Who sent you?"

"The Leader of the City Beneath sent me." His voice had an odd tone.

"Where is the City Beneath?" Daewen asked. She knew exactly where it was but needed the fairy to confirm it.

"The City Beneath was once the Citadel of Morfinnel, the Dark Prince." The fairy clamped both hands over his mouth to stop the words from coming out.

"Who is the Leader of the City Beneath now?"

The fairy made a strangled sound as he fought to keep the words in. "The Leader... of the... City Beneath is... is... no...ow!"

The bars tightened again and he pulled his wings in close to his back.

"The... Leader... is..." he gritted his teeth.

"Come now," Daewen crooned. "You know you want to tell us."

"Want to tell you..." he tried stuffing his whole hand in his mouth. "The Dark Prince's favoured General, Einhard."

"I don't recall anyone by that name," Sardo said. "Make him tell us if he had another name, one that I might recognise."

"What name was this man originally known by?" Daewen asked.

"General Einhard of the Mighty sword was once Master of the Dark Prince's horses. His name was Huon."

"Huon! I remember him." Sardo spluttered with contempt. "He was never Master of the Horse. He mucked out the stables... was a shit-shoveller. Oh, pardon my language ladies."

"Oh, tell it like it is lad," Daphne chuckled.

"We should have the spy removed from our presence, my love, before he has a chance to say anything further and cause himself too much damage," Branchir suggested.

The fairy knelt in the centre of the cage with his wings pulled in as tight to his body as he could get them and was rocking to and fro with his head in his hands. Strange keening sounds came from him as he tried to stop any more information leaking out.

Chapter 35

With Fyr's wrists locked into shackles, the one called Barda dragged him out of the throne room, along the screens passage and down a flight of stairs into the cellars. Most of the visible space was taken up with a large cache of weapons and barrels of provisions. It looked like they were preparing for a siege. Barda prodded him towards a heavy wooden door at the far end of the cellar. Taking a large iron key from his belt, he unlocked the door and gave Fyr a hard shove. He went sprawling into the filth of the dungeon floor.

A pair of flaming torches gave a little illumination but it was enough to tell that the contents of this room were the stuff of nightmares. Odd shapes loomed menacingly in the gloom. Before Fyr could pick himself up Barda had grabbed a hook and attached it to the chain between his shackles. Winding a crank handle over by the door, the rope pulled taut through a series of rings set into the ceiling and slowly drew Fyr's arms above his head. It kept going until it hauled him to his feet. Pain shot through his wrists and shoulders as they took most of the weight of his body.

Barda turned the handle slowly, listening for the clicks of the ratchet and watching Fyr intently. He continued slowly, one click at a time, until Fyr's toes were only just touching the ground.

"Make yourself comfortable. We could be here a while." Barda's grin was unpleasant. He appeared to only have three teeth in his head.

"So let me see. His Most Regal Highness said to show you my playthings... now, where shall I start?" He walked slowly to the corner where a brazier sat; he lit it with one of the torches. The barrel beside the brazier seemed to interest Barda more. He reached in and began pulling out a horrific array of implements which he placed almost lovingly on a wooden bench.

"Right so! I got pinchers and squeezers, rippers and gougers, nippers and cutters …" He held each one up in turn and mimed its use. Tremors ran through Fyr's strained muscles but he made no sound – which annoyed Barda. "Okay, then we got these: branders and flayers, jabbers and crushers…" There was still no sound from his victim. Barda frowned. They usually began sobbing and begging by this point. He clicked his tongue in irritation and gave the crank handle one more click of the ratchet. Fyr's toes left the ground and all his weight was suspended from his wrists. He let out a gasp as the metal cuffs bit into his flesh. That got a nod of approval from Barda who went back to his show and tell.

"Ah, now then, this is quite fun." He dragged the dust cover off a wooden chair that was studded all over with sharp metal points. "See, what we do is, have you sit there all nice and comfy-like, then we do up these straps… wouldn't want you to move… we can add weights to press you down… we can even light a fire underneath it... heats up the metal points a treat, 'specially on the seat." He was almost drooling with excitement as he rubbed his hands and whisked the cover off a large table-like shape.

"I call this little beauty my bed of pain... See what you do, is lay down here and I put these on your wrists and ankles..." He demonstrated the shackles at either end of the table. "Then I turn this handle..."

He picked up a metal pole and slotted it into a wheel at the side of the table. The thick ropes wound onto rollers underneath the table. "We can do it slowly ... a little bit at a time see..." Again, he demonstrated. "Or we can do it a bit quicker..."

More demonstrations.

"Or we can put another roller under you... bends you see... eventually you get so stretched out of shape that yer joints and muscles don't work no more or..." and he gave a wheezing snigger, "We can go all the way, stretchin' and pullin' 'til... pop! It rips yer arms and legs right off... I ain't never been allowed to go that far yet." He gave a nasty wet sounding chuckle that had foam gathering at the corners of his mouth. He turned back and looked at Fyr and his face fell. "Oh now look at you... look what you've gone and done. His Most Radiant Majesty said no blood but it's all running down your arms. You really should've waited a bit longer to bleed... 'E ain't gonna like that..." He seemed to be talking to himself rather than Fyr. He grabbed Fyr's hair and pulled his head up. "Don't you go passing out on me now fella... we ain't done yet."

A click and a rattle and the chains slackened enough for Fyr's feet to touch the ground. His arms were on fire from his shoulders to his wrists. He locked his knees in order to remain standing even though his legs threatened to collapse. He did not want to put any more pressure on his strained muscles.

"Don't you go nowhere now... I'll leave you to ponder what I've shown yer... back soon..." Then Barda left and locked the door behind him.

Fyr managed to look around him in the hope of finding something to lean on and relieve the pressure. There was a wall behind him but it was just too far away to reach. Little rains of dirt and dust trickled out of the joints between the stones all around him but it barely registered as he tried to cope with the pain.

A larger chunk of masonry hit the floor by his feet. He looked up to see what new agony they had planned for him. Tiny white filaments were pushing their way out between the huge stones of the building's foundations. Some spread across the surface to act as an anchor while others pushed out, weaving their way blindly towards him. He could do nothing to avoid the waving tendrils. Then the first one touched him. It was only a slight, tentative brush against his cheek but he had to smile despite his pain.

Now that the roots had found him, the fine white filaments became thicker and surrounded him, forming a cradle that supported his weight and took the pressure off his tortured limbs. These roots belonged to a willow tree that Fyr had not even noticed in the grounds, but the tree knew about him. It sent an apology that it was unable to free him yet but, never fear, the trees were working on it and would be back to get him as soon as they could.

After too short a reprieve, the roots apologised and began to recede into the wall. They warned him that the bad man was returning. Fyr was surprised to note that the holes the roots had made were almost unnoticeable and the fine root hairs had swept most of the dust and debris out of sight before they disappeared and Barda's key sounded in the lock.

"Come on then, let's be 'avin' yer." Barda came in with two other men. "Spoilin' my fun…" he muttered under his breath.

The two guards supported Fyr as Barda released him from the chain and his legs finally gave way. Gritting his teeth as the men draped his arms around their shoulders; he stumbled as they half dragged him out of the dungeon and back up the stairs. Barda clicked his tongue in irritation. Neither he nor his toys had had the opportunity of getting better acquainted with Fyr yet and he had been looking forward to making him scream.

Fyr expected to end up in the hall again but they exited the building and he was dropped into a small cart with high barred sides, almost a cage. It trundled through the grounds and out onto the village green where they came to a halt beside the pillory.

Even through his haze of pain, Fyr could not fail to notice the low stage that had been erected close to the pillory where he was now restrained. It was almost as though it had been put there to give him a good view of the show. He watched through pain-blurred eyes as an audience began to arrive. Well dressed, obviously wealthy people took up their places in the seats at the front and lowly villagers hung around at the back to watch the spectacle. There was a mass murmur as Hedeon and his entourage arrived, dressed in all their finery. He stopped beside Fyr and leaned in close to speak.

"I do hope you will enjoy the show. However, we can't have you interrupting or spoiling the proceedings, so..." He gave the guard at his side a nod and Fyr was gagged. Hedeon patted him on the head and went to take his seat.

The curtain twitched and a man dressed in long, black robes stepped up onto the stage.

"My lords... Gentlemen and commoners. May I welcome you all to our latest auction. Today we have four lots for your perusal and delectation: four prime specimens who are fit and well and each one is able to function in whatever capacity you deem fitting."

The seated crowd applauded politely but the villagers, standing at the back behind the rope barrier, all looked on in stunned silence.

"And here we have the first lot for your approval," the Auctioneer went on, "Hebe here, at a mere nineteen, is the youngest of our auction lots today." Hebe was pushed through the curtains and up onto the stage where the Auctioneer drew her front and centre. He gave her arms a squeeze and tilted her chin up. "Observe. She is clean and tidy, well-kept and she has all her own teeth. By all accounts, she is also a very good cook. She has been keeping house for her father and three brothers for the past four years but they are no longer in a position to afford her services. Who will open the bidding?"

No one offered anything until the Auctioneer whispered something in her ear and the girl looked up and out over the sea of faces with a weak, forced smile.

"Do I hear twenty crowns for this delightful, hard-working creature?"

"Twenty crowns," a voice called out."

"Twenty two," called a second.

"Twenty five," said the first.

"Thirty," the second bidder shouted.

"Thirty three."

"Thirty five."

Then there was a pause.

"Do I hear Forty? No? Thirty eight?" The Auctioneer scanned the faces in the crowd. "Very well, I have thirty five... thirty five crowns... any more bids?"

The first bidder shook his head.

"Very well, going once at thirty five crowns... going twice at thirty five crowns ... going three times at thirty five crowns... sold for thirty five crowns to the gentleman in red." He clapped his hands to seal the deal. "Immediate payment please. Come up and claim your goods."

From a seat near the back, a grey haired man in chain mail and a red surcoat with a boar's head emblazon made his way to the front. He pulled a leather money pouch from his belt and tossed it up and down in his hand, pleased with the chink of coins inside. He threw the pouch up to the Auctioneer and held his hand out to the girl.

"Let's go." He grabbed her arm and led her away in tears while he chuckled to himself.

"And the next lot..." the Auctioneer carried straight on. "This is Rosa. She is very well domesticated, having spent the last ten years caring for her sick mother who has recently passed away making this delightful creature available."

There was only one bidder for her, a fat, warty old man. He leered at her as he went up and paid his thirty seven crowns. He had been the one to buy her house too.

Lobelia was the third lot. Her size and build made her ideal for the owner of the livery stables. He paid thirty two crowns for her to work alongside his farrier. Now there was only one 'lot' left. Fyr held his breath as the curtain moved and Kesia was pushed up onto the stage.

Chapter 36

Having listened to the spy's talk of the citadel, Sylvestri offered to investigate. Thinking about that place made her feel guilty now though. She had drifted through the halls of the citadel many times in the past. How could she not have seen, not have known what Morfinnel had been up to for all that time? This time she would make sure to blow through every hidden corner of the place, nothing would remain concealed from her, not this time.

She arrived at the ancient tombs almost within the blink of an eye and remained unseen whilst she roamed up onto the moors. She knew exactly where to find the entrance, well-hidden though it was. She drifted around the outside of the prehistoric megaliths taking note of every tiny change and alteration. In Morfinnel's day, the way into the citadel had been a closely guarded secret. There had been false trails and traps for the unwary and unwanted. Now, a well-worn path ran between the village, a few miles away, and one particular tomb. Morfinnel would never have stood for that. It gave away the entrance.

As gentle as a summer breeze, she drifted between two of the giant upright megaliths that supported the roof slab. Once inside, she followed the tunnel down and around to a point where it split into three. In Morfinnel's day, unsuspecting visitors had a one in three chance of taking the correct path. Now, large stones blocked two of the three entrances, leaving a single option. Sylvestri drifted on down into the cavern below where, incongruously, a moated stone castle had been built into the wall on the far side.

Sylvestri remembered the stiff sentries of old. They had been everywhere: wary, alert and always on guard. Morfinnel would not have had it any other way. His guards were highly motivated to follow orders – pain and death were definitely motivating forces. These few men though, sat about playing card games, dice and dominoes... and drinking. Morfinnel would have had them flayed alive.

The men wore armour of a sort but their blades were dull, rusty and left on the floor in a pile by the door. Sylvestri was not sure what she was seeing here. The fairy-spy had led them to believe that this was a force to be reckoned with. She turned as a small boy came running full pelt down the tunnel and up onto the open drawbridge. He peered up to the top of the gatehouse battlements where, presumably, someone was on sentry duty after all.

"Da!" he shouted.

"Who is it?" a man leaned over to peer down at the boy. "Oh, It's you scamp, ye da's been called away... to the privy..." Laughter echoed round the cavern. "What d'ya want?"

"Da said to keep watch an' tell you if strangers come round. They's four of'm an' they's nearly here...."

"Righto lad. I'll let Himself know. You get

yerself off 'ome. Don't you be gettin' in the way. Run along now."

As the boy ran back up the tunnel, the men began to stir themselves, gather up their weapons and assemble outside. For all the fuss and noise they made, Sylvestri was surprised to discover there were only eight of them. There had to be more of them inside, surely. She sped in through the gate and breezed through the whole building, including the previously secret dungeons and there was only one other person in the whole place.

This had to be Einhard. He was not quite what she was expecting after the way the fairy-spy had spoken. A short, fat man with thin hair combed over his bald head and a weak chin... make that chins. She watched him as he fidgeted about and tried to find a suitable pose that would make him look important. As far as Sylvestri could see, he was an idiot, probably set up by the others to take the fall.

First, he stood with his feet apart and his

arms crossed over his belly but that took effort so he sat down. Then he was up again with his fists on his hips and his nose in the air. Then he was down again. In the end, he sat on Morfinnel's throne and tried to keep still. Suddenly, he twisted sideways and thrust his weak chins in the air, presumably thinking it made him appear more regal. Sylvestri wanted to laugh; she thought it made him look as though he had a bad smell under his nose. Was this really the so-called Leader of the City Beneath? He was just too ridiculous for words.

The sound of heavy boots, marching in unison, thundered across the drawbridge. Sylvestri drifted around to watch. The first two to enter were Einhard's men judging by their unkempt appearance. The next four she recognised, with some surprise, as Hedeon's men. Their surcoats were in Hedeon's rather garish colours but each man had his own emblem emblazoned across his chest: a boar, a rat, a bull and a wolf. The simpering idiot on the throne did not impress them.

"Welcome friends," the man on the throne stood. "I am General Einhard, Leader of the Great City Beneath. What can we do for you fine gentlemen?"

"I don't see a great city. Just a bunch of idlers hibernating down here like dormice," the rat murmured to the bull.

"Hold your tongue Tobran," Jarin, the bull muttered back. "We don't want to put their backs up before we've had a chance to set out our case."

"Well I hope they're quick about it. I've a new purchase at home and I'm eager to get back. Ain't had a chance to break her in yet," the boar murmured to them.

The wolf, stepped forward. "General Einhard. I am Major-General Merek. We come bearing greetings and salutations from the Highest, Most Eminent King, Hedeon of the Boroviche."

"Much appreciated," Einhard simpered. "What can we do to help you?"

"We have eyes and ears in many places

and it has come to the attention of our Most Excellent and Illustrious Highness that there is a certain amount of enmity between your people and the... Pretender to the Elven throne," Merek said.

"If you mean Prince Branchir, there is certainly no love lost there. We don't recognise his claim to the Elven throne," Einhard said.

"I hate to be the one to disillusion you my lord, but I don't think his court is even aware of yours." Cedric the boar said.

"We have been biding our time and regrouping after the coup that deprived us of our Prince. He was betrayed by the one person he thought he could rely on. That same person is now all high and mighty... all comfy and cosy with the pretender. He even kidnapped the Prince's sister."

"Is that so?" Merek said. "Then I believe we have a common cause and in the spirit of mutual agreement and understanding we have come to offer our support so that we may work together to reach our shared goal.

Are you willing to enter into a contract with our Most Eminent Highness, King Hedeon?"

"Er..." Einhard was not sure what they were asking of him or what they offered in return. "Are you saying you'll help us get rid of Prince Branchir if we help you?"

"Indeed. It would also benefit our Most Gracious Leader if the pretender to the throne was removed," Merek said with a smile.

"So you'd like us to work together?" Einhard looked excitedly at each of the strangers.

"We would," Merek confirmed. "If you are in agreement we will return shortly with the contract and further information. How many men can we rely on you to provide?"

This time Einhard looked warily at each of his own men.

"Oh, well... right at this moment I can't give you numbers. It will take a few days to arrange for the gathering."

"Good. You have seven days." And with that, the strangers all turned and marched back across the drawbridge and out of the citadel.

Einhard's men stood around shuffling their feet and staring at the ground. None of them were quite sure what they had just agreed to.

"Fuck me... we're really going to do this?" one of them asked.

"We're finally going to get revenge for our Prince," said another.

"And a chance at the throne for ourselves?" said a third.

"And about time too," Einhard nodded, feeling quite proud of himself. "Has our agent returned from the pretender's castle yet?"

"Not yet, but it's been less than a day. I'm sure he'll be back with plans of the castle soon."

Oh, no he won't, Sylvestri thought, but they don't need to know that.

"Right!" Einhard rubbed his hands together eagerly. "Time for the gathering... Round up the women and children and get them locked up. And don't forget the gnomes."

That last comment made Sylvestri do a double-take. The gnomes could not be in league with this bunch of clowns. She needed to find Hob. If anyone knew, he would. He may be the Earth Elemental but he was still supposed to be the King of the Gnomes. She sped back up the tunnel out of the citadel and headed for the Gnome Homes.

Chapter 37

Simon and Marianne made their way down the garden and through the Faerie gate with Eleanor's help.

"So where do we go from here?" Marianne asked as they stood on the other side of the gate and contemplated the long journey in front of them.

"I can get us through the trees fairly quickly but once we reach the edge of the forest we'll have a long walk across the plains to the Gnome Homes unless Hob, in his usual enigmatic way, knows we have arrived and sends help." Simon knelt down on the leaf-strewn ground and delved with his fingertips into the soil. "Ah! I feel a faint vibration," he said just before two small gnome heads popped up through the ground and made Marianne scream.

"So sorry Missus. Didna mean ta scare ya." Digger whipped off his cap and bobbed up and down as he tried to bow and apologise at the same time.

"We bin sent to bring yers 'ome," Dibbler said copying his brother's bobbing about.

"Could you two please keep still? You're making me feel dizzy," Marianne winced.

"Oh, sorry Missus, sorry again." They were both about to start bobbing again when Simon stopped them.

"Come on then lads," he said. "Let's get this over with."

Digger held out a surprisingly large hand to Marianne and Dibbler took hold of Simon's hand. Just as in Simon's dream, he felt himself slipping and sliding down into the earth. Beside him, Marianne screwed her eyes up tight and held her breath until he grabbed her hand to reassure her that she was safe. She made no sound as the ground closed over her head then he felt her relax against him in relief as she realised they were standing in a tunnel.

"I don't want to do that, ever again,"

she shuddered.

"It wasn't that bad," he said putting his arm around her and pulling her in close.

"Just... no!" she gave another shudder and they started walking.

They had not been walking for long when Simon began to get a feeling of déjà vu. They emerged from the tunnel into a huge domed cavern. Walkways ran around the walls of the dome with openings arrayed at uneven intervals. At the level they were on, all the openings were shops, just as Simon had seen in his dream... and there was the bar, complete with raucous singing... and then they were in the tunnel that he knew led to Hob's throne room.

"What's been keeping you lad? I've been waiting for ages." Simon blinked as Hob leapt down from his throne. "And Marianne, it's lovely to see you again lass." And just like that, the sense of déjà vu vanished. The throne room and everyone in it were still there and there was no abyss or strange tunnels threatening to trap him. Simon gave a sigh of relief.

"Why don't we go somewhere a little less public? There'll be another damned school party wandering through any minute and there's only so much gawping I can stomach," Hob said. He led them through a door behind the throne and along a service corridor housing kitchens, store rooms, work rooms and other such essential offices.

He opened the door to his private suite.

"Cosy," Marianne smiled. The room was circular with three further doors at the compass points. In the centre of the room, armchairs were set out around a low, circular table.

"I modelled this on Branchir's library, only without the books. He went to a cabinet and took out a bottle and three silver wine cups which he placed on the table.

"Might as well make ourselves comfortable," he said sitting down. Hob poured a little of the pale amber liquid into each cup and handed them to Simon and Marianne. "We should... what is it you humans say… make a toast?"

Simon and Marianne nodded together.

"A toast then… to my successor." And Hob knocked back the contents of his cup in one gulp.

Neither Simon nor Marianne had as much as sipped theirs yet.

"This was what the dreams have been about, isn't it?"

"Dreams?" Hob said with a raised eyebrow.

"Are you telling me these dreams I had, had nothing to do with you?" Simon asked.

"What sort of dreams?" Hob asked.

"I watched as each one was given… took on… accepted… their element. I saw Salamander as a scared little boy, bullied by his grandfather into taking on the role of Fire Elemental because his father didn't want the responsibility. Undine had to pay a debt to the Water Elemental who saved her from drowning as a child. Young Aurora thought she was going mad because of all the people's emotions constantly bombarding her. Sylvestri had been an abandoned and abused child who... should I go on?"

"What about me? Did you see the mantle pass to me?" Hob asked.

"No, you were the one person I saw trying to get rid of the task... job... duty... whatever."

"It's a gift lad," Hob smiled. "At least, I thought it was. I can see that other people might see it differently. I know it is time for the gift to move on now. I've had it for longer than most.

"And in my dream you tried to persuade your son, Erek... but, just like Salamander's father, he didn't want it."

"Not quite. I loved Erek dearly but he was too flighty to ever shoulder the gift. It would have become a burden and I couldn't do that to him. He was far too much like his mother. She was a nymph you know," Hob's eyes had a faraway look. "They are both long gone now and for a long time I thought all I had left was Alsea... she is far too much dryad, too much nymph and not enough gnome... and then you appeared."

"Are you saying Simon is more gnome than...?" Than what? Marianne was not sure. "Look at him. He's well over six foot and your gnomes are less than half that."

"And sometimes we are not," Hob smiled. "You've seen me in my other form." And he changed. In this form he looked like Simon's brother – only Simon did not have a brother.

"I'm not sure how it all works but our family line seems to be a little more mixed than most. There's even some human way, way back," Hob shrugged. "The thing is I have been feeling it slipping away for a while and it had to go somewhere. There has to be free will in accepting it but I think the powers that be think you are the best candidate for the job. You can accept it, or not, but ultimately your hand might be forced if there is nowhere else for it to go."

Simon and Marianne lifted their cups simultaneously and took a sip. It slipped down Simon's throat smoothly, like warm honey.

It made Marianne choke and her eyes water. "Wow! That's strong stuff," She managed to croak as Simon patted her back.

"So, what do you say lad. Are you up for the challenge?"

"I guess so. I can't say I wasn't expecting it after all those dreams leading the way."

"Good." Hob shook Simon's hand, sat back in his chair and promptly passed out. Moments later, all three were slumped unconscious in their armchairs as the Elemental magic wove its gifts around Simon… and strangely, Marianne.

Chapter 38

Kesia had no choice but to follow their orders and step up onto the stage. They had caught Fyr and he was their prisoner. They said they had their eye on her father too but at least he was still free, for the moment.

"Come on my dear. We don't have all day," the Auctioneer said through a toothy grin. "Smile nicely at all the good people."

She walked slowly towards the Auctioneer but her eyes were on the pillory and Fyr.

"Please... don't hurt him," she begged.

"Eyes front and centre," the Auctioneer gave her a nudge. "He has nothing to do with me. Maybe if you can prove you're willing to behave..." He turned back to the audience.

"No... not my little girl..." her father's faint cry came from the back of the crowd where he was being held up by two armed men.

"Here we have, last but by no means least, lot number four. You may recognise her as Kesia, daughter of Ori Lukash, the chandler. As you just heard, he just vouched for her." The Auctioneer gave a nasty leering smile. "I wonder… would someone be so kind as to escort the poor man home? It would be unfortunate if he had a … turn for the worse. I'm sure he would not want to disrupt the proceedings."

"Please…" Kesia begged, but she knew it was pointless. "Don't hurt him."

"Oh!" He looked from the back of the crowd to the pillory. "And which 'him' are we talking about?" His grin was cruel. "Be a good girl and behave yourself and maybe…" He left it hanging there and turned back to the crowd. The seated audience were getting impatient for proceedings to resume.

"Right, who will open the bidding? Do I hear thirty crowns?"

"Forty crowns," the first bidder called.

"Forty five crowns," shouted the second.

"Fifty," a third bidder offered.

"I'll double that..." the new bidder, from the front row, stood up and tossed two leather coin bags up to the Auctioneer by-passing all the auction conventions, but no one disputed it.

"Sold to his Most Eminent Excellency." The Auctioneer shoved Kesia to the front of the stage so that one of Hedeon's men could grab her arm. Hedeon and his entourage began to file away across the green. As they neared the pillory, Hedeon indicated that Barda should remain with Fyr.

"See how long you can keep him alive... he's her incentive for good behaviour. However, persuade him to give up the whereabouts of his two missing friends. Just don't cause too much damage... nothing too fatal!"

The guards dragged Kesia away but she kept turning to try and get a look at Fyr as he struggled with the gag and the pillory. He kept her in sight for as long as he could but Barda stepped in front of him and blocked his last view.

"These people 'ere ain't no fun," Barda complained, mostly to himself because Fyr was not listening. "You'd a thought they could at least 'ave chucked some rubbish... but not a one!" He unlocked the pillory and yanked Fyr's arms behind his back, locking them into shackles. "Walk nice now... or not... it'd give me a good excuse..." he laughed and spittle flew.

There was no sign of Kesia as Barda dragged Fyr back into the house and down to the dungeon. The door at the far end stood open, as though waiting for them. Fyr would have given almost anything to be able to escape from these restraints, knock this grinning thug out and search the place for Kesia but he knew, after the promise the tree made, that he would have to bide his time for just a little while longer. He could do that. He only hoped that Kesia could too.

The guards reattached Fyr's shackles to

the hook and Barda turned the handle to raise his hands above his head again. This time he allowed Fyr to keep his feet firmly on the ground so that the metal cuffs no longer cut into his flesh.

"His Glorious Majesty said no blood, so no blood it is," he muttered to himself. "Keep you alive, he said. So I will. Here, you must be thirsty, have a drink." He gave a nasty smile as he waved a cup of noxious smelling brew under his nose. Fyr squeezed his lips together and turned his head a way.

"Go on then laddie, fight it... it's more fun when you fight... for me, not you... but I 'aven't got all day. 'Is Most Excellent Highness wants answers an' I'm goin' to get 'em, one way or another. So..." He nodded to someone behind Fyr. One guard grabbed Fyr's head while Barda pinched his nose and forced him to open his mouth. Barda managed to pour some of the thick, brown liquid in and then forced Fyr's mouth closed. The taste was so bitter and without being able to spit it out, he had no option but to swallow.

"There's a good lad. Thanks for your help boys," Barda said to the guards as they left the dungeon. "It's just thee and me now lad. This shouldn't take long."

Barda was whistling tunelessly while he made a big show of gathering the equipment he might need. He pottered about in no particular hurry as he then began to add coals to the brazier, singing tunelessly to himself.

"Floggers n' flayers n' squeezers n' crushers..." the sound became a discordant hum in Fyr's ears as though the place swarmed with hundreds of angry bees. Fyr blinked. His eyesight had become blurry but he could see no bees.

The fire in the brazier expanded to an enormous size, the heat of it reached him all the way from the other side of the room and made his skin burn, then it began to itch and he had no way to scratch it. It was driving him mad. If only he could get his hands free then he could strip off his clothes... The room began to spin and his blood pounded in his chest and his head. His jailor had disappeared and in his place, crouched an odd misshapen creature with arms that were too long and a head that was too small for its body. It was hunched over the white hot brazier.

"Wherethetrees?" Fyr slurred. His mouth was dry and his tongue would not work properly.

"Trees are all outside lad, where they belong," the monster gurgled. His voice came from a long way off and then bounced around the walls. Fyr closed his eyes but that did not help either. The room began to tip and he felt himself falling and falling and falling… any moment now he was going to hit the ground… but something was biting at his hands.

Barda came over to Fyr and lifted his head by his hair. He pried open his eyes to examine his pupils. They were so dilated that there was barely any iris visible. Barda chuckled, knowing it would not be long before he got those answers for His Most Illustrious

Leader. He went back to his brazier to check on his tools.

"Gotta be sure it's 'ot enough," he chuckled waving a branding iron over his head. He was off in his own little world now, not taking a blind bit of notice of Fyr. He heard Fyr mutter about the trees again but ignored his drug-induced ravings.

Barda was so involved in his preparations that he was unaware of the roots that pushed their way back through the joints in the stone and enveloped Fyr. They worked their way between the metal cuff and Fyr's wrist, pushing out until they had weakened and bent the metal. Once his hands were free, the roots took him inside the tree and whisked him away.

Barda knew he had only been looking way for a minute or two, but when turned back to his prisoner he was no longer there. Where could he have gone? He could barely stand, let alone walk. The drug he had given him would have left him disorientated and confused and quite possibly, hallucinating. The door was locked and the key firmly attached to his belt, still he double checked. With no other way out, he checked behind, under, inside every possible nook and cranny but the only sign of him was the dried blood on the metal cuffs still hanging from the ceiling.

Where could he have gone?

The only thing out of place was a small amount of dusty mortar and grit that had crumbled from between the stone joints. He made his way around the walls, tapping and pressing, stone by stone. Maybe there was another way. If there was a secret tunnel after all, and no one had bothered to tell him... and now the prisoner had made him look stupid. He was seriously pissed off.

Regardless of his orders, there might just have to be an unfortunate accident with the prisoner when he caught up with him. He was just grateful that his King - Hedeon the Almighty – had already left, taking his auction purchase back to his fortress.

Hedeon and his men had returned to the campsite they had used on their outward journey. They planned to camp overnight and resume their journey to the fortress at first light.

"Borin! Are you sure this is the same place?" Hedeon demanded. His tent and belongings stood in the centre of the clearing exactly as they had left it. However, the clearing seemed somehow smaller.

"Nothing has been moved Your Greatness. It's all here, your tent, our bedrolls, the cooking pots, the provisions..." Borin said.

"Well, get a fire going and some food sorted out girl," Hedeon gave Kesia a shove towards a stack of firewood. "And Borin...?"

"Yes your Highest Excellency..."

"Don't let her out of your sight, for anything. She cost me a lot of money so I need to get the most out of my investment. She is going to be the first of my stable and give me lots of sons so make sure to keep your hands to yourself, or you will lose them... am I making myself clear?"

"Yes, yes, Your Most Wonderful Excellent-ness," Borin bobbed up and down and gave Hedeon a salute.

"See to it quickly girl," Hedeon said as he climbed into the large, ornate tent.

Kesia did as she was told, hoping that this could save the life of her father and Fyr. She knew non-compliance would not be tolerated and would probably result in terrible consequences for all of them. So far, this man had only wanted her to cook and clean... she could do that much but her mind would not let her contemplate anything else... not so soon after the demon... If he touched her... if he tried to force her... she would scream and scream and scream and until she could not stop.

The wind rustled the leaves all around her and for a split second Kesia imagined she heard a voice, just a whisper, calling her name. She did her best to show no reaction but she kept listening. There it was again. She had not imagined it... a whisper on the breeze, sighing her name. Had Fyr come to rescue her? But she knew it could not possibly be him. He was still a prisoner in Hedeon's dungeon. Hedeon had told her that himself. He said that if Fyr gave up the whereabouts of his friends they would let him go. Kesia did not think either of those things was likely to happen. Fyr would never give them up and they would never let him go. She bit her lip to stop herself crying.

The guards had heard nothing, not even Borin who was standing right beside her. They all seemed oblivious to the sound. With the stew cooking in a large pot over the fire and flat breads ready to be slapped onto the hot stones, Kesia stood up and stretched. She turned to Borin but kept her eyes cast down to the ground.

"Please sir... I need to..." she pointed out into the trees.

"What do you need? You ain't goin' nowhere."

"But I have to... you know... go," she shifted from foot to foot and squirmed with embarrassment.

"Oh!" The penny dropped. "You need to pi...pee?"

She nodded.

"Well I can't let you go out there on your own. I ain't s'posed to let you out o' my sight."

"But I... won't be able to go if you are watching me," she gasped, horrified.

"Tell you what. I'll tie a rope around your wrist and the other end round mine. That way I can keep a hold of you while you take care of things." She nodded and allowed him to tie the rope around her wrist. "Come on then, and be quick about it."

They walked out of the clearing together and into the trees under the watchful eye of one of the other guards.

"Here you go," he said.

"I can't go there... it's too close... everyone will see me."

"What about over there?"

"Oh no, they'll all hear..."

They moved deeper into the trees.

"Oh dear... too many nettles here. Can we go a bit further?"

"Here?"

"Thistles."

They moved a bit further into the forest.

"What about here?"

"Brambles."

"Oh for the love of... what about over there by that big tree... the one with all the ferns near it? No one will be able to see or hear you way back here."

"Perfect." It was what she had been counting on.

"Right! Be quick," Borin said, "No funny business. I'll be waitin' here."

She gave him a shy smile and ducked behind the tree. Borin waited and whistled, all the while keeping a tight grip on the rope.

"You done yet?" he called.

"Almost," she called back.

"What are you doing?" The other guard came over to see what was taking so long.

"Women..." Borin rolled his eyes. "Call of nature." He held up his wrist with the rope tied around it. "She ain't going nowhere. See?" It was still taut.

The two men stood and waited for another couple of minutes.

"It's gone very quiet," the other guard said. He walked along the length of the rope to where Kesia had gone behind the tree.

"BORIN!"

Borin went cold. Had the stupid girl done something to herself? Was she hurt? Still holding onto the rope, he rushed over to see what the other man was looking at.

Whilst they had been searching for a suitable site, Kesia had been following the whispering voice, the one only she could hear. It drew her to the ancient oak and told her not to be afraid. A twig brushed along her arm and wiggled under the rope. This tree reminded her of the ones they had met in Aldamar. That felt like such a long time ago. Another twig joined the first and they loosened the knot enough for her to slip her hand out and then hooked the loop over a sturdy branch. She felt herself embraced by the tree, taken inside and then whisked away from this place.

"Safe… safe… safe…" the trees whispered to her.

"But I have to go back… for my father… and Fyr… I have to try and save them," she wept.

Safe… safe… safe…" the tree whispered again.

She knew she was moving. The trees were taking her somewhere, but she had no idea where and no idea how to make it stop.

Chapter 39

Simon awoke just as Marianne and Hob were beginning to stir.

"What on Earth were we drinking? Did you spike it with something?" Simon demanded of Hob.

"Don't... not so loud, lad," Hob groaned, holding tightly to his head so that it did not fall off or float away.

"Urgh!" Marianne winced. "We only had a tiny sip. How can we be so hungover? Must have been potent stuff."

"Twern't the mead at fault. I can vouch for that. It is strong stuff but you'd need more'n a mouthful to be passin' out drunk," Hob said very quietly.

"So it was spiked?" Simon frowned.

"No! Ooh!" Hob's hangover seemed to be worse than Simon's; he and Marianne were recovering quickly.

"Simon, you're hurt." Marianne leapt out

of her seat and knelt in front of him. She grabbed his collar and dragged it down. Blood was seeping through his shirt just over his heart but there was no hole in the material – no evidence of shooting or stabbing. She pulled the fabric down further.

"It looks more like claw marks or scratches or... how the...?" she reached into her ever present carpet bag for a small first aid kit. Cleaning the blood revealed a strange design tattooed into his skin. It was not very big, no more than the palm of Marianne's hand. "Someone came in here while we were unconscious and tattooed him? Who would... why?"

"It's not just him lass. You've got blood on your shoulder-blade," Hob told her.

"Do you know what's going on, Hob?" Simon demanded.

"Let me get a closer look at these marks lad." Hob got up from his seat and moved very carefully. He was still not sure how well his head was attached.

Marianne looked at the cleaned tattoo. "It's a bit of an odd design… sort of random…"

"That's not random," Hob grinned. "Not at all random. It a mark of acceptance, a mark of power. It's the mark of an Elemental. It only looks random because it's an amalgamation of several different symbols, each one having its own meaning. This is your badge of office and shows where your strength comes from."

Hob found a pencil and scrap of paper and copied Simon's tattoo down so he could see it more clearly.

The triangle, circle and horizontal line were all a dark, reddish brown colour.

"So that part is the symbol for earth," Hob said.

Inside the circle, there was a leaf above the horizontal line and roots below, both in green.

"I'm guessing this shows your dryad heritage."

"So I take it you have one of these too?"

Marianne asked Hob.

"Oh, aye," he said as he drew his on the paper beside Simon's.

"The triangle is the same colour, muddy brown but I have a cross like this," and he drew a horizontal and two vertical lines. "But they're grey. They represent the stone and rock of the earth because I'm a gnome."

"What about Marianne?" Simon said. He stood up behind her and eased the fabric away from her shoulder.

"What does it look like?" she asked, peering over her shoulder at Simon.

He drew the symbol on the paper that Hob had used.

Like Simon's tattoo, the triangle and circle were an earthy brown but the swirling symbol inside the circle was green like Simon's leaf.

"Yes, indeed," Hob nodded. "She has the earth symbol but it's missing the horizontal line. Not sure what that means. But this triple spiral, it's the symbol for healing. I'm guessing it's green because you use plants in your potions and such."

"I don't understand. If these are the marks of an Elemental, why have I got one?" Marianne asked.

"Don't rightly know!" Hob shrugged. "Never happened before that I know of." He frowned at one and then the other. "Maybe it's because you two are so closely linked… you've sort of come as a pair. Simon is the Earth Elemental but you are his soul-mate so your powers complement one another. It's all about balance."

"I'm sure I've seen Salamander without his shirt when we've worked together at his house. I'm sure he doesn't have a tattoo like this," Simon said.

"I can assure you Salamander will have a tattoo. It won't be exactly the same of course because his would represent fire. They appear in different places on the body for each Elemental."

"You know, I think I did see it… in my

dream. It's on the side of his neck, probably covered by his long hair most of the time," Simon said.

"And I'm sure Evie would have told me if she'd suddenly got a tattoo," Marianne said.

"I can only assume that whilst you are a magic user, Evie is not. You support Simon when he works his magic." Hob gave a sudden shiver.

"Are you all right?" Marianne asked him.

"I think someone just walked over my grave," Hob said.

"Don't joke... that's not funny," Marianne said with a grimace.

"Don't fret, lass. It's just a saying... but there is a bit of a draught in here. Is that you Ves?" he shouted.

The door burst open with a sudden gust of cold air and then Sylvestri stood in the room.

"Hello darlings. Can't stop. On way to Branchir's place. Just thought you should know. You might have a little bit of a problem," she said turning to Hob.

"Problem?"

Sylvestri told them what she had seen and heard at the citadel – which was now being called the Great City Beneath.

"I'm sure none of my lads would willingly do anything to hurt Branchir or his family. I would have heard something."

"You have been a little distracted lately, darling," Sylvestri told him with a smile.

"True, but I'll investigate. Leave it with me," Hob assured her.

"And you're sure these other men came from the Boroviche?" Simon asked.

"That's what they said. I've no reason to suppose they lied."

"I find it hard to believe. Most of the people I met there seemed content with their lives. Although, I seem to remember there were one or two who were not happy with the changes when they came out of the door. Some of them had a hard time with the magic and couldn't believe in it even when it exploded over their heads... but a war...

really?"

"It would seem as though much has changed while I've been preoccupied with my own troubles," Hob muttered to himself.

"Keep your people safe, Hob darling." Sylvestri kissed his cheek. "Must dash!" she vanished and blew out of the room on a stiff breeze.

"I should have asked her about her tattoo," Marianne muttered to herself distractedly. "Not the time, I suppose."

Chapter 40

The trees were passing him between them, from one to the next, at high speed. Without control of the process, it was seriously disorientating... or it might have been the drug still in his system. Every time Fyr attempted to stop and find out where he was, the trees whisked him on again. Most of the trees ignored him and just pushed him on to their neighbour but every now and then, he encountered one that could communicate. It was not words, or even pictures, it was more akin to emotions that the trees projected. He knew they were trying to keep him safe and were taking him to a place where he could find help.

The final tree held on to him briefly before spitting him out. The sudden stop made his head spin and he staggered a few steps. He had no idea where they had taken him and it took a few moments to get the lie of the land. The forest was at his back, ahead of him were high rocky peaks, a river ran along to the right of him through a narrow gorge and he stood on a paved road that followed the river into the high peaks. The tree behind him gave a shiver of its branches and seemed to be pointing along the road and he knew where it would lead.

He walked along the road, the landscape becoming increasingly familiar, until he came to a deep pool and a small waterfall. He knew if he climbed up behind the waterfall, he would find the gate that would take him to another place. He and his companions had been here before and travelled through this gate to Aldamar. This was the land of the dryads, distant kin, who had taught them how to travel through the trees. They knew that not all Boroviche were driadi and until that point, it had not been particularly significant. That was when they discovered that each Boroviche member of their party was driadi.

The group had help the first time they

went through the gate but the homeward journey had been easy. Fyr hoped that the trees knew what they were doing and that he would be able use the gate on his own or they had just wasted their time in bringing him here. He followed the steps cut into the rock up to the narrow ledge behind the curtain of water. Moss and spray from the thundering water had meant the steps and ledge were slippery but, taking it slowly and carefully, he made his way into the cave without out any mishaps.

A faint glow emanated from the rear of the cave. "Well, here goes nothing," he muttered to himself and walked towards the gate. At the last moment, he closed his eyes and held his hands out in front of him in anticipation of walking into the solid rock of the cave wall but after four or five steps, he stopped and opened one eye. He was still in a cave but it was a different cave and the gate was behind him.

"Ha! What do you know? It worked," he laughed. "I'm in Aldamar." Now all he had to do was find this person the trees had assured him knew what to do next.

As before, he felt there was something calm and peaceful about Aldamar but it would not do to let his guard down. He was on high alert.

"Hello?" The prickly feeling on the back of his neck told him someone was watching him. He stood in the middle of a clearing, that was carpeted with bluebells, and cast his eyes about. He could not see anyone - although if they were dryads, he would not expect to see them. He tried calling out again.

"Hello. I'm Fyr of the Boroviche. I come from Faerie seeking aid from the dryads of Aldamar."

"What are you afraid of?" a small voice called out.

"Beg pardon?" Fyr looked for the speaker and noticed a small patch of bluebells quiver.

"You said you fear something... what are you afraid of?" they called out... followed by a whispered conversation with another, presumably a companion, unless they were talking to themselves.

"No, my name is Fyr. I am of the Driadi Boroviche from Faerie."

More whispering. Fyr turned this way and that. He scanned the trees high and low but there was no sign of the speaker.

"Please... can you come out so that we can talk?"

Another patch of bluebells, this time at the far side of the clearing, shivered and parted to show two little faces peering up at him. They did not look like dryads.

"You don't look afraid," one of them said.

"Don't be daft," the other one said. "He said his name was Fear not that he was afraid. Maybe it's we who should be afraid. Maybe he eats nymphs."

"Oh, no... really... look... I came here looking for the dryads..." he began in desperation.

"No, we're not dryads," they said together.

"I got that!" he muttered under his breath as the nymphs carried on speaking.

"I'm Acantha and this is Acacia."

"Nice to meet you I'm sure... but I really need to..."

Fyr tensed up suddenly as he heard something heavy moving at speed through the forest. It was heading towards them by the sound of it. The two nymphs did not appear to be unduly concerned but that did nothing to reassure him. He retreated a few steps until his back was against the trunk of a larger tree. It would be bad manners to enter a tree uninvited but he would face that problem if, and when, the creature thundering towards them decided it wanted to eat him.

"Hey Joe, wadda ya know?" Acacia sang out as an orange and black blur leapt over their heads to land in a crouch on all fours between him and the two little nymphs. The creature... no, person... had his back to Fyr but he recognised him.

"What are you two little nitwits up to now? Go home and stop tormenting the poor man," he growled. "And my name is Joseph, not Joe, as you well know."

The two nymphs ran off giggling. Joseph stood and turned to Fyr.

"I apologise for the welcome, or rather, lack of." Joseph stood up on two legs and held out his hand in what Fyr recognised as a human custom. Fyr took his hand and shook it. "It is good to see you again, but this is not a social visit is it?" Joseph said.

Fyr shook his head. "When we arrived home there was a huge problem. For one thing, we'd been gone much longer than we thought and everything had changed…. They took Kizzy and now they're selling women and forcing men to fight. I was in a tight spot when the trees came to my rescue and they told me there would be someone here who could help us." It all came out in one breath. He felt shaky from the last traces of the drug in his system and unnerved by the conversation with the nymphs. "And now I wonder if I've done the right thing by coming here. I don't know exactly what sort of help I'm asking for."

"Try and breathe... be calm," Joseph put a hand on Fyr's shoulder. "Maybe we should visit my mistress. She'll know what to do."

Joseph led Fyr through the forest but it was all a blur; every path and clearing began to look alike. They crossed streams and walked trackways that followed hills and valleys until they reached a clearing that felt subtly different to all the others. Two great trees stood alone in the centre and, although he could not see it, Fyr knew this was another gate.

Joseph held out his hand. "We will go through to my mistress's home. I should warn you, it is an uncomfortable place and we must be very careful not to be seen."

Fyr nodded, took Joseph's offered hand and they passed through the gate to emerge in a small copse of trees near a low, white palling fence.

"What is wrong with this place?" Fyr asked. "The air feels bad… and smells even worse. I can almost taste it. It feels… unclean."

"I told you it was uncomfortable," Joseph wrinkled his nose. "This is the human realm. Magic is almost non-existent here, usurped by machines. They use up resources without replacing anything and fill the air and water with poisons. There is no balance in this world because the humans are destroying it. It's a good job that the humans know nothing of the other worlds or they would be despoiling them too." Joseph was speaking very quietly whilst crouching behind a holly bush close to the fence.

"What are we doing?" Fyr whispered.

"Just making sure the coast is clear. Most people here would find my appearance rather alarming. You could probably pass for human, at least you don't have pointed ears or the hind quarters of a goat."

Fyr was wondering, not for the first time,

whether he was doing the right thing.

"Okay, we can move now. Mistress Eleanor knows we are here. She will meet with us through there." Joseph led Fyr through the fence and into the garden. "Just one thing," Joseph stopped him. "Don't be too surprised if I suddenly change; I can't always control it when I get over excited."

Fyr stared at the tiger-man. Just what was going on here?

"What's that sound?" Fyr whispered.

"Sorrrry, that's me... purring... can't help that eitherrrrr."

Eleanor was waiting for them at the bottom of a large hole. Before anyone could speak, Joseph took a flying leap, changed mid leap into a small, sandy coloured cat and landed in her arms. He purred and rubbed his head against her chin.

"Okay Joseph, calm down," she chuckled. "I've missed you too. Hello... it's Fyr isn't it?"

"Hello." He was stunned by the sudden

change, even though Joseph had warned him, it was still a surprise. When Joseph said he might change this was not what he had imagined. "I thought Joseph said there was no magic here."

"True, there isn't much. This house is one of the few pockets left. It is especially concentrated down here... but that's another story. What can I do for you?"

"Well..." Fyr poured everything out in a jumble just as he had with Joseph but Eleanor did not seem to mind. She listened carefully to everything he said, asking questions every now and then. Suddenly Eleanor looked up as a figure appeared at the top of the hole.

"Alsea," Eleanor smiled.

Alsea hugged Eleanor and then turned to Fyr. "I've been following you through Aldamar. If Eleanor says you're good people, then of course we'll help you. I think you know my son, Simon... so that's good too. I contacted Ibur. He's a Tisu-lidé dryad, that's a Yew tree dryad. He said any friend of the

Forest Mage is a friend of the Tisu-lidé."

"Oh, right," Fyr said and could not think of how best to respond. It was difficult to follow Alsea's butterfly mind. "Well, thank you. It's more than I could hope for."

"Ibur and his people are expert archers," Eleanor added.

The sudden high pitched, warbling sound made Fyr leap up in alarm but he was the only one to move.

"Don't worry," Alsea patted his arm. "It's human machine magic."

Eleanor gave a little chuckle. "It's not magic, it's technology… or science or…"

"Silly, of course it's magic," Alsea gave her a little smile back and leaned over to Fyr. "With that little tiny box she can see and talk to people over great distances. It's the human version of scrying and scrying is magic, so…"

Fyr nodded slowly at Alsea because he had no idea what scrying was but Alsea obviously believed it was magic. He watched as Eleanor took a small, flat, glowing object from her pocket and frowned at it. She tapped it a few times and then gave a sigh.

"I'm really sorry," she said to Joseph. He was still a small cat, curled up on her lap. She stroked her hand along his back and then gave him a scratch under the chin. "I have to go and so do you." She looked up at Alsea and Fyr. "James's mother has decided to come looking for me and she can't know about any of this. She wouldn't understand. I'll head her off while you leave. I don't know what I can do to help right now but I'll be here if you need me. Dorcas or Branchir will know how to contact me."

Joseph leapt from her lap and returned to his tiger-man form.

"I shall assist Fyr in getting the dryads and their little friends through the gate but then I must return to the tasks I have set myself in Aldamar. Unless you would rather I..."

"No, your work in relocating all those people is important." She gave him a smile as he bowed then led Fyr and the dryads back to the gate, and to Aldamar.

Chapter 41

It did not take Simon and Marianne very long to reach the castle using the trees as their transport system. Marianne did not mind it as much as the trip through the earth but she held on to Simon and kept her eyes screwed up tight. When they arrived, they discovered that Sylvestri had beaten them to it. Finding the sisters and their familiars in residence was something of a surprise though.

"Aunt Addie," Marianne hugged her. "I had no idea. How did you get here?"

"Long story my love, King Branchir invited us, but... let me look at you," she said changing the subject. She held Marianne at arm's length and scanned her from head to toe and back again. "Something's changed." She pursed her lips with her head on one side while she appeared to be considering what it could be.

"Well that's another long story. Remind

me to tell you someday," Marianne said with a smile. Two could play at that game. "But we came to see if there was anything we could do to help with the threat from the Boroviche."

"It's not all of the Boroviche," Branchir said as he came over the greet them. "A faction has arisen that threatens the stability of all of Faerie."

"Arisen from where?" Simon asked.

"Good question," Branchir said. "Two of the people, drawn here to aid you not so long ago, escaped and came to warn us, which was the first we knew about it."

"Escaped?" Simon frowned. "Escaped from where?"

"Our homeland is now virtually sealed off and under the control of a man named Hedeon and his supporters..." The man stepped forward and bowed.

"I recognise you... sorry I don't remember your name but you were with Fyr and Kesia... how are they?" Marianne asked.

"Ah," Thorn sighed. "That is part of the

problem. We don't know. They were split up when we arrived home. She was taken back to her father's village as far as we know. Last conversation we had with Fyr was that he was about to set off and rescue her."

"Why would he need to rescue her if she was just taken home?" Marianne asked. The faces of those around her said they knew the answer, it was not good, and so they recounted the story for their benefit.

"But that's... that's..." she was too shocked for words.

"Positively medieval," Simon held on tightly to Marianne.

"Never mind medieval," Dorcas said. "It's beyond prehistoric and totally unacceptable. The ordinary folk have been forced to submit to serfdom which is slavery by any other name. It's probably just as well our magic doesn't work here or we'd be tempted to intervene, and then we'd be the ones in trouble."

"I'll bet Mousey here could find a way

and avoid the three-fold return, he's been doing it for centuries," Daphne said, giving the small box on the floor a poke with her toe.

"Mousey?" Marianne peered down at the creature in the box. It looked like a mouse but a rather odd, anthropomorphic version of one. It was sitting upright, using a cotton reel for a stool with its back legs crossed one over the other and its front legs, or arms folded across its chest. A seriously disgruntled look contorted its face – which was not easy for a mouse.

"What... who...?" Marianne looked up at Daphne.

"Definitely a who." Daphne's smile had a wicked edge.

"We thought it would be the easiest way to get my father into Faerie," Emma sighed. "But of course, we can't turn him back again, now."

"And Faerie magic won't work to counteract their magic either," Branchir added.

"You need Eleanor," Marianne suggested. "She could probably do it with her mixture of magic."

"But she would still be faced with the same problem of the three-fold return," Emma said. "Anyway, he's the least of the problems at the moment. Our Boroviche friends here have the more pressing need."

"Whatever we do, avoiding all-out war is a priority for the sake of all of Faerie," Branchir said. "This Hedeon character is surrounded by a band of ruthless allies who are prepared to go to any lengths and he has set himself up as their king. Thanks to Sylvestri's discoveries, we know that some of Hedeon's people have made advances towards the people who still inhabit the old Citadel... and they have another would-be king. The last conflict on our soil was difficult enough. We have very little in the way of offensive or defensive armaments and if it hadn't been for Eleanor and James and the chalk giants... well, it doesn't bear thinking about."

"Who are the chalk giants?" Simon asked. The mention of them gave him a strange shiver of recognition, a flash of something half remembered but tucked out of reach.

"They're carved into the hillside below the Lake of All Souls. We don't know by whom or when... sometime back beyond living memory... figures of men and animals. The grass never seems to grow over them so they stand out. Eleanor and James's magic called to them and they awoke. The Great Chalk Giants were our saviours, especially against Morfinnel's enormous war machines," Branchir said.

"Is it possible that the people in the Citadel still have some of those machines, or the plans and resources to make more?" Hermes asked. The familiars were back in their human forms as soon as they knew there was a possibility that the sisters could be in danger.

"Possible... there are a couple of deep caverns stacked with huge piles of worked timbers and forged metal parts. I don't know if the men there are aware of it all or what they're for... but yes, it's possible," Sylvestri said.

"Might I make a suggestion?" Emma said with a glance at Daphne.

"By all means, dear lady," Branchir nodded.

"Daphne has a room in her old nest in Aldamar. We only discovered it recently. It's where we found the jewels and where my father hid all of the Treasures of the Heroes of Old, collected by your ancestor. We have no idea exactly what is in there but we recognised one or two things. Like your chalk giants, these artefacts have slipped into the realms of myth and legend in the world of humans and the people of Aldamar have no use for them. We could return to Aldamar and bring them back to Faerie."

"Surely though, these treasures truly belong in the human world. Is that not where they should be returned?" Branchir said.

"I fear the human world has enough

ways to destroy itself without adding powerful ancient artefacts into the equation," Emma said.

"Besides they would all fight over who had the rights to them or want to put them in a museum," Daphne frowned.

"We should be able to access the Aldamar gate under our own steam but need assistance to return to Faerie with the artefacts," Emma said.

"I could come with you," Sylvestri suggested.

She recognised Sylvestri as a kindred spirit.

Chapter 42

Hedeon forced a smile and looked at the two men, strung up by their wrists, before him. They were in the very dungeon from which the spy had miraculously disappeared. "Dear me... I really should execute you but Merek has persuaded me otherwise, besides, execution would be too quick... too merciful... too easy. You shall both stay here overnight and if you can get yourselves out and escape like the spy, you can go free." He gave a nasty chuckle and began to paw through Barda's toys. "On the other hand, if you are both still here in the morning... you'll be going with Merek. I'm sure you'll both be very... useful."

Borin had struggled to free himself but Barda knew it was pointless. He had devised the restraints himself and still could not work out how his prisoner had managed to escape from them, never mind get out of a locked room, right from under his nose. The more Borin struggled, the tighter the bonds became but with the gag in the way, there was no way Barda could tell Borin to keep still.

Periodically throughout the night, more prisoners were pushed and prodded into the cell. All women and children, some were gagged and some were blindfolded but they were all in chains. The new prisoners were far too quiet... and drowsy. Borin guessed that they had all been given something to keep them docile and malleable. Barda knew exactly what it was because he had helped to develop it. At some point during the early hours, it was going to wear off and it was going to get very noisy in there.

When Hedeon reappeared the next morning he was looking very pleased with himself.

"Still here I see... time to go." He gave his guards the nod and they dragged the two men outside. Still bound in chains, they were hauled up onto horses. Most of the other men around were on foot, shifting uneasily, their eyes darting this way and that until Merek and Hedeon appeared. It was obvious they not want to be there but they were afraid.

To show just how ruthless he was prepared to be, Hedeon was sending Borin and Barda into the fight with Merek as an example of what would happen if he did not get what he wanted. They had once been his shield bearer and his torturer, but they had failed him and now they had to pay the price. That they both managed to lose their prisoner was beyond careless and could not go unpunished.

Hedeon stood on a box to address his troops. He had a manic look in his eye that Barda had not noticed before... until last night.

"Noble knights and men of the Boroviche," he addressed the men gathered before him. "I stand before you, your true and only King. The man who sits upon the throne of this land is nought but an imposter, a False King. A King of lies and trickery. I am a true descendant of Good Queen Orlagh who saved our people from destruction generations ago.

For all these years, we kept to our borders, kept our own council and did not stray. We kept ourselves true to our name. Then the strangers came, with their lies and their false promises and their talk of magic. My people, this so-called magic is not real and I despise any who are gullible enough to believe in it.

I tell you this now. We were no more locked inside a door then than we are now. They came with lights... smoke and mirrors, expecting us to roll over and what... worship them? Be grateful to them? I tell you... this land... all of it is mine.

I am the True King. I shall wear the crown and sit upon the throne of this land. The False King's head shall be displayed upon a pike above the castle walls for all to see... a castle that will soon be mine ... alongside the dead bodies of his family and friends. That is what their false magic will get them. From this day forth, I have outlawed magic. Any and all talk of magic or belief in magic is banned. Breaking these laws is punishable by death. Now go and fight for what is rightfully mine." His voice had risen from strident through to hysterical and as if on cue a great moaning and wailing rose as the women and children cried out in anguish as the drugs that had kept them quiet began to wear off.

Merek stood in his stirrups. "Men, those are the cries of your families, your wives, your children. If you wish to ensure their safety then you will follow the orders of his Most Magnificent Majesty. Follow me unto the fray and we shall return victorious." He had to shout to be heard over the sounds of crying and wailing. The Knights rounded up their companies, drilled them into order and set out on the long march.

Chapter 43

Sylvestri accompanied the sisters and their familiars to Aldamar. She had only offered to go with them to Daphne's nest to satisfy her own curiosity.

"Let's face it," she told them. "I'm just plain nosy. I was with Hob when you were all trying to get that door open. I tried too but the spells wound around it were so tight that it wouldn't even let the smallest of breezes inside. So... now you've got it open... I'm intrigued."

Arriving at the nest, Verdigris ignored them, pretending to be asleep. Daphne was about to grab a hold of the knocker in the green man's mouth and give it a good hard rap but Emma's touch stopped her.

"May I?" she asked. Daphne shrugged and nodded. "Good afternoon, Verdigris," Emma said politely. "I hope we find you well today. I am very sorry to disturb you, but I wonder, might we enter please?" She laid it on thick and appealed to the door-knocker's sense of self-importance. He opened one eye and squinted at them. He took one look at Daphne and gave a rude snort but he smiled at Emma. He liked Emma. She was always nice to him.

"Dear lady, it is my pleasure to be of assistance to you today," he said.

"Why thank you," Emma gave him a little bow of the head in thanks as the door swung open. They all walked in and, as Daphne passed, she stopped, smiled and patted him on the top of his head.

"Well done Verdi. Keep that up and I'll be having you melted down and turned into something that's actually useful."

Verdigris would have gasped with indignation but that would have meant letting go of the knocker. So he did his best eye roll and tried to stick his nose in the air – not easy when you are made of brass.

There was no difficulty in finding or

accessing the room now. Although locked, it was Daphne's spell. She did not trust John Dee as far as she could throw him, even though he was now a mouse, in a box, in Faerie... no one knew where his poisonous little side-kick, Ivy was. So, just in case....

With her spell disabled, they opened the door and peered inside. The room appeared to be just as they had left it. Dumped in a great hurry and left in a chaotic muddle, pieces of armour, weapons and other miscellaneous items were stacked around the room in a jumble of boxes, barrels and hessian sacks.

"We still have the same problem," Dorcas said. "We've no idea what is safe to touch,"

"Well, I for one am not touching that little scythe," Daphne shuddered.

"Maybe we could cast a protection spell," Addie suggested.

Emma looked thoughtful. "I'm not sure that would help. It might actually work against us and protect the wrong people, or stop the weapons from being used at all."

"What about a seeking spell, worded to help us find the pieces that'll be of most use?" Addie said.

"It might work," Emma nodded. "We can't take everything, and there is no point in taking those." She pointed to a sack that held Zeus's thunderbolts.

"Could they not be thrown, like grenades?" Addie asked.

"Like my father, they are mostly noise; all flash and bang but little substance. All bluff and bluster and essentially useless. Even so, I wouldn't want him to get his hands on them."

"The bows could be useful, but not the arrows," Apollo said. "Eros's love and hate darts or my name-sake's death and disease bringers would only make a bad situation worse."

"I've got an idea," Dorcas said. "Let me scribble a few lines while I focus on casting for what we need." She left the room and sat on the floor in the passageway.

As fast as she was writing the lines, she scratched them out again. Scraps of paper disappeared in puffs of white smoke as she destroyed the words that could be dangerous in the wrong hands.

"Daphne," she called a while later. "Do you have such a thing in your nest as a needle and thread?"

"Metal or bone needle?"

"Metal, please."

Dorcas threaded the needle, tied the two ends of the cotton thread together and made her way back into the cluttered room.

"Right, I'm as ready as I'm ever going to be," she said, holding the thread by the knot and letting the needle dangle freely. She held her pendulum out at arms' length and began to recite her spell.

"Open my vision, clear my sight,
Bring the objects into the light.
Let me divine those that we need,
So the enemies we may impede.

Keep safe from danger and stay my hand,
>   We help our friends to defend their land.
>   Guide me and aid us in this quest,
>   North to South and East to West.
>   Seek and find and show to me,
>   As I will, so mote it be."

Standing in the centre of the room, the pendulum moved in large sweeping circles as it searched out the items they could safely take. The thread stiffened as she felt the pull towards something. Dorcas took a couple of steps and the needle pointed directly at a pile of sacking. As she carefully drew the sacking back, the pendulum vibrated and the needle flew to an object where it stuck, like a magnet.

"It's a helmet," Addie whispered. She had no idea why she was whispering, but it seemed appropriate. She carefully lifted the helmet up in both hands. It looked familiar.

"Didn't we give this to Perseus once?"

"I believe so..." and so it went as they gathered each piece very carefully and laid it out in the hallway.

Strangely, the pendulum only pointed to one weapon. It seemed to be seeking out armour and protection, defensive rather than offensive artefacts. By the time they finished they had several breast plates, helmets and shields. The only weapon was a sword made by Hephaestus for Peleus, father of Achilles, it had the power to ensure the wielder won every fight.

Transporting their haul was easy enough; some of it they could carry in the sack in which they were found, the rest they could wear.

"You did a good job there, Dorcas," Daphne said.

"Not bad for an hour's scribbling," Dorcas smiled.

Hermes carried the Caduceus that once belonged to his name-sake. It was not a weapon as such but a staff of healing. However, while it had the power to send people into a healing sleep or wake those from the sleep of death, which Addie assured them was probably a coma, it could send people into a sleep from which they would never wake.

Sadly, Sylvestri found the room to be something of an anti-climax - the promise of secrets being far more exciting. Having satisfied her craving to be nosy within the first ten minutes, she left and went to wait for them by the gate. Choosing to be invisible while she waited, she was surprised to see groups of people arrive. The new arrivals were unaware of her presence. Here was a little more intrigue to pique her curiosity.

The nymphs and a few satyrs arrived first. They sat themselves down to wait quietly – which was highly unusual. Next came a group of dryads, and then another. They all sat on the grass and waited. Usually, a gathering like this would have been an excuse for a party but the atmosphere was solemn and subdued. Who or what were they waiting for?

After a while, another group arrived.

These were clearly dryads too, but looked very different from the Aldamar contingent. These dryads were taller, leaner and dressed in tight leathers rather than leaves, twigs and acorns. Sylvestri recognised them as members of the Tisu-lidé – the Yew People. They each had a long bow strapped across their back and a quiver of arrows at their hip. These were dryads from one of the other worlds outside of Aldamar, battle-hardened and used to protecting their borders against the darkness beyond.

Sylvestri did not attempt to communicate but drifted around the groups as a gentle breeze, listening for information, but it was a little unnerving. They were all too still, too quiet.

Sylvestri noticed Joseph first. His appearance usually sent the nymphs into a hysterical twitter but even his arrival did not lighten the mood. He had Alsea with him and a stranger. At a guess, this stranger was yet another dryad. He was taller than those from

Aldamar were, but not as tall as the Tisu-lidé. A third type of dryad...

'Interesting,' Sylvestri thought, especially when Joseph and the stranger began to help the various dryads and nymphs through the gate to Faerie. By the time Emma and the others returned, the great gathering had disappeared.

"Sylvestri, are you here?" Emma called out.

"Right here darling," she whispered. "I'm holding the gate open. Can you see it?"

They made their way up to the gate to find Sylvestri outlined by the golden glow of the gate.

"Welcome," she grinned. "You just missed all the excitement."

Chapter 44

Safe, safe, they assured her as she hurtled along at break-neck speed, pushed from tree to tree. Just as she was beginning to feel the effects of motion sickness, all movement stopped and they deposited Kesia beside a tiny cottage deep in the forest. While she was deciding whether or not she should knock on the door, it opened and a dark-haired woman of indeterminate age smiled at her.

"Are you lost, dear?" she asked. Her voice was firm but not unkind.

"Yes," was all Kesia could manage. Her stomach rolled, her throat felt tight and prickly as she fought back the tears.

"How did you get here? This is not a place to be taking an afternoon stroll," the woman said. "You'd better come in before the ogres come sniffing about."

"Ogres, what are they?" Nothing good,

she assumed.

"You've not heard of ogres, where are you from child?" She held out her hand. "Come in, quickly."

The cottage was little more than a single room. Every shelf was crammed and every surface covered in pots and jars, books and bunches of herbs and flowers. Filled as it was, everything had a place and it was clean and tidy. Just visible behind a curtain at one end of the room was a narrow bed and at the other end, a large table above which, suspended from the roof timbers, was a rack. More bunches of dried herbs, pans and ladles and other equipment hung from hooks. A large cooking pot, sat over the fire pit in the centre of the floor, bubbling away to itself. Kesia noted that many of the shelves were full of books, more books than she had ever seen in her life, let alone all in one place.

"Come and take some tea with me. I don't get many visitors out here," The woman said, placing a kettle of water on the fire beside the cauldron. "Now then, tell me how you came to the house of the Maení."

Kesia did not know whether to trust the woman but there was something serene and soothing about her manner. The trees had assured her that she would be safe and they had left her here. She trusted that they knew what they were doing so Kesia told the woman her story. When she finished she shuddered and wrapped her arms around herself.

"Well, I assume the trees had a reason for leaving you off here," the woman said. She did not seem surprised that they had helped Kesia. She knew of the Great Mage after all and it was rumoured that he could travel through the trees the way the gnomes travelled through the earth. "I am Maení to King Branchir…. It means Wise woman," she added when Kesia looked blankly at her. "My name is Zofia. It is probably best if I take you to meet with the King. I'm sure he will want to hear your story."

"How far is it to the castle?"

"About a day's journey through open countryside. There are many dangers, not least ogres... huge bristly, knuckle dragging creatures with tusks that prefer their meat fresh, preferably still wriggling," she smiled, then realising that Kesia did not understand her humour added, "I apologise, I should not tease. There is a much quicker way to the castle that avoids all the nasty things thanks to a tunnel dug by some very helpful gnomes many years ago. Come, follow me."

Kesia put her teacup down on the table and followed Zofia behind the curtains at the end of the cottage. Dragging the bed away from the wall revealed a trapdoor that gave onto a ladder and then into a tunnel. Lighting their way with a storm lantern, Kesia jumped as the trapdoor closed and something heavy scraped across the floorboards above.

"The bed moves back into place once the trapdoor closes," Zofia explained. "Few people know about this tunnel and I'd like to keep it that way."

The tunnel sloped down gently for a few hundred metres before it began to rise again. After another hundred metres, they came to another trapdoor above their heads. On the wall beside the ladder, a handprint had been carved into the rock. Zofia placed her hand into the shape and a loud clunk sounded from above as a bolt slid back and the trapdoor opened.

Leaving the lantern at the base of the ladder, Zofia led the way up into a small space that might have been a small cupboard but the curved walls around them made it feel as though they were inside a large barrel lying on its side, which is precisely what it was. Indeed, the door was the round end of the barrel. It opened up close to a wall and into a room filled with identical barrels, lined up in rows. They had arrived in the buttery, in the cellars of the Elven King's castle.

"Secret passages are so exciting, don't you think?" Zofia grinned.

Kesia was not sure how she should

respond and gave her a shy smile.

"So then, let us make ourselves known before they arrest us as spies. That might be a little embarrassing." Zofia was enjoying this just a little too much. Kesia felt sick. She knew she had met the King before and wondered if he would remember their party of travellers.

Oddly, despite what Zofia had said, no one showed any surprise at their presence. Maybe it was more of her odd sense of humour. In fact, many of the people they met gave them a little nod or wave in greeting as they passed. One man thanked Zofia for some medicine and a woman stopped to show her how well her sore hands had healed.

They had just reached the servery when the King's Chamberlain came upon them.

He bowed low "Good day Madam Maení…" then he bowed to Kesia "Mistress…" She began to wonder if there was more to Zofia than met the eye. What had she said her title was… wise woman? There must be more to it than wisdom.

Thanir led the way up the back stairs to the King's library. He opened the door without knocking and introduced them.

"Welcome ladies, do come in," Branchir said with a smile.

"I think he was expecting us," Zofia whispered to Kesia with a little smile. She gave a reluctant Kesia a little push further into the room.

"It's Kizzy, isn't it?" the King asked. Apparently, he did remember her.

"Yes Your Majesty," she whispered. She gave a little gasp of surprise as the Queen stood up and took her hand. "Come and sit by me child," she said softly. "We have two of your travelling companions here. They are anxious to know how you fare." She nodded at Thanir and he left to fetch Thorn and Gould.

"You're a sight for sore eyes lass," Thorn said as he pulled her up into a hug.

"What happened to you? Where did they take you? Are you all right?" Gould asked when it was his turn. "Fyr went looking for you.

Did you see him?"

Kesia could only nod or shake her head. Words did not want to come out. Talking about Fyr to Zofia had been easier - she did not know him and she let her talk without interruption. She knew Thorn and Gould would have all sorts of questions that she was not sure she would be able to answer without falling apart.

Daewen patted the seat beside her again and took hold of Kesia's hand. Immediately, she felt calmer. She owed these two men some sort of explanation. They were Fyr's friends. Once she had told them all as much as she could the two Boroviche men were eager to go rushing off to his rescue but the King stopped them.

"Gentlemen, let us not be too hasty. Come and join me at the map and we shall see what it can tell us."

Kesia had never seen anything like this map before. It was like a tiny model that showed all the fields and hills and rivers, even tiny individual trees.

"Can you show me where your village is?" Branchir asked her.

"I think my village is there." She pointed to a small, dark spot nestled close to a river out to the west.

Branchir held a hand out over the map and made a pulling and then spreading movement with his fingers. The spot rose up out of the map and hovered above it. There was her village, in miniature, with every detail: all the buildings, and the village green where she had last seen Fyr. Moments later, tiny people were moving around the miniature landscape as people came out of the inn.

"How is this possible?" Kesia looked up at the King.

"Magic," he smiled. "We may see anywhere we need to, although not inside buildings."

"Would I be able to see my father? He ... if he is still well enough… he will be working. His workshop is at the back of that building." She pointed to his shop. Branchir enlarged the image further and twisted it so that she could see into the garden and the open rear of the building. There were three men working, making candles, one of whom was her father.

"He's alive," she cried. "Oh thanks be… I was so worried. At the auction, he collapsed and they carried him away. They wouldn't let me see him or tell me anything." She moved around the map to get a better look at the village green, or rather, the pillory. There was someone locked into the device but it was not Fyr. Before they moved on, she pointed out New Place, the house where she had been held prisoner with the others, prior to the auction. As far as she knew, the only ones left now were Posey and Petal.

"Is there any way to locate a particular person?" she asked.

"I can try." Branchir held out both hands over the map and moved them slowly over the village but there was no indication of Fyr at all. He collapsed the village back down to a spot and continued to move his hands over the landscape. He had not got very far before they were distracted by a small peal of bells. Turning, Branchir whipped a cloth from a small round table with a polished mirror top. To Kesia it was just a mirror but she could tell that he saw something other than his own reflection. He was using it to communicate with someone. Their conversation did not last long and he spoke too quietly for her to catch what he was saying. After a few moments, he said his farewells and turned away from the mirror. Kesia had no doubt that it was more of the King's magic at work. He looked up at Kesia and smiled.

"That was my cousin Eleanor. She lives in the human realm but I believe you have met her already." He smiled when she nodded. "She had a visitor." He gave her another smile. "I am sure you will be relieved to know that Fyr is just fine and is on his way here. He should be with us very soon with a large group of people from Aldamar." He took her back to the map and moved his hands over a mountainous region to the north. He located and enlarged the area around the waterfall. The large group of people had already come through the gate and were slowly moving away from it. Kesia squinted at the tiny figures and let out a small squeal.

"There he is… I see him… that's Fyr." She looked up with tears in her eyes. "

"He will be here before you know it." He collapsed the map back down.

"But they have so very far to travel. It will take days to come that far."

"They will travel the same way you did. The dryads will bring the people through the trees. I have seen it done. They will be here within the hour, I don't doubt."

As expected, the dryads headed towards the forest and disappeared.

Chapter 45

With the return of the sisters and their familiars, things were beginning to feel inevitable.

"It was difficult to know what we could and what we should not touch," Emma told him as they began to unload their treasures.

"I set up a seeking spell and this is what it gave us," Dorcas added. "I'm sorry that there are very few weapons. Only one, in fact; this sword will guarantee success to whoever wields it."

"Everything else is some form of armour or protection," Daphne said.

"For which I am very grateful," Branchir bowed in thanks.

"We can explain what these artefacts are fabled to do in the human world," Hermes said. "But we have no idea if they work the same way here. That is yet to be discovered."

"This is known as the helm of Darkness,"

Emma said as she held up a polished helmet. "It was made for my uncle, Hades. He disappeared long ago and no one knows where he is or even if he's still alive, so he won't be wanting this back. It grants the wearer invisibility. Hephaestus's workshop made most of this armour. It's all supposed to endow a certain level of invulnerability to the wearer but none of it is fool-proof. Like Achilles, there is always a small flaw in the design."

"Thank you for collecting it," Branchir said. "But as you so rightly pointed out, we have no way of knowing whether it will work here."

"There is one way to find out," Daphne said as she picked up the Helm of Darkness, placed it on her head and disappeared. "Well?"

"That one works," Belus confirmed reaching out a hand to make sure she was still there.

"Maybe I should add an extra layer of Fae magic to them, just in case," Branchir wondered aloud.

"Sire," Thanir broke into Branchir's thoughts. "There are a great many people appearing just beyond the castle…"

So many people were arriving that Branchir had to move from the library to the Great Hall to await the rest of the approaching crowd. Aurelia pulled her husband, Sardo to one side.

"I know you feel that you have to do this…"

"You know I do."

"Yes, but as your wife, it is my duty to remind you that you have other responsibilities to consider. You have a family."

"What if I am the best person for this job?"

"That is yet to be decided. All I am saying is that I don't want you to do anything reckless. Keep yourself safe too."

"I will always have the King's back and he will always have mine."

"Just so long as you keep my words in

mind," she smiled at him and tied her ribbons around his bicep.

"I thank you my lady, my wife. As always, I wear your colours with pride." He bowed over her hand and kissed it and then, as he stood, he pulled her in close for a proper kiss.

"I should go and join the other ladies," she smiled when she got her breath back. "They are waiting for me over there."

Marianne and Addie had suggested to Queen Daewen that it would be prudent to set up a place for the wounded, should it come to that. It was always good to be prepared, and it gave them something to think about, something to do while the men held their council of war.

The women had set up a long table just inside the doors to the Great Hall. It was gradually being stocked with fresh and dried herbs, vegetables and other plant materials which Addie sorted and catalogued. They had a small brazier in which to boil up potions and sterilize equipment. It was impossible to know just what potions or poultices they would need until the time came but they were determined to be as prepared as they could. Mattresses and bedding were also being stockpiled close to the great fire place. There was no fire yet but it was laid and ready to go as soon as it was needed.

Daewen, Aurelia and Kesia sat side by side on a long bench and rolled strips of cloth, torn from sheets, turning them into bandages and dressings. Kesia was feeling more and more anxious as time went on; every little movement near the doors had her almost jumping out of her skin.

As each group of dryads arrived, they settled themselves into small groups around the hall. Considering there were so many people in one place, it was oddly subdued. So quiet that everyone spoke in whispers. Kesia was beginning to think that she had imagined seeing Fyr on that map. After all, the figures on the map had been so tiny… it could have been anyone... probably wishful thinking... not him at all... Her eyes stung and her throat felt too tight as she fought back the tears threatening to undo her; if she started crying now, she would not be able to stop. She swallowed hard and concentrated on helping the Queen and the Duchess with their tasks.

"Don't worry," the Queen leaned in and whispered. "He'll be here soon, I'm sure of it." She smiled and Kesia did her best to smile back but her heart was just not in it.

Yet another group poured in through the door to the Great Hall and Kesia tried not to get her hopes up, knowing they would only be dashed - again. She was not going to look this time; she would keep her eyes on her task. At least, that had been the plan but she could not help it. Her gaze took in yet more dryads bringing more of the tiny people she had heard called nymphs. They were followed by a group of very tall people dressed in dark leather with bows strapped across their backs. And then, behind them...

"Fyr!" She leapt to her feet, dropping her roll of bandage, and ran to throw herself into his arms. She could not help it. She burst into tears – happy tears.

"Come and sit down lad." Addie appeared at their side. "You don't look so great."

"What did they do to you?" Kesia took his face in her hands and looked into his eyes. They were red-rimmed and glassy. He seemed to be having trouble focussing.

"They made me drink something… made me see things. I thought it was out of my system. The trees sent me to Aldamar and I was fine for a while. Didn't notice it while I was there, but when I came back here…" He sat down heavily on the chair that had somehow appeared behind him. There were voices floating around him but he could not concentrate enough to work out what they were saying… something about time difference.

"Here, drink this." A flagon appeared in

front of his face but when he reached out a hand to grasp it, he missed. He tried again... and missed again. He felt something touch his lip and realised that someone was holding the cup to his mouth. Suddenly he was very thirsty.

"Slowly does it lad. We don't want you to choke."

"Where's Kizzy?" he managed to ask.

"I'm right here," he felt someone squeeze his hand and knew it was her. He felt the world start to lean sideways and had to go with it.

"Best take him over there to lie down before he falls down," the voice that was not Kizzy said. He felt strong hands lift him and help him a few steps across the floor before lowering him to lie on something soft.

"Give him time to sleep it off and he'll be fine in no time, you'll see," Addie said to Kesia once Hermes and Helios had placed Fyr on one of the make-shift hospital beds. "We'll call you if we need help but you're better off here, looking after your young man."

Kesia was at a loss for words so she gave a startled Addie a hug and then sat down beside Fyr to wait.

Chapter 46

The next morning Branchir stood at his map and watched the two enemy forces approach. One came from the east, led by a character who called himself Einhard. He and his men may have emerged from the late Prince Morfinnel's citadel but that was where the comparison ended. Einhard was not Morfinnel and his men were an undisciplined rabble.

"The little shit-shoveller has certainly given himself airs and graces," Sardo said through gritted teeth. "I can't imagine how he managed to get himself into a position of power."

"However he managed it," Branchir said. "They're almost here now. There may not be that many of them but they have those large covered wagons. Do you suppose they are the giant weapons they had before?"

Sardo nodded.

The other group came out of the west. They were a different matter entirely. They marched steadily, in formation, with a discipline missing from Einhard and his men. Neither force was aware that they were being observed.

Meanwhile, Merek, who was currently leading the western force, was quietly and grudgingly grateful to the False King; his long straight road made the long march to the castle so much easier. All through their march, he anticipated meeting with resistance. They should have encountered road blocks, scouting parties, skirmishes and ambushes. He eagerly awaited a minor scuffle or two but, disappointingly, there was nothing. They had virtually walked up to the front door of the castle without any opposition.

Could the False King be so out of touch and unaware of what was happening? Maybe he was just so arrogant in his belief that he could win. He was looking forward to wiping the smug smile off the False King's face.

When Merek and his men came upon Einhard's small group, they were driving wagons heavily laden with enormous timbers, coils of rope, great chains and other metal pieces that made no sense to him. Two of the wagons held smaller loads: large crates covered with tarpaulins.

"What've you got there?" Merek demanded to know.

"Secret weapon," Einhard's grin was smug. He tugged the tarp from one of the wagons to reveal – not crates but cages, crammed with little people. Some sat on the floor with their heads in their hands while others were trying, and failing, to gnaw their way through the metal bars.

"Iron's one of the few things they can't chew their way out of." Einhard gave the closest little person a poke with a stick. Teeth clamped down on the end of the stick and wrenched it out of his grasp causing him to leap back with a yelp. He gave a self-conscious chuckle as though he had planned for that to happen.

"Feisty little buggers, ain't they?" Merek said with raised eyebrows. "What are they?" He had never seen anything like them before.

"They's gnomes, an' they gotta do exactly what I tell'm cos I got their children locked up tight in my dungeon an' if they ever wanna see'm again..." he said over-loudly as he leered in at the gnomes with a nasty grin.

"And just what is it that you're expecting them to do? They're hardly big enough to hold a knife, never mind a sword." Merek frowned. He did not suffer fools gladly and was looking forward to disposing of this fool at the earliest opportunity... but not until they had built the machines. Until then, he would pass the time considering his options: he could run him through with his sword, he could string him up from the nearest tree and watch him dance or maybe just lop his head from his shoulders and watch it bounce on the ground. He was sure he would be able to come up with something much more creative. Merek suddenly realised that the fool had stopped speaking and was waiting for a reply.

"Beg pardon?" Merek did not really care whether the fool thought him ill-mannered but he knew he should at least be aware of the man's plans.

"I said, we're gonna build the battle machines here behind the hills and then move 'em into place; they got wheels."

"Yes, yes. I got that part, but what is it you are intending to do with these... gnomes?"

"They're gonna dig us some tunnels under the castle walls and bring 'em down so we can walk right on in and take it. Digging tunnels is what they do."

"Is that so?" He really wanted to wipe that smug look off the fool's face. "So how long will it take for your men to build these machines?"

"Dunno, couple of hours I guess... can't be that difficult. An' while the men are at that, these gnomes are gonna do their stuff and dig."

Merek ground his teeth. "Very well. I will begin to distribute my men to surround the castle. We eagerly await your assistance and the deployment of your armaments."

"Yes... good..." Einhard nodded, not quite sure what he meant but the man turned and walked away before he could ask.

Inside the castle, Branchir and Sardo studied the enemy's movements on the map. Simon and Sylvestri came over to join them.

"I don't understand how they managed to seize so many gnomes?" Sylvestri said. "Where is Hob in all this? Does he even know?"

"My great grandfather has been a little preoccupied of late. He hasn't been himself for a while and I fear I am partly to blame," Simon said quietly.

"Great grandfather! Well, you learn something new every day," she blinked at Simon, looking for a resemblance. "I knew there was something amiss with him but you'd have thought that something this serious would have caught his attention?" She looked up at the men. "I'm going back to that citadel. The dungeon was empty when I last blew through but I need to double check..."

"Wait," Simon stopped her. He was staring at the map and the area around the old tombs. "I think we can do this a different way. May I try?" He looked up at Branchir and held out his hand.

"I don't think your dryad powers are going to help here," Sylvestri shook her head sadly, as Marianne appeared at her husband's side.

"That's okay. It won't be dryad powers that he'll be using," she smiled and took Simon's hand whilst holding out her other hand. Branchir took both their hands, closing the small loop. He had travelled over the map like this before, with Eleanor.

"Should I make a wish?" he asked.

"It might help. We need to see what is happening to the gnome children in those dungeons. We'll combine our magic with yours and see where it takes us," Simon said.

"I'm not sure we have enough power between us to do this," Branchir began, especially if they were going to travel underground.

A strange buzz vibrated though Branchir's spine. It spread through their joined hands, down his back, through his legs and feet and up into his skull where it spread like warm syrup up his neck and over his scalp. He almost expected something to run into his eyes. It was an effort not to jerk his hands away when everything went black but his eyes soon became accustomed to the darkness and he could see minerals sparkling in the soil all around them. The illumination grew and they found themselves faced with a row of prison cells built into the rock and surrounded on three sides by iron bars. The cells were empty and the wall of rock at the back of each cell was riddled with small holes: tunnel entrances.

"I believe they all went that way," Simon smiled. "Shall we follow and see where it leads?"

They crawled into one of the tunnels and arrived, via a worm hole, at the Gnome Homes, in Hob's throne room. All the missing children were there, surrounding Hob. A few of them sobbed quietly but most of them looked up to their King in expectation as he tried to find out where they had all suddenly appeared from. It was difficult with so many of them trying to speak at once.

"You lad, you tell me what happened." He picked the tallest child who was able to explain with a little help from his sister. He let them speak without interruption, mostly because he was speechless with anger and did not want the children to think he was angry with them.

"Don't worry little ones," Hob did his best to assure them. "We'll set your parents free. They'll be home before you know it."

Yes, they would. A bright light flared all around them and Branchir found himself beside the map again, still holding hands with Simon and Marianne.

"Welcome brother... sister," Sylvestri grinned at Simon and Marianne. "Welcome to the club."

"Which club?" Sardo asked.

"Now I understand why Hob was so distracted. I should have seen it coming," Sylvestri said.

"Seen what coming?" Sardo was gazing from face to face with a frown.

"We have a new Earth Elemental," and she bowed to Simon. "Or I should say Elementals." And she bowed to Marianne too.

Chapter 47

Fyr was feeling well enough to sit up now. Kesia sat on the side of his bed holding his hand. Her sobs had quietened but every time she tried to speak, her breath hitched and the words seemed to get stuck.

"Did they ... hurt you?" he asked.

"No, not really," she said as he stroked her hair. "It was humiliating. They treated me as though I was no longer a person. The man who bought me was their leader. He calls himself a King. I heard him tell one of his men that he was going to start a stable and I would give him sons." She gave a shudder and Fyr wrapped his arms around her.

"It's all over now. You're safe. They won't be able to get you here," he told her.

"How did you get away?" she asked. "How did you get here?"

He decided not to tell her the whole story just yet. "Like you, the trees helped me," he said, then, "I should probably go and speak to the King." He would, very soon but he was not ready to let her go yet.

"You stay right there lad." An old woman came over and patted him on the shoulder. "The boy knows you're here. He'll come and find you when he's ready, when you're ready." Then she walked away, followed by a white and ginger cat.

"Who's that?" Fyr asked.

"Daphne! She and the other old ladies are sisters I think they said." Kesia and Fyr turned to follow Daphne with their eyes and watched as she joined a group of women who were chatting and rolling bandages and mixing potions.

"I can't keep up with them. Sometimes they're old and sometimes they're young and sometimes Daphne looks like one of those little people over there," Kesia nodded at the group of nymphs that were sitting in a circle on the floor by the fire. "And no one seems to think it at all odd..." She shook her head.

"I can't tell you how relieved I am to have found you again," Fyr said, tightening his arms around her once more. "And I don't want to let you out of my sight but I have to speak to the King and offer my service. It's only right. I can't sit back and do nothing and let others fight our battles. As much as I don't want to let you go... this is about more than just us."

"I know... but I can't help being afraid all the time. I don't want to lose you again."

He hugged her even tighter because there was nothing else he could say. He looked up as the King moved away from his map. He strode to the centre of the Hall with a man he recognised as General Sardo and Simon, the Great Forest Mage.

"Good people," Branchir said. He did not shout or raise his voice but was heard by every single person present. It was as though he spoke to each of them individually. "Welcome to Faerie and the Hall of the Edhelaran." There was a brief hum of greeting in return before they waited for Branchir to continue. "Right now, two separate forces have converged on this castle from the east and the west. We can only guess at their intentions as they have not yet sent heralds with any declaration or messages nor have they requested a parley. They are attempting to surround the castle and therefore we must assume their intent is hostile. We do not know whether they will attack or attempt to besiege us but we must be prepared." Branchir looked to Sardo to continue.

"From the intelligence we have gathered, we know that the eastern faction hold a group of gnomes captive. We believe their strategy is to force the gnomes to tunnel beneath our walls causing them to collapse thus giving the enemy access to the interior of the castle. They were using the children as leverage and holding them hostage in the dungeons below the citadel."

A buzz of outrage rose but ceased as Branchir raised his hand.

"The gnomes are good people and we

have always been friends and allies and this is still the case." Branchir held his hand up and continued. "The leader of the eastern army did have the children imprisoned – note I used the past tense. The children are no longer there. They were able to take the initiative and free themselves and returned home. The Lady Sylvestri – the Queen of the Four Winds – was able to move unseen amongst the enemy troops and whisper the glad tidings to the gnomes. They have a new plan. They intend to tunnel as instructed… just not beneath our walls, and have promised to lead the enemy on a merry dance."

"This will take some of the troops away but not all," Sardo took up the address again. "Our plan is to create an outer ring of natural defences beyond the enemy's current position which will trap them and cut off their retreat should they attempt it."

"Might I speak?" A tall, leather-clad dryad stood and raised his hand.

"By all means, brother," Branchir said.

"My name is Ibur," he turned to Simon. "Greetings to you Great Mage. We have met before."

"I remember," Simon nodded.

"You say you wish to create an outer ring of defence. This is a good idea, but possibly a little too late. On our way here, we had to cross a large expanse of open ground, as there is little cover available. Whoever goes out there to dig these defences will be in great danger. With the trees many miles away, how do you propose to deploy the dryads?"

Branchir nodded. "You are quite correct sir. This is the current situation. However, we have access to something that the enemy does not, magic – the knowledge and use of. We also have the Elementals on our side. Earth and Air are already with us." He turned and bowed to Simon. "Fire, Water and Spirit are on their way here to help."

"If you have this magic, why do you not use it and just send the enemy back where they came from?" Gould asked the question that many others were thinking.

"If only it was that easy. Magic does not work quite like that. There are always consequences for any magic done. If we merely sent them home, what is to stop them from picking up arms and simply returning to begin again?" Branchir explained.

"No, we have to teach them a lesson without harming the rank and file of people forced into a fight they do not want," Sardo added.

There were mutterings of agreement all around the hall until Simon stepped up beside Branchir.

"Those of you from Aldamar will know of the cottage where our friends live. It is surrounded by a protective hedge that has the power to grow extremely fast in order to protect those within."

A ripple of acknowledgement went around the hall.

"What we propose is to construct something similar but on a much larger scale.

We will use full grown trees rather than bushes so that the dryads may conceal themselves and travel at will."

The whispers began to get louder and Gould voiced their concerns again.

"How will planting trees now help? It will take years and years for them to grow big enough... and someone is still going to have to go out there and plant them."

"This would normally be true, but this is a far from normal situation and will require a helping hand," Simon said. "No one will be put in any danger while we create this protective ring. I will combine my green magic with that of the King and use his map to transplant trees of a good size and age from the Great forest and replant them around the castle."

"Ah!" Emma smiled at her sisters and whispered, "I wondered what Hob had been up to. Now I see." She came over to Simon and took his hand. "May I offer my congratulations, Earth Elemental."

"Thank you, but as ever, Marianne and I

are a team. We are both... or together, the Earth Elemental. The others will arrive very soon. I can feel it in here." He tapped his chest over his heart. "Once we have everything in place, I will request the support of the Chalk Giants."

"They came to our aid once before and smashed the huge war machines. Let us hope they are willing to wake and help us once more," Branchir said to those around him.

Chapter 48

Once they reached the castle, each Knight took up a position around the castle, well out of firing range and waited for their orders and the arrival of the promised war machines. Their men sat in dejected groups while they too awaited their orders.

Unfortunately, Einhard's men from the citadel and surrounding town had very little idea what their machines were supposed to look like and they were having difficulty reassembling them. There always seemed to be too many parts... or not enough. Wagons trundled around the castle and deposited bits and pieces in piles. They had a few vague sketches but they bore little or no resemblance to the bits and pieces and gave no indication as to how they should be put together. This was going to take more than a few hours work.

So focussed were they, it was some time before anyone noticed the vibrations that rumbled through the ground.

"I'm guessing that this is the work of your little gnomes in their tunnels," Merek said to Einhard. The fool had given a good talking to the gnomes before they left, with threats of dire consequences to their children should they fail in their task or refuse to comply with his orders.

As each of the gnomes came out of the cage, they had an iron band bolted around their ankle. Luckily, thick, leather boots protected them from the iron's harmful effects. Ropes were tied to the leg-irons to act as leashes, each one held by one of Einhard's men; the men were going to follow them into the tunnels, the gnomes were only going to be trusted so far.

As far as Einhard knew, he still had the upper hand with the gnome families under lock and key but Sylvestri had already blown through with the good news.

"Don't let on that you know," Sylvestri had warned.

"Don't you worry Mistress, we'll dig 'em tunnels right enough. Just not the ones they want. We'll make sure they end up far away from 'ere. Many thanks for getting the message to us."

As good as their word, as soon as they were given the go ahead, the gnomes began to tunnel. They disappeared underground, closely followed by their handlers. Sylvestri watched as Einhard folded his arms with a smug grin.

"Now we just have to wait awhile and the walls will come a tumblin' down," he bragged. Sylvestri blew an icy blast around him and he shivered.

"Someone walk over your grave?" one of his men asked with a chuckle.

"Just get on with it and get those things built," he grunted and waved his hand in the direction of yet another pile of timbers and rope.

Back in the Great Hall, the other Elementals had arrived, just as Simon had said and were waiting for Sylvestri to join them. As she came in Salamander was slapping Simon on the back and Aurora was hugging Marianne in congratulation.

"But I don't understand how these people managed to get this far without any of us being aware of their intentions," Undine whispered as she and Sylvestri greeted one another. "I've checked with the water sprites and they had no warning of either group."

"This does seem to have come about rather rapidly, but when all is said and done, we cannot be in two places at once. There is nothing for you to feel guilty about," Sylvestri said to her.

"Quite right," Aurora added as she came to join them. "I've felt a slight shift in the ether, but I couldn't get to the bottom of it. This must have been it."

Branchir called the group together, including the sisters and their familiars.

"Simon, Marianne and I are about to start work on the perimeter defences. We have heard from Hob and the children made it home. They're all unharmed. So let's get the first phase underway," Branchir said.

He stood at his map with Simon and Marianne, just as they had done earlier but this time they did not hold hands.

"I really hope this works the way I think it should," Simon said.

"I wish you success with this endeavour," Branchir said.

"Oh, I felt that," Marianne shivered as the magic flowed across the map towards her. "What would you like me to do?"

"Think of this map as a seed tray and the trees are seedlings that need pricking out. We should take random trees from the densest places, we don't want to damage the surrounding areas or leave bare patches. Then we can transplant them in a loose ring around the castle."

"I understand in theory. I've helped you with real seedlings many times but we're trying to pull up fully grown trees here," Marianne frowned.

"As you grasp each individual tree don't tug or pull, try and concentrate on the ground around their roots. Imagine it loosening and releasing them. Then pass them to me and I'll plant them the same way." Simon was studying the map, looking for the best trees to move.

"I imagine the best course of action would be to begin by spacing them widely so we can surround the castle quickly. Then you can fill in the gaps and the dryads can start on their phase of the operation," Branchir said.

As Simon had said, the task was just like pricking out seedlings. They had done this together so many times that the ring of trees soon began to take shape. As he placed a tree where he wanted it to grow it felt as though the ground welcomed it and the soil sucked the roots back under the ground.

"I think we'll be okay with this now," Simon told Branchir, knowing that he was eager to set the dryads' phase in motion.

Branchir approached the large group of

dryads, nymphs and satyrs.

"Follow me up to the walls. We'll get a good view of the tree tops from there. Will that be enough for you to be able to travel or do you need to touch the trees?"

"I can only speak for my people," Ibur said. "If we are familiar with an area, we merely concentrate on where we wish to go and it is enough. These trees are new to us so a visual target is a good idea. Physical contact is not necessary."

"It is the same for us," Alsea agreed.

They followed Branchir through a maze of alleyways to the inner curtain wall, the tallest of the three concentric walls. Branchir and the Yew dryads were tall enough to see over the battlements but the Aldamar dryads and their small companions were not.

"I think we're going to need something to stand on," Alsea suggested.

"Just so you know," one of the satyrs looked up at Branchir apologetically. "We ain't got no fighting skills, apart from a few squabbles amongst ourselves... we don't usually fight."

"But we're quite good at nipping in and out of places without being seen by the bigguns," another satyr added.

"With the dryads help, we can nip out, grab tools and weapons and stuff and pop back in," one of the nymphs explained. "They'll never know where it all went."

"Very well, let phase three begin." Branchir had some boxes brought up so that the dryads could climb up to get a visual on the tree. Each of the Aldamar dryads paired up with a nymph or satyr and together with Ibur and his people, they began to disappear.

Once the dryads and their companions had gone, Branchir continued to stand on the wall a while longer, watching in awe as the trees appeared all around them. Below him, he could hear the panicked voices of the enemy troops as they ran around like headless chickens because, every few minutes, the ground shook and a new, fully-grown tree appeared out of thin air. Branchir gave a grim smile and went back to the centre of operations in the Great Hall.

Merek rode from group to group, observing the men as they attempted to build the machines. He threatened and cajoled to chivvy them along but it made little difference. Building these giant machines was a slow business, especially as they were constantly looking over their shoulders at the trees that kept appearing. Trees did not just appear, therefore, it could not be real.

"Ignore them. They're not really there," he ordered, referring to the trees. "It's nought but a parlour trick. Get moving with those infernal devices."

"Aye sir," several voices around him called uncertainly.

"But those trees…" one man could not help himself. "They weren't there earlier."

"Smoke and mirrors," Merek said by way of explanation. It was what Hedeon had told him and he saw no reason to disbelieve him.

He got down off his horse and prowled around a couple of the groups to get a closer look at what they were doing. Each group had their own building project: trebuchet here and a ballista there, and to each group he said the same thing.

"Take no notice of the trees, they are not really there. It's merely trickery. It can only fool the truly stupid. Get on with the job."

The men were doing their best to ignore the trees that kept popping up; after all, they did not want to appear stupid or to be seen believing in something that had been outlawed.

The building projects were not going well. Something was seriously wrong. Odd things were happening... even more odd, if that was possible. Tools and parts kept going missing. Some of them turned up in strange places and some had disappeared altogether.

The dryads sheltered the nymphs and satyrs within the safety of the trees. When the builders' backs were turned, they would dart out, grab something - a tool or a part and disappear back inside again.

"Did you move it?" one of the men building a ballista grumbled.

"Move what?"

"You know damn well what... are you winding me up?"

"What? No! I don't know what you're... wait, where's my hammer?"

"Same place you put my spanner I 'spect."

The same argument was going on at every group Merek visited. The men were beginning to fight amongst themselves. Merek and his knights were spending all their time breaking up fights and scuffles amongst Einhard's men and their own. However, they were not averse to breaking a few heads to make sure they got the job done.

Inside the castle, a small crowd had gathered around Branchir's map to keep an eye on the activity outside the walls. The nymphs, satyrs and dryads worked well as a team. Their snatch and grab petty thefts looked as though they might work for a while but all too soon the enemy Knights had threatened and intimidated their builders into cannibalising parts of several machines until they had one of the machines complete. Still, there was no way of knowing whether it would actually work. So far, there had been no real engagement with the enemy. There was still hope that the dryads and nymphs had time to influence the outcome.

"What are they doing?" Sardo pointed out a small group of men hauling on ropes.

The giant trebuchet began to move very slowly across the open ground. They were about to find out whether or not it would work.

"About fucking time," Merek grumbled. "So how does this thing work? Demonstrate." He pointed at the trebuchet. Einhard gave the man the nod to continue. The man directed his crew. It needed several men to haul on the ropes and walk the treadmill wheels to raise the huge counter-weight box. It was the size of a small house, filled with rocks, and weighed as much as a hundred men. At the other end of the long arm was a sling which was brought down and locked into place. One of the men loaded the sling with a rock the size of a small cabbage – or a man's head, and hurriedly stepped back.

"You might wanna step back too m'lord. These things can be a bit unpredictable." Merek was warned. The brakeman stood to one side, hunched and ready to yank on the rope.

"Prepare to release," the foreman shouted.

"Ready!" the brakeman shouted back.

"Let fly." The order was given, the rope was pulled and the counter-weight box dropped causing the arm and the sling to fly up and over, sending the rock over the first two curtain walls before disappearing. The sound of it landing somewhere inside the castle was a little muted.

"I'd say that was a successful hit,"

Einhard said smugly.

"So you say. How do you know it actually hit anything?" Merek turned back to the foreman. "Can you aim at the outer wall so that I may better judge the efficacy?"

"You heard the man," Einhard almost leaped on the foreman. The man looked worried but he nodded and began to bark orders.

"Shorten the sling... get to the ropes... You two, get to the wheels..."

It was a long, slow process; nearly ten minutes before the counter- weight was once again raised and the sling could be loaded with another rock.

"Prepare to release..." All the men moved away and the brakeman took up his position with the rope.

"Let fly."

The brakeman gave the rope a hard tug and the second rock went sailing over the moat and hit the top of the outer-most wall. The semi-circular damage looked as though a stone-eating giant had bitten a great chunk out of the stones.

"I see," Merek nodded. "Loading and preparing this weapon is very slow. How do you suggest we may speed this up?" He looked from the foreman to Einhard.

"Well m'lord. We usually work with a bank of three machines together: one preparing, one loading and one loosing. But there were so many bits missing that we had to cannibalise just to get this one made."

"Whatever," Merek waved his hand as he walked away. "Just make it happen quicker." Timbers groaned and creaked and men grunted with the strain as they set about priming the weapon again. Shouts of "Let fly!" could be heard periodically as the projectiles hurtled towards the castle.

"Get people down there to check on the damage, make sure no one is hurt," Branchir called out and three of his men dashed out of the Great Hall.

"We felt the ground shake," Daewen

appeared at her husband's side. "What happened?"

"They managed to get one of their machines working," Sardo explained as Branchir held his hands out over the map and enlarged the castle. He turned the image around full circle and tilted it from side to side, forward and back.

"There, there" Sardo pointed, "and there."

The first projectile had landed between the two outer curtain walls. Luckily, there was nothing there for it to damage. The second hit was to the outer wall. Large chunks of masonry fell in but it fell into empty space. The third one hit the outer wall but bounced off and dropped into the moat. It appeared as though they were using trial and error to range find and now they had a target. The projectiles still came one at a time with a long gap between them but they were now hitting the same place in the wall, gradually chipping away at the hole. Huge cracks were beginning to spread.

"It won't be long before we have a gap big enough to get through," Einhard grinned at Merek.

"That maybe so, but how do you intend to get across that moat?"

"We'll build a bridge..." It looked as though the idea had just occurred to him and he ran off in the direction of a group of his men to get them started on the new project.

"You're certain there will be a fight?" Branchir asked Aurora.

"I fear it is inevitable. Neither of the enemy's leaders will want to give up. They will force their people to the bitter end unless there is some intervention," she told him.

"Thank you. I wish to minimise bloodshed and injury... I had hoped we could avoid an all-out battle this time but it is not to be." He gave a deep sigh. "If everyone is ready, it looks like we're moving on to phase two. Move out."

AN ELEMENT OF CHANGE

Thank you for reading this book. I do hope that you enjoyed reading it as much as I enjoyed writing it.

If you loved it… or didn't… or anything else in between, please go to the Amazon website, leave a review and let me know what you think.

Thanks again, Linda

<u>Tales of Otherside</u>:

Book 1 – Eleanor's House.

Book 2 – In Sickness and In Health.

Book 3 – Lost and Found.

The story continues in…

<u>The Otherside and Beyond</u>:

Book[1] 1 – Time and Again.

Book 2 – All The King's Men.

Book 3 – It All Comes Round Again.

Book 4 - Hidden in Plain Sight.

Book 5 – Before the Fall.

Book 6 – A Matter of Time.

Printed in Great Britain
by Amazon